M_cN A L L Y'S

Dilemma

LAWRENCE SANDERS

M_cN A L L Y ' S
Dilemma

DOUBLEDAY DIRECT
LARGE PRINT EDITION

G. P. PUTNAM'S SONS

NEW YORK

G. P. Putnam's Sons
Publishers Since 1838
a member of
Penguin Putnam Inc.
375 Hudson Street
New York, NY 10014

The publisher and the estate of Lawrence Sanders have chosen Vincent Lardo to create this novel based on Lawrence Sanders's beloved character Archy McNally and his fictional world.

ISBN 0-7394-0484-9

Printed in the United States of America

**This Large Print Book carries the
Seal of Approval of N.A.V.H.**

McNALLY'S
Dilemma

1

I WAS PERUSING the lunch menu at the Pelican Club when I let out a howl, which was a bit uncouth even for that unpretentious lodge. This brought forth our waitress, Priscilla, a phenomenon as unusual as my outburst. To get Priscilla's attention is tantamount to hailing a taxi in the rain, as she would rather be gliding down a couturier's runway than punching the parquet at the Pelican.

"Steak tartare?" I exclaimed, still in a state of shock. The cuisine at the club is far from haute, and while I don't mind indulging in one of Leroy's thrombotic blue-plate specials, I draw the line on courting mad cow disease.

"Leroy is upgrading the menu," Priscilla explained.

I should say here that chef Leroy is Priscilla's brother and, along with their father and mother, Simon and Jasmine, the Pettibones are the African-American family of great charm who keep the Pelican aloft, as it were.

"What happened to the hamburger?" I asked. Leroy's hamburgers are among the best in Florida, if not the world.

"Like I said, we're upgrading."

"Before you reach the zenith, may I still order a hamburger, medium rare?"

"Sure."

"How, if it's not on the menu?"

"You order the steak tartare, medium rare."

"But that's a hamburger."

Priscilla put ten beautifully manicured fingernails on her slim hips and spoke as if instructing a not-too-bright child. "Well, a hamburger is what you want, isn't it?"

Leading with my chin, I countered, "Why should I pay fourteen ninety-five for a hamburger that cost seven-fifty, with *pommes frites,* yesterday?"

"Why? Because if you want to mutilate a perfectly good steak tartare, you have to pay for the privilege, that's why."

And with that, Priscilla moved away with a smile, a nod, and a promise. "I'll be back when you've made up your finicky mind."

My finicky mind was already made up. I'd have the steak tartare, medium rare, though the expensive choice was contingent upon the arrival of my luncheon companion, Vance Tremaine. The meeting had been suggested at breakfast that morning by my father, Prescott McNally, rendering the cost of our lunch a bona fide item for my expense account.

I toil for the law firm of McNally & Son; he is the *père,* I am the *fils.* Despite my unceremonious ejection from Yale Law, my father was willing to set me up in a sideline at McNally & Son, known as Discreet Inquiries, where clients who prefer their private affairs be kept private—and who can afford to sidestep the police—are guaranteed prudence. Here in Palm Beach, discretion is the better part of valor and *sotto voce* is our motto. Ergo, Discreet Inquiries is as vital to Palm Beach society as are the sun and surf.

"Do you know Vance Tremaine, Archy?" the Master of the house had inquired after dabbing at his mustache with a linen napkin. Although we breakfast in the kitchen of our faux Tudor manse on Ocean Boulevard my father dressed for the occasion in a gray worsted suit with vest and a cravat of pale blue silk.

"I know of him, sir. He married Penny Brightworth, who's not very bright but is worth a zillion pennies." My wit is exceeded only by my charm.

"Penelope Brightworth Tremaine is our client, Archy."

"Yes, sir." *Mon père* is seldom impressed with my wit, especially if it's at the expense of one of our rich clients.

"I received a call from Mr. Tremaine last night and he expressed a desire to consult us on a matter not related to law, per se."

"Discreet Inquiries, sir?"

He nodded. "It would appear so, Archy. He did not want to come to my office so I suggested that you would call him this morning and set up a meeting at a mutually agreed upon venue."

As Vance Tremaine obviously did not want to be seen by his peers consulting with McNally & Son, that would be my Pelican Club—as different from the Bath and Tennis and the Everglades as *mousse au chocolat* is from chocolate pudding. Father is not amused by my membership in the Pelican but is not oblivious to its usefulness to Discreet Inquiries.

"I suggest you do a little research into the life and times of Mr. Tremaine before the meeting, Archy."

"Yes, sir."

After our coffee and chat, I retreated to my micro third-floor suite: bedroom, sitting room, dressing room, and bath, tucked beneath our copper mansard roof. You can't beat the rent: the big O, and I don't mean Jackie.

I called Lolly Spindrift, gossip columnist for one of our local rags, who could tell me everything I wanted to know about Vance Tremaine, most of which was none of Lolly's business—or mine. Lolly is a man of vitriolic tongue who fills his Mont Blanc with acid and his bed with men.

"Lolly? Archy McNally here."

"Archy, what can I do for you? It had better be something naughty, or you can stop wasting my precious time. Lady Cynthia gave one of her charity benefits yesterday that was about as interesting as watching paint dry, and I still have to find a way to make it all sound gushingly chic for the late edition. But I have a feeling you had a reason for calling. Tell me, Archy, what do you want to know?"

"A few intimate facts re: Vance Tremaine."

"Size thirty-four boxer shorts and he dresses on the left."

"Good grief, Lol, not that intimate. Just the facts, please."

Vance Tremaine was from old money, so old the well had run dry. Penny Brightworth was from new money, so new it bordered on the vulgar. Daddy founded a fast-food franchise that enabled the Brightworths to dine elsewhere. Vance graduated from Yale some twenty-five years ago, a young Adonis forced to choose between going to work or marrying money. Penny graduated from Sarah Lawrence at about the same time, a plain Jane with marriage to an Adonis as her post-graduate goal. Theirs was a match made in heaven.

Vance had an eye that roved with the speed of the Concorde; it was said he cheated on Penny two days after the wedding, his *amore* being the stewardess on the flight that took the honeymooners to romantic Roma. This, to be sure, is PBR, Palm Beach Rumor, as opposed to PBF, Palm Beach Fact. "However, the only PBF I would swear to in a court of law," Lolly once admitted, "is the one that decrees the sun rises over the Atlantic and sets behind West Palm."

Penny doesn't like sharing her husband or her bank account, and for twenty-five years has been threatening divorce every time Vance is caught with his size thirty-four boxers on the wrong side of his knees. Penny has vowed that Vance's next bimbo will also be the proverbial straw. One more time and Vance will be tossed out of their faux Spanish hacienda—ten acres, ocean view—and onto the A1A with nary the proverbial pot in which to wee-wee.

"Why the interest?" Lolly asked, poison pen surely in hand.

"I think he's in hot water, Lol."

Lolly laughed. "Last I heard it was cold water that was Vance Tremaine's undoing. Want to hear about it, Archy?"

Vance arrived ten minutes late. A slim, handsome man with a Palm Beach tan, he looked a good ten years younger than a guy approaching the half century mark. He sat, pulled out a white handkerchief and wiped his forehead, despite the fact that it was cool for November. Vance Tremaine was up to his *cojones* in cow dip, and I had no doubt that it was them *cojones* that had gotten him there. He wore a lightweight blue suit and rep tie. I wore jeans, Bally loafers (no socks), a lavender button-down dress shirt, open at the collar, and my tweed blazer with bone toggles instead of buttons.

When Priscilla decided to pay her respects I ordered a Bloody Mary and Vance went for a Scotch on the rocks. "Rather lethal for high noon," I preached.

"I need it, Mr. McNally."

"That bad, eh? And if you're going to bare your soul, the name is Archy."

There is something pathetic about

watching a grown man squirm in his chair. "Do I start from the beginning, Archy?"

"Cut to the chase, Vance, and begin with her name."

Aware that his reputation had preceded him to the Pelican Club, Vance sighed the word "Ginny." He continued with, "A little black dress, sable hair, dark eyes—imagine a young Audrey Hepburn with a bit more meat on the bone."

I refused to imagine any such thing, but the reference and the black dress begged the question: "Givenchy?" When I got a blank stare, I explained, "Givenchy is the guy who designed all of Audrey's *lovely* black dresses."

"I don't think so," Vance said thoughtfully. "Ginny is strictly off the rack."

Priscilla arrived with our drinks and, fearing we would never see her again, I ordered my steak tartare, medium rare. "But that's a hamburger," Vance cleverly observed.

"Don't ask," I cautioned.

He ordered the tossed green salad with Leroy's special dressing, which I have long suspected to be Creamy Italian via Kraft. Tossed green salads and jogging after thong bikinis on our beach is what must keep Vance Tremaine "fit as a fiddle and ready for love." (If that sounds familiar, you saw *Singin' in the Rain,* MGM, 1952.)

"Off your feed?"

Vance downed his Scotch as if it were a tonic that would improve his appetite. "I'm off women," he answered with little enthusiasm for the proclamation.

I sipped my drink and encouraged Vance to tell me more.

He picked up Ginny (or vice versa) at Bar Anticipation in West Palm. In case you don't know the establishment, Bar Anticipation gives new meaning to the word "sleaze." Perhaps to justify his patronage, Vance interrupted his tale to say, "You'd be surprised at how many people we know bend their elbows at Bar Anticipation." He waved his hand around the now-crowded room to bring home his point.

Anticipation turned to fulfillment at a local motel, where Vance knew Ginny in the biblical sense—both Old and New Testaments, according to Tremaine. They dozed off; Vance awakened to the sight of a fellow, hard of muscle and soft of brain, looking through the viewfinder of a 35mm Nikon, the little blue bulb flashing *pop, pop, pop.*

"I get the picture, Vance."

"So did the guy with the Nikon, and if my wife sees them . . ." Vance polished off his drink and once again made like Satchmo with the handkerchief.

"How much in return for you *in flagrante delicto,* in glorious color?"

"Five thousand."

Just as I thought. Amateurs. A couple of punks who had cooked up a scam as old as a Milton Berle gag. Palm Beach, especially in season, is invaded by these con artists, and their scams run from the sublime to the ridiculous. My cases have included a self-styled financial consultant peddling a Fabergé egg and kidnappers who called in their ransom note to a phone line with caller ID giving me, and the police, the culprits' phone number and their exact location.

Ginny and friend needed to be taught a lesson and Archy McNally was the perfect teacher for the job. "Leave it to me, Vance," I said as Priscilla brought us our lunch. Vance was so relieved he eyed my hamburger—née steak tartare—with envy.

Upon returning home, I called my friend and occasional partner in fighting crime and pestilence, Sergeant Al Rogoff of the PBPD, then spent the remainder of the afternoon cataloging my beret collection.

That evening, I sacrificed cocktails with the Lord of the Manor and his mate, something I quite enjoy due to the fine quality of his Lordship's potables, in favor of Bar Anticipation. Ginny was there, as I knew she would be. You see, their type of sting is one that requires hitting two or three marks in quick succession and then scampering off with the loot. Word gets around fast, and even the proprietors of Bar Anticipation have their limits.

Sable hair, dark eyes, and a little black dress. If the hair and eyes were the ones she wore last night, so, I assumed, was the dress. I could see what Vance meant by "more meat on the bone." Ginny was more Elizabeth Taylor than Audrey Hepburn, but I'm not complaining.

I wore a three-button blue suit and rep tie, à la Vance, and Allen-Edmond cordovan kilties. Except for the kilties the look was very un-Archy, but business is business.

Commandeering the stool next to Ginny, I opened with, "Givenchy?"

The lady was quick on the uptake. "How kind," she cooed. "But no. It's from a shop in South Beach. They call it a knockoff."

"A knockoff for a knockout," I retorted, wishing I had a waxed mustache to stroke. "May I buy you a drink?"

Ginny giggled. "I have always depended upon the kindness of strangers."

For this, Vivian Leigh and Tennessee Williams should have risen from their graves and strangled her.

One word led to another, one drink led to another, and Ginny's hand led to my thigh, a territory she seemed to know rather well. All of this led to her motel room, where she plied me with cheap gin and suggestive gestures. When her cavorting failed to arouse her supposed mark, Ginny grew a bit frantic and announced that she was going to adjourn to the bathroom and "slip into something comfortable."

This was my cue to bring down the curtain on this farce. "Forget it, my dear," I told Ginny, "your Richard Avedon ain't showing up tonight."

That got her attention. "What are you talking about?"

"Snap, snap, pop, pop, five grand, and Bob's your uncle."

"Are you a cop?"

"No, but as we speak, your partner is handing over his photographic endeavors to one of Palm Beach's finest."

The sudden realization that she had been set up caused her to lose her cool and she shouted, "You skunk. You . . ."

I held her wrists in a firm grip to keep her ruby-tinted claws from gouging out my eyes. "The fix was in all the while," she ranted. "What do you want from me?"

"Your cooperation."

To a woman in Ginny's profession, my retort had but one meaning. Her little hands stopped fighting my grip and she was once again ready to slip into something comfortable. "I wouldn't let him take your picture, Archy," she purred.

"Why not?"

"You know why not." She actually blushed as she spoke. Mata Hari, meet your master. "I like you, Archy."

Al Rogoff was not going to arrest her friend, for it would serve no purpose. Vance would have to press charges, and he might as well have the pair show the photos to Penny as do that. Al was going to put the fear of God in the guy and tell him and the lovely Ginny to get out of town.

But Ginny didn't know this, so when I said, "And I like you, Ginny. That's why I'm going to walk out of here and forget we ever met, if you hand over the negatives of last night's 'shoot'—and while you're at it, any other negatives you might be hoping to turn into ready cash."

Knowing a good deal when she heard one, Ginny complied while continuing to make suggestive gestures in hopes of a last minute reprieve. "Can I keep the ones from Disney World?" she asked.

"Absolutely not," I scolded.

I left with my cache, wondering if I had saved Mickey a lot of grief.

Father was in his den. I knocked.

"Come," he called.

He was sitting in the swivel chair behind his enormous desk, reading Dickens. "Yes, Archy?"

"The Tremaine case is closed, sir."

"Very good, Archy."

"Would you like to hear about it, sir?"

"No, Archy. Would you like a glass of port?"

"I think I would, sir."

And that, as they say, was that.

2

THE FOLLOWING DAY I was back at the Pelican, lunching with my fiancée, Consuela Garcia, to whom I am true in my fashion. Connie is social secretary to Lady Cynthia Horowitz, a labor that keeps Connie on the telephone longer than Barbara Stanwyck in *Sorry, Wrong Number*. Connie is a handsome woman of indeterminate age—"Don't ask, don't tell" is a policy Connie and I embrace wholeheartedly. She is also a woman of great patience which I put to the test more often than may be prudent.

While waiting for Priscilla to deliver our turkey clubs, we sipped Molson Ale and munched the garlic pickle spears. Connie wore a beige Donna Karan pants suit and black shoes with those thick, chunky heels that do nothing for me but are all the rage. I wore my belted-back chinos, left over from my days at Yale; a pale yellow and white striped shirt with a navy silk ascot; a powder blue linen jacket; and, unlike Connie's chunky heels, my blue canvas tennis shoes were more for comfort than show. I do not take my position as the Beau Brummel of the Pelican Club lightly.

Spearing a spear, Connie ventured, "I hear you lunched with Vance Tremaine yesterday."

"Is nothing sacred?" I ventured back.

"Sacred? In this joint? You must be kidding."

To defame my club is to defame me. And it's also her club. Yes, we opened our doors to women some time back, and I now wondered at the generosity of this rash egalitarian gesture. The Pelican was founded by a group of like-minded gentlemen who find the traditional clubs stuffy and, in numerous cases, unobtainable.

We are also a charitable group whose jazz combo (I play the kazoo) performs relentlessly, one might say, for those less fortunate. Our last gig was at the Senior Citizens' Center in Delray Beach. We opened with a bouncy rendition of "Enjoy Yourself, It's Later Than You Think," and closed with a rousing "Nearer My God to Thee." In retrospect, perhaps poor choices, but we received a standing ovation from those seniors who could stand. The Center's hostess, Ms. Magdalena Fallsdack, assured us that most of our audience was stone deaf, adding, "God protects the elderly."

"You've been talking to Priscilla," I said, just as Priscilla arrived with our turkey clubs and a single order of *pommes frites.*

"I don't talk to anyone around this place who isn't ordering food," Priscilla announced, then left us to ponder the statement.

"No," Connie said, spooning mayo out of a plastic tub that, I'm sure, once held margarine. "Lolly called to check some facts for his piece on Lady Cynthia's cocktail reception and mentioned the Tremaine connection."

I find it almost impossible to eat a club sandwich in the manner a sandwich should be eaten without doing serious damage to my jaw. Therefore, I discard the top piece of toast, remove the lettuce and tomato beneath it and I am left with a perfectly manageable turkey and bacon sandwich with a side helping of lettuce and tomato. Archy, Gourmand Engineer.

"It was a business lunch," I informed Connie.

"Discreet Inquiries?"

"Discreet, my dear, is the operative word."

"You confide, Archy, only when you need my help."

This is true. Lady Cynthia Horowitz is a leader of Palm Beach Society (note the capital S), and as the clients of McNally & Son and Discreet Inquiries are from that same social strata, their comings and goings and doings are of the utmost interest to me. Connie, in her capacity as Lady Cynthia's secretary, is privy to much that matters on Palm Beach Island. What matters is Love, Hate, Envy, Sex, Bank Balances, Genealogies, and whose Versace is genuine and whose ain't.

The only people more privy to this crowd than Connie are, of course, those who "do" for them. Our housekeeper and houseman,

Ursi and Jamie Olson, along with their brethren up and down Ocean Boulevard, have a communications network that would give NASA pause.

I have shamelessly used Connie in my endeavors, and never more so when I was called upon to investigate the theft of Lady C.'s stamp collection, one that was insured for half a mil and worth zilch. But if you've been paying attention you know that story.

"I like to think of us as a business couple," I told Connie, forking a *pomme frite* from a plate we were supposed to be sharing, but the hand (Connie's) is quicker than the eye (mine).

"Was the black dress at Bar Anticipation also business?"

I tried to raise one eyebrow, a gesture *mon père* has mastered, and failed. I knew Lolly Spindrift didn't tattle that one because Bar Anticipation is not a place Lolly would enter if chased by wild dogs. This begged the obvious question. "Who, among Lady C.'s crowd, frequents Bar Anticipation?"

"Discreet, my dear, is the operative word."

Touché.

Hoping to divert Connie's attention from the black dress to matters more pressing, I asked her what info Lolly was seeking regarding Lady C.'s cocktail reception. Lolly, I always assumed, knew everything, and what he didn't know he simply made up based on evidence as solid as quicksand.

"Actually, he wanted a young man's name."

"That figures. Who was the guy?"

Connie shook her dark hair. "I have no idea. So many people bring a date or houseguests to these charity receptions I'm not always aware of who's who, and neither is Lady C., but she couldn't care less as long as no one smokes anyplace on the property."

"Was the lad with Phil Meecham?" I asked. Meecham, owner of the *Sans Souci,* a yacht that gives new meaning to the term "pleasure craft," is a buddy of Lolly Spindrift when they aren't simultaneously mad about the same boy and at each other.

"You mean, was he one of Phil's boys? I don't believe so. In fact the few times I was able to survey the crowd I think the young man was talking to Veronica Manning."

I tried again, and failed again, to raise one eyebrow. Why do I persist? "Are Melva and Geoff down for the season?" Melva and Geoff are Veronica's mother and stepfather.

"I guess so. I know Veronica was there but I don't remember seeing her parents and I'm sure they weren't on our guest list, so I imagine someone brought Veronica."

Veronica's mother is Melva Manning Williams, née Ashton, an old friend of mine. Her second husband, Geoffrey Williams, is a handsome pain in the butt whom I suspect of being a gold digger and know for certain is a womanizer, second only to Vance Tremaine. Though Geoff Williams is not the light of my life, I've never let this interfere with the high regard I harbor for Melva.

"And knowing the very young," I added, "Veronica brought the lad." None of this really mattered, but it was diverting chitchat.

In fact, so innocuous was the subject of Veronica Manning and the lad, Connie answered by breaking our date for that evening. We were supposed to dine at Connie's condominium. She's not a bad cook if rice and beans are your thing. They are not mine, but then dinner is not the main attraction at Chez Garcia.

I was to bring my collection of lady song-birds, on vinyl, please, for an evening of connubial bliss between consenting adults. Who better than Chris Connor, Jo Stafford, Lena Horne, Billie Holiday, and "Her Nibs" Miss Georgia Gibbs to set the mood?

"Lady C. is giving one of her intimate dinner parties," Connie explained. "Thirty, under a tent, poolside. I know she'll want me to stay until dessert, at least."

"Does she ever spend an evening alone?"

"Not if she can help it."

"Connie," I said, taking her hand across the table and around the tub of mayo, "the black dress meant nothing. I mean, you do have to work tonight, or . . ."

"That's for me to know and you to find out."

Touché, again.

The weather continued sunny but cool, which didn't prevent me from changing into my cerise Speedo trunks, stepping into a pair of sandals, and donning a mini terry robe printed with a portrait of Donald Duck before crossing the A1A for my daily two-mile swim. Risking the wrath of the PB

Chamber of Commerce, I will say the temperature this November afternoon was more brisk than tropical, causing me to trod the sand sans my pith helmet.

I had a "thing" (briefly) for hats when I was at Yale Law (briefly) that bordered on something of a fetish. The pith is part of that collection that has recently expanded to include linen berets in white, puce, and emerald green, courtesy of a custom hatmaker in Danbury, Connecticut. They cause Seigneur to look upon me with misgivings and make mother giggle.

We dined that evening on Ursi's *caneton à l'orange* served with a perfectly chilled *meursault* and ended with a *crème caramel* as smooth as velvet. Those who wonder why I have never left home have never tasted one of Ursi's culinary endeavors.

Mother, who would like to see me married, asked after Connie. Mother is a lovely woman whom I cherish dearly. As often happens when we cross that line between middle and old age, mother is now sometimes forgetful and her mind is apt to wander now and then. It is a trait that renders her more, not less, precious to father and me.

Mother is what might be called "pleasingly plump" or "stylishly stout," and I use both of those archaic but kind descriptions in their best possible connotation. She suffers from high blood pressure, which may account for her florid complexion and shortness of breath. The latter causes father and me great concern. Last, but far from least, she dotes on sweets, her garden, and her son, Archy.

I told her Connie was working late that evening and mother opined, "Well, perhaps when she marries she can leave the employ of Lady Cynthia and enjoy life."

"Are you implying," the Master asked, "that working for Lady Cynthia is less than enjoyable?"

Lady C. is one of *mon père*'s richest, if not *the* richest, clients.

"I don't think so, dear," his wife cooed.

Alone in my third-floor digs, I lit my first English Oval of the day, poured myself a small marc, and put Chris Connor on the phonograph. "These Foolish Things Remind Me of You." Of whom was I reminded? Consuela Garcia, or Ginny, whose dress was "off the rack"? I honestly didn't know. Was it my fate to be forever cast in the role of the student prince who loves the girl he's near when he's not near the girl he loves?

I blew smoke rings and watched them drift toward the ceiling in slow motion. I imagined myself in tails, hand in hand with a girl in a beaded gown (Archy and Ginger?), skipping through the ethereal hoops. Ethereal, alas, is as real as my love life gets.

I sat at my desk and dutifully recorded *L'Affaire Tremaine* in my journal. Recording my experiences as CEO, Office Manager, Secretary, and Mail Boy for Discreet Inquiries is a chore I adhere to faithfully and one I enjoy. My jottings this evening, and my cool dip in the Atlantic earlier, reminded me of Lolly's remark about cold water being Vance Tremaine's undoing. The story played out thusly.

Vance was in New York on business— what business will soon become clear— and stopping at the Yale Club, as they say. This twenty-one-storied limestone edifice, solid as the Rock of Gibraltar, is situated most conveniently on Vanderbilt Avenue between Grand Central Station to the east and Brooks Brothers to the west. After a hard day on Wall Street, an Eli on the run can purchase a pair of cashmere socks, sip a tall Scotch and soda, and still make the seven-fifteen to Greenwich with time to spare. That the school and club are now both coed went a long way in attracting the patronage of Vance Tremaine when in the Big Apple.

We open with Vance sitting in the football-field-size second-floor lounge, furnished with leather chairs, couches, and mahogany tables. Two fireplaces, towering windows, and oil paintings of presidents who went from Yale to the Oval Office with nary a backward glance complete the picture of a gentlemen's club favored by New Yorker cartoonists. The bar is also on the second floor, enabling the late-afternoon crowd to amble between bar and lounge, toting their drinks and little glass bowls filled with peanuts or other tidbits.

Having been introduced to Vance's predilection, it will not surprise you to learn that he struck up a conversation with a charming recent Yale grad wearing a very tailored aubergine skirt, white blouse, Hermès print scarf knotted in the fashion of a man's necktie, and carrying a Coach brief-case. All this, and especially the briefcase, was the ultimate turn-on for Vance, for reasons known only to his analyst. Her red hair was the cherry atop the sundae.

When he asked her if she was free for dinner, she didn't say yes and she didn't say no. Neither did she say Vance was old enough to be her father, but stated demurely that he, Vance, had graduated Yale the same year as dear old Dad. Vance, who is quick on the snappy retort, said, "Then he married in prep school or you are the most precocious ten-year-old I've ever had the pleasure of meeting."

"I'm twenty-two, Mr. Tremaine."

"I'm forty-seven, and the name is Vance."

For the record, it's a PBR that this year marks the third anniversary of Vance Tremaine's forty-seventh birthday.

Next he hinted, none too subtly, at the expertise an older man brings to a relation-ship. He ended with, "If you've never dated a man of my vintage, consider the allure and the mystery of the unknown, Allison," for that was indeed her name. "Shall we meet here at seven-thirty?"

Employing the skills she had learned in four years' rigorous study, Allison didn't say yes and she didn't say no.

Invigorated, Vance retreated to the fifth floor of the Yale Club, which houses the men's locker room, the men's showers, the men's steam room, the men's sauna, the men's masseuse, and, the target of Vance's mission, the swimming pool. An inside staircase leads to the gym and squash courts on the sixth floor. Vance was pleasantly surprised at the vast changes he encountered on the fifth floor. The old open stall lockers had been replaced with modern, slim closets with, of all things, doors. The floor was carpeted and upholstered chairs and odd tables formed a comfortable lounge area around a television set.

Vance approved of the renovation. He signed in for a "steam and plunge" ("swim" being too pretentious a word for a pool of rather modest proportions). He hung his clothes in a new, slender locker and walked into the shower area, off which were the steam, sauna, and pool rooms.

He peered through the windowed door of the sauna but was put off by the sign that cautioned men with heart problems from entering. This was reminiscent of the notice Dante had posted on Hell's Gate: *Lasciate ogni speranza, voi ch'entrate!* (Leave all hope behind, ye who enter here!) Moving right along, he ventured into the steam room, a six-by-ten-foot rectangle, where he singed his behind on the marble bench before fleeing in favor of a cold shower. Ready for his plunge, Vance grabbed a towel from a stack conveniently placed by the entrance to the pool, draped it around his neck, opened the door, and marched right in.

One swam at the Yale Club, as the French say, *au naturel* or, as the boys at Yale say, bare-assed. So, imagine Vance's surprise when he came face to face with Allison and another young lady in territory that only a few years ago was sacrosanct to those poor little lambs who had lost their way—*baa, baa, baa.* Vance gasped and turned the color of Allison's hair. The girls, being well bred, did not gasp but stood their ground and kept their eyes above Vance's waist. If he turned and ran to from whence he came, he would be exposing his rear flank, and reasoning in a nanosecond that one exposure per viewing was sufficient, he took a giant step forward and leaped into the pool, losing his towel in midair.

Perhaps in anticipation of such an occurrence, the pool's designer had positioned the deep end nearest the portal from the men's showers, so Vance was spared a broken leg or two. However, upon surfacing, Vance was more the color of Allison's blue eyes than her red hair. As usual, those in charge of such things had neglected to press the button marked "heater," rendering the pool's water temperature a degree or two above frigid.

Hugging the pool's tiled perimeter, Vance shouted at his audience. "What the hell are you doing here?"

"We, sir," said Allison, "are here to swim and, as you can see, are properly attired for the sport." Referring, no doubt, to their smart one-piece swimsuits. "What did *you* have in mind?"

"Since when are you allowed to use the pool?"

"If by 'you' you mean 'women,' we gained entrance to the fifth floor seventy-five years after being granted the right to vote."

Good God, Vance thought, women's libbers. Next thing you know they'll have us doing the backstroke with Democrats. "Would you please hand me that towel," Vance said, clinging closely to the tiled wall. The pool water at the Yale Club, besides being often cold, is always clean and clear, the better to see the mosaic tiled Y that graces the pool's floor.

The girls, laughing, made their way to a door opposite the one from which Vance had entered. A door that had been a solid wall on his last visit just two short years ago.

"How the hell am I going to get out of here?" Vance wondered aloud.

"The way you got in," Allison called over her lovely bare shoulder before making her exit.

At this point, the lifeguard entered from the men's lockers and at a glance noting the situation, picked up the towel and helped Vance out of the water. The boy's name was Jesus. He was Cuban, as was most of the help at the Yale Club; however, being saved by Jesus did not cause Vance Tremaine to be born again. In fact, he had the temerity to show up in the lounge at seven-thirty, only to see Allison on the arm of a recent Yale graduate who looked like the cover boy of a Brooks Brothers catalogue.

"I thought we had a date," Vance protested.

"Sorry, Vance, but you blew the cover on the mystery of the unknown," Allison retorted.

This amusing reverie was shattered by my ringing telephone. I checked the time on my desk clock; I have a policy against taking calls after midnight, especially if it might be bad news. Bad news can wait until morning. It was one minute before the witching hour, and, being a purist, I picked up and said, "Archy here."

"Archy? It's Melva. Melva Williams."

"Melva? How nice to hear your lovely voice. I heard you were down for the season."

"Yes. A bit early, but I'm here."

"How are you, Melva?"

"As well as can be expected under the circumstances."

Now there was an opener if ever I heard one, and this poor fish nibbled at the bait. "What, Melva, are the circumstances?"

"Geoffrey is dead."

I gave that the obligatory beat and then responded with the requisite condolence. "My God, I'm sorry. When? How?"

"When?" Melva Williams said. "About a half hour ago. How? I shot him, that's how."

I glanced at my desk clock. It was one minute after twelve.

Well, the season had certainly started off with a bang!

3

I KNEW MOTHER WOULD have retired to the master suite, just as I knew *mon père* would be in his den, reading Dickens. If you are beginning to believe that Dickens is all the man reads, you would be correct. For as long as I can remember this has been his sole leisure pursuit, rendering my father either a very slow reader or one who has come full circle and is on his second, or perhaps third, time through. Whenever I lament my given name, Archibald, I also remember to count my blessings. I could have been christened Ebenezer McNally.

"You're still up," my father stated after permitting me to enter.

"Yes, sir. And on my way out."

"Trouble, Archy?"

"I'm afraid so, sir. At the Williams manse."

"Melva Ashton Manning? They're here?"

The Ashtons and Mannings are New York's version of Boston's Cabots and Lodges, hence father's refusal to be amused by Melva's second marriage to Geoffrey Williams, who, PBR has it, came into the world as Jeffrey Wolinsky. When Ted Manning was killed in a polo accident, father would have liked Melva to remain a widow rather than marry beneath her. A latter-day Victorian, father often refers to divorce as "an unfortunate separation," not unlike a surgeon telling a patient, "Sorry, old chap, but I must unfortunately separate your right arm from your shoulder."

Father will no doubt be delighted to learn that Melva has finally performed the ultimate unfortunate separation from Geoff.

"Yes, sir, they're here."

"And?"

"Geoff Williams has been shot, sir. I believe he's dead."

Did I see him smile at the news or was he recalling an amusing passage from *Bleak House*? "An accident, Archy?"

"Melva shot him, sir."

The pater executed a perfect one-eyebrow lift, which was as ruffled as Prescott McNally's feathers ever got, and asked hopefully, "Justifiable homicide?"

"I don't know the details, sir, just what Melva said on the phone not five minutes ago. I believe 'I shot him' were her exact words."

"I see. Well, Melva Ashton Manning will need a lawyer, Archy."

One doesn't become the proprietor of the McNally Building on Royal Palm Way by being shy about soliciting trade. "I believe she called me as a friend, sir, and I imagine she has a New York lawyer."

"Who is most likely not admitted to practice in Florida. They will need a firm to liaise between their client and the court. Tell me, have the police been notified?"

"I don't think so, sir. Melva seems to be in a state of shock, so I'd best get there and do what has to be done."

"Very good. Express my sympathy to

Melva and assure her that we are at her disposal. And keep me posted, Archy."

"Yes, sir."

Jamie and Ursi occupy the apartment over our three-car garage but no lights emanated from their quarters. As I approached, our dog, Hobo, ambled out of his gabled dog house, sniffed the cuffs of my trousers, and wagged his tail. Hobo is part terrier; his brown and white spots suggest one of his parents was a Jack Russell and the other a one-night stand. I patted Hobo's head and he ambled back into his canine abode.

My red Mazda Miata convertible is the type of car one should leap into in the manner of Tom Mix mounting Pal. But when it's garaged and the top is up, I recommend a more conventional approach, such as opening the door and sliding into the driver's seat. Comfortably if not dashingly ensconced, I sped south on the A1A, recalling the events in the life of New York's erstwhile "Debutante of the Year" that brought her to this sad impasse.

Melva Ashton was as top drawer as one can get without sitting atop the family's pedigreed highboy. Miss Porter's was followed by Radcliffe, which was followed by a trip to Hollywood for a screen test, when it was fashionable for debs like Melva and Gloria Vanderbilt to be screen-tested. Their names never appeared in lights, but Gloria's, for a time, graced the derrière of many a jeans-clad lady.

Her first late husband—I'm not quite sure how one can be "first" and "late" at the same time—Teddy Manning roughed it at St. Paul's and Harvard, where he majored in polo. He and Melva took dancing lessons together when she was ten and he twelve. They danced their way to the altar a dozen years later, took up residence in a triplex on Fifth Avenue, summered in their Further Lane mansion in East Hampton, and wintered in a palatial rental in Palm Beach. They produced a daughter, Veronica, and when she was thirteen Teddy fell from his pony during a match in England he attended annually as the guest of the royal family. Teddy Manning died with his boots on and in the company of gentlemen.

Geoffrey Williams arrived on the scene

as, of all things, tennis instructor to Lady Cynthia Horowitz. He resembled Wallace Reid of the silents and, unlike past "gorgeous" tennis instructors on Lady C.'s payroll, he actually knew how to play the game. In addition, Geoff filled a pair of tennis shorts, as Lolly Spindrift put it, "with remarkable efficiency."

Melva and I met on the Palm Beach tennis beat and made a good team both on and off the courts. We enjoyed our easygoing relationship too much to ruin it with even a hint of romance, and when Veronica came down from prep school on long weekends, we made it a jolly threesome, munching hamburgers at the Pelican Club. "I like this much better than the Bath and Tennis," precocious Veronica declared. Out of the mouths of babes . . .

When Geoff started courting the widow Manning and she encouraged the attention, I kept an open mind and a closed mouth regarding the affair. PBR had it that Geoff was a tennis pro, but I couldn't find him listed on any of the tennis pro circuits. He was also touted to be a golf pro, and although he was usually under par, I couldn't find him listed on any of the golf pro circuits. He was also reputed to be Geoffrey Wolinsky, minor Russian nobility, whose ancestors made it out of St. Petersburg a minute before the Bolsheviks marched in.

Finally, it was put about by those who had tried and failed to win the heart of Melva Ashton Manning, that Geoff was one Jeffrey Wolinsky of Russian Jewish lineage whose family made it out of Kiev before the Cossacks marched in. Take your pick of any/all of the above. One thing we do know: Geoff was, and this is PBF, a man who found women irresistible, and the ladies, too often, returned the compliment.

The gate was open and the blinking red light told me the alarm was turned off. For me, or did someone neglect to put it on this evening? I drove up the circular drive to the front door and saw Hattie, Melva's housekeeper, awaiting my arrival. Hattie was a short, plump woman with gray hair pulled tightly back from her face and knotted into a bun. She wore black dresses with white collars and cuffs. Hattie had been with Melva from before Veronica was born, and Veronica had to be twenty, at least.

"Mr. Archy. Thank God. It's terrible what has happened. Terrible. We must help Missy, Mr. Archy. She said, 'Call the police, Hattie,' but I said, 'No, call Mr. Archy. He will know what to do.' " She rambled on in that vein as she led me into the house and to the drawing room, where Melva was seated in a wing chair, smoking a cigarette. She wore a robe over her nightgown and her feet were bare.

"I gave these up ten years ago, Archy, remember? I said if I ever again took one puff I'd be back to two packs a day, and look at this . . ." She pointed to an ashtray overflowing with butts smoked down to the filter. A glass and a bottle of Dewar's stood beside the ashtray. "Would you like a drink, Archy?"

"I don't think so, Melva. The cigarettes won't help, and neither will the Scotch."

Her eyes were glassy, like those of a china doll, and just as comprehending. A small woman, Melva now resembled a child trying to fill a grown-up's chair. Her fashionably short hair was beginning to gray, and I doubt if she would ever attempt to hold back the tide. "Would you like to view the remains, Archy?"

Hattie let out a gasp and covered her mouth with her fist. This was only going to get worse before it got better.

"Where?"

"The solarium," Hattie answered.

I made my way down a long hall to a glass-enclosed room overlooking the pool and furnished with potted plants, exotic flowers, wicker furniture, and Geoffrey Williams lying on his back, stark naked, his chest covered with congealed blood. Pants, shirt, and a pair of briefs stood in a heap on the floor not far from his tousled head of hair. A pair of abandoned Gucci loafers completed the inventory of Geoff's outer- and underwear on his last day in our vale of tears. A gun lay beside the body. How like Melva, to abandon the weapon like a toy that no longer pleased her. There was always someone to pick up after Melva Ashton Manning Williams.

The only thing I learned from the scene of the crime was that Geoffrey Williams was definitely not Jewish.

Back in the drawing room Melva was still smoking and Hattie was still crying. "Why, Melva?" I asked, taking an English Oval from my shirt pocket and lighting it. When in Rome, and all that.

"Why what, Archy? Why did I marry him, or why did I shoot him?" She sounded less hysterical, more lucid. Was the shock wearing off, or the Scotch taking effect?

I shrugged. "It's your call."

"I married him because I was lonely and he was handsome and charming and the best lay in town. Does that surprise you?"

It didn't, but poor Hattie had her fist in her mouth once again.

"I shot him because I caught him in there, with a woman. A young woman. They were screwing."

"He was never faithful, Melva, and I don't think he ever pretended he was."

"But he never flaunted it, Archy. We had an understanding. He could do as he wished as long as he didn't frighten the horses on Main Street. What I mean, Archy, is that it was something he did in the dark. I was his wife, and he never so much as looked at another woman in my presence. Oh, I heard the rumors, but I could never prove them, and that suited me just fine. It didn't diminish his looks, his charm, or his performance in bed, and I liked the envious glances of other women when I appeared on the arm of Geoffrey Williams. Then tonight, in our home, he shattered our delicate balance."

"Where was he tonight?"

"A dinner party aboard Phil Meecham's yacht."

That accounted for Geoff's informal attire. Meecham's invitations always said, "Don't Dress," hoping everyone would take him literally.

"I refused to go and went to my room to read," Melva continued. "Geoff made some calls and then came up to tell me Lolly Spindrift was going to pick him up and drive him home after Meecham's party. He left the Rolls so I wouldn't feel marooned. Hattie wasn't feeling well and went to her room to lie down shortly after lunch. I didn't see her again until—until it happened."

"That's right, Mr. Archy. I was not well. I think it's the change of climate. I always have to adjust to the new climate."

"I heard a car pull in around eleven and waited for Geoff to come to bed," Melva was saying. "A half hour later, I was still waiting. I never heard Lolly drive off, so I grew concerned. I took the gun from my night table—."

"Why do you keep a gun?" I interrupted.

"Why? I don't know. For just such an occasion as this, I guess. I thought there was a burglar in the house. It was Teddy's gun. We've had it for years. I wasn't even sure it was loaded."

"So you came down here . . ."

"Yes," she said. "Here to the drawing room. All the lights were out and I lit lamps as I went from room to room. Then I heard voices coming from the solarium. I went there and saw them. Geoff and a woman. A very young woman, I believe. They were on the floor and she—she was on top of him, riding him, you might say. I think I screamed. She—the woman—stood up, grabbed her clothes and fled.

"Geoff turned toward me and started to get up. I was shouting, hysterical, blind with rage. He was laughing. Yes, laughing, as if we were actors in a French farce. The more I ranted, the more he laughed. I was incensed. I heard her car drive off and wondered if she was still naked and what a scandal there would be if she were stopped by the police. Then I think he noticed the gun I was pointing at him. He raised a hand toward me and said something, I don't know what, all I could hear was my own voice deafening me to any other sound—including the gunshot. I didn't know I had fired until I saw him fall back, saw the blood . . ." She buried her face in her hands and sobbed. Hattie went to her and stroked her head. When the weeping and trembling subsided she looked up and said, "Veronica."

"Veronica," I repeated. "Where is she?"

"That's why I called you, Archy. Veronica. I want you to find her and keep her with you until things quiet down. Once we notify the police, this place will be a zoo. The local *paparazzi* and television crews will set up camp on Ocean Boulevard and as soon as the New York boys get wind of it they'll come down by the planeload."

"Where is she?" I asked again.

"At a house party. I have the address." She withdrew a piece of notepaper from the pocket of her robe.

"When did she leave here?"

Melva shrugged. "Before Geoff left, I think. She came up to say she was going."

"She has her own car?"

"Yes. You'll do it, Archy. You'll find Veronica?"

"I will, don't worry about that. Call the police as soon as I leave. If they find me here they'll detain me." She nodded her understanding. "One more thing, Melva. The alarm system. It was off when I drove in. Did you turn it off?"

"No. We never activate it during the day, only at night. First one to drive out the gate for the evening sets the alarm. It's a house rule and it's usually Veronica who does it. She's been out every evening since we arrived."

"So if Veronica went out first this evening, she set the alarm. But who shut it off if you didn't?"

"Perhaps Geoff. To give his lady friend a quick exit."

"You have to know the digital code to drive in, Melva. To drive out all you need is two hands to open the gate."

"I don't know what you mean, Archy."

"I'm not sure I know either." I gave her a peck on the cheek. "A proper Bostonian named Crowninshield once said married men make lousy husbands. He was right."

It didn't get a laugh, but it helped. "Chin up, lady. McNally and Son are at your service."

And because the rich are different from you and me, Hattie escorted me to the front door as befits a housekeeper come hell, high water, or murder. "Can you tell me anything more, Hattie?" I probed.

"Like Missy said, Mr. Archy, I was in my room most of the day. The room over the kitchen, up the back stairs. The shouting woke me. It was after eleven. I listened but I couldn't hear what they were saying. When I heard the gun go *BOOM,* I thought we had been robbed. I was afraid, Mr. Archy. I thought the crooks had killed Missy. Then the getaway car making so much noise, just like in the movies. I came down and . . . and . . ."

"Okay, Hattie. Take it easy. The police will be here in five minutes. Stay with Mrs. Williams as long as you can. I'll be in touch in the morning."

I put the piece of paper Melva had given me into my jacket pocket and drove off in the Miata. I wanted to get as far from the murder scene as possible before the PBPD moved in. I turned south on the A1A because I knew the police would approach from the north. My Miata is not exactly indiscreet, especially if Al Rogoff happened to be working the graveyard shift this chilly evening.

Well, I thought, Palm Beach can now boast a society *crime passionnel,* or crime of passion, which clever defense lawyers often equate to "temporary insanity," getting their clients off with being placed in psychiatric care at most. However, murdering one's husband was not new to high society. Regardless of Melva's fate, when the media quotes her saying, "She was riding him," Melva Ashton Manning Williams will kick off a *cause célèbre* unparalleled in Palm Beach's short and audacious history.

4

AT ONE IN the morning I had very little company on Ocean Boulevard. Were my fellow travelers—besides exceeding the legal speed limit—hurrying to or from dangerous liaisons? Under a starry Florida sky, wrapped in our mobile suits of armor, we were a landlocked version of ships passing in the night. I assumed mine was the only ship fleeing a murder scene, but life in Palm Beach had taught me to assume nothing, expect anything, and look to the morning papers to reveal what exactly it was that went bump in the night.

When I thought I was a safe distance from Melva and her police escort, I pulled off the road and into a driveway, stopping just before the security gate. This one, unlike the Williamses', I was sure would be armed. Except for the cadenced roll of the surf on the other side of the highway, a sudden break in the light traffic rendered the spot eerily silent. A full moon completed a scene more suitable to lovers and werewolves than poor Archy in search of Melva's offspring. I removed the penlite from the Miata's glove compartment and dug the piece of paper Melva had so conveniently given me from my jacket pocket.

Reading it, I was seized with what the French call déjà vu and what I call being goosed by the fickle finger of fate. The address so carefully recorded by Melva was instantly, and distressingly, recognizable. Hillcrest! A decaying mansion on Lake Worth.

The fact that there was not a hill within sight of the place made the abode's name as ludicrous as its vaguely Spanish architecture. I saw Hillcrest as clearly in the penlite's circular gleam as I did the day I followed Lady Cynthia Horowitz to the house that proved to be her rented love nest. A nest she was sharing with my father, Prescott McNally.

Rusted wrought-iron gates, grass sprouting from a brick driveway, and more then a few red tiles missing from the roof was the Hillcrest I knew—and abhorred. The fact that I had been following Lady C. in the line of duty—trying to find her missing stamps—did not lessen the shock and fury of my discovery.

I convinced the lady to dismiss her lover in exchange for not telling her insurance company that her precious stamps were phony. I also returned the stamps that had never been stolen but given, by her, to the guy who was trying to sell them. Lady Cynthia Horowitz, in spite of her title, was far from noble. The lesson I learned, with relish I must admit, was that even Prescott McNally had an Achilles' heel, even if in *mon père*'s case, the weak spot proved to be a tad higher. Later, however, I did wonder if father's affair with that oft-married septuagenarian with the Miss America figure was the result of Eros's dart or the abundance of Lady C.'s gilt-edged securities. In father's case I refused to give love the benefit of the doubt.

To this day, father does not know that I was the cause of Lady C. giving him the brush-off, and Lady C., when she's not trying to seduce me, treats me with a mixture of distrust and respect but not, alas, fear. It would take more than Archy McNally to put the fear of man or God in that woman.

I drove south until I came to a winding road below Manalapan Beach. This spit of land, between the Atlantic Ocean and Lake Worth, is so narrow that a kid with a good arm could toss a ball from the beach into the lake. I made a right, entering Hillcrest's driveway, and came to an abrupt halt. Mine was the last in a line of cars parked on the brick driveway which I knew meandered down to a garage and a turnaround at the rear of the house. The noise coming from Hillcrest told me that there were probably more cars parked on the back lawn—a green expanse overlooking the lake and a decaying dock.

On my last visit the place had been as silent, deserted, and mournful as a crypt. Now, with the lit windows and the sound of music, or what some call music, Hillcrest was more Studio 54 in its heyday. But unlike Studio 54, where many came but few were chosen, there was no guardian of the velvet rope to banish the many and welcome the few.

At Studio Hillcrest all I had to do was turn the knob and walk in. The music was pure disco, the beat of which has always reminded me of how the ogre's heart must have sounded when he chased Jack around the beanstalk. I found myself in a huge entrance foyer, facing a broad staircase. The center hall was flanked by archways to reveal two enormous rooms nearly devoid of furniture but overflowing with humanity. Rather young humanity. I could see makeshift bars set up in both rooms, their surfaces crowded with wine bottles that never knew a cork. The air was so thick with the aroma of funny cigarettes, one could get arrested for breathing.

It was a scene out of *Our Dancing Daughters,* and I half expected to see Joan Crawford doing the Charleston on a grand piano while wiggling out of her panties from beneath her crepe de chine gown. What I got, alas, was Binky Watrous.

"Archy, what are you doing here?"

"I came for the cuisine. *Et tu?*"

"I came to cohabitate."

Binky's statements of fact often defy the snappy retort. This was one of them. "Whose house is this?" I asked.

"Beats me, Archy."

Need I say here that in order to be heard Binky and I, hands cupped about our lips to simulate megaphones, were shouting into each other's ears?

"Who invited you?" I asked next, knowing I might as well have asked Binky to define the theory of relativity. Binky has always reminded me of a grown-up version of the child actor Claude Jarman Jr. Limp blond hair, limp blond mustache, and large, limpid eyes not unlike those of the fawn poor Claude toted about in *The Yearling.* Binky, in fact, could have been cast as both the boy and his pet—an all-time first, even for Hollywood.

"No one invited me," came the not surprising answer. "Who invited you, Archy?"

"Same guy."

"Who's that?"

"Never mind, Binky. Did you just happen to drop in? I mean, it's a bit off the beaten path for gate-crashing, or were you rowing down Lake Worth when you saw the lights and heard the enchanting music of the Sirens?"

"Neither, Archy. Hillcrest is the talk of Palm Beach." Then, after a pause, "With the young set, that is."

I am on the good side of forty, by several years, and Binky, I'm sure, is in clear view of thirty. So, if Hillcrest was the talk of the young set, I could have asked Binky Watrous how he heard about it. I didn't because we would then have to play this painful scene again.

But mention of the young set did inspire me to look more closely at the boys and girls—gyrating, imbibing, and puffing—now that my eyes had become more accustomed to the lighting that was on par with the radiance of my penlite. They looked barely old enough to drink, let alone gyrate. It all appeared illegal and immoral, but then I'm neither the law nor the guy able to cast the first stone.

"Fill me in on the talk of the young set," I shouted at Binky.

"This is a party house. Something going on most nights of the week. Everything is very loose and no one asks for ID."

There was nothing loose about the way these modern-day vamps clung to their Valentinos. "And the booze is compliments of the house?"

"It's BYOB, Archy. Bring your own bottle. But the ice is on the house."

But not, I was certain, the cannabis and any other mood enhancers being offered to our young set. I did know, from my afore-mentioned investigation of the place, that Hillcrest had been built many years ago by a man who had made his money manufac-turing portable johns. That product's partic-ular odor, it seems, was destined to haunt Hillcrest. I also knew the man had left it to his wife, who, when her time came, left it to her alma mater.

Their children contested the bequest, and while school and progeny did battle the house was available on a month-to-month basis with the rent going into an escrow account to be presented to the winner. I also knew the rent was five thousand bucks a month. The present tenant either had a thick wallet or had come up with an odious scheme to pay for his keep.

All speculation, I know, but I thought it wise to caution my young friend. "I don't think I would make this place a habit, Binky, unless you enjoy riding in paddy wagons."

"You know I'm not into anything heavy, Archy." Poor Binky was offended.

"I know," I assured him, "but guilt by association in a joint like this is still guilt."

The G word made Binky wonder, "Are you on a case, Archy?"

"Actually, I'm looking for Veronica Manning."

Binky smiled, revealing a fine set of teeth. Here was a topic to which my friend could instantly warm. "Some dish," he informed me.

"Like I said, Binky, I came for the cuisine."

It takes Binky a few moments to get the drift of my verbal acumen, but when his brain made the connection he let out an appreciative chuckle and patted my shoulder. "Is she here?" I asked.

"I talked to her a while ago and then I saw her go off to one of the chat rooms."

"The what rooms?"

"Private chat rooms, just like on the World Wide Web. In case you haven't noticed, it gets a little noisy in here, so if you connect with someone and want to get it on, one-on-

one, you just slip off to a chat room. I tell you, Archy, this place has everything."

Another Watrous statement better left undisputed. Instead I queried, "Was Veronica with someone when you saw her head for a chat room?"

"You don't go to a chat room alone, Archy."

"What about people who like to talk to themselves?" Before Binky could utter yet another profound observation I told him to point in the general direction of the chat rooms where those connected could get it on, one-on-one. I am proudly computer illiterate, but I know the difference between a World Wide Web and a spider web.

Moving in the general direction of Binky's protruding forefinger, I walked down the dark passage beyond the staircase and came to a small hall and three closed doors. What I guessed was the dining room was to the right, and what must have been called the sun room, with a panoramic view of the lake, to the left. Another door, directly under the staircase, I was sure would open to reveal a flight of stairs leading down to the kitchen and pantry. I would wager my weekly stipend that the kitchen was connected to the dining room by a device once known as a dumbwaiter, a label that has surely been deemed politically incorrect for obvious reasons.

I chose the dining room, opened the door, and looked in. The room was lit by a chandelier hanging from the center of the ceiling and dimmed by a rheostat to feign the warm glow of candlelight. Veronica's hair, blond and shoulder length, shimmered in the flattering light, and her slim body was silhouetted against a curtainless window.

"Room's taken," a masculine voice belonging to the shadow facing Veronica advised me.

"I'm looking for Veronica Manning," I advised the voice.

"What do you want?" The shadow was annoyed.

"Archy?" Veronica spoke. "Is it Archy McNally?"

"In person." I advanced into the room. The chandelier looked large enough to have once graced a table that could seat twelve. Someone had removed the table but had left the accompanying chairs and placed them haphazardly about the room. Much to my relief, there was not a bed in sight.

"Archy?" Veronica called again. "What are you doing here?"

"If I said I was here for the cuisine, would you believe me?"

"Who is this guy?" Veronica's one-on-one was not pleased with my presence.

I couldn't see his face clearly enough to pick him out of a line-up, but the voice told me he was young and cocky, and his outline suggested someone tall, and (by de facto reasoning) dark. I wondered if he was the young man Connie had seen Veronica with at Lady C.'s reception.

"He's Archy—" Veronica began, but I interrupted. I didn't fancy my name resounding through the unhallowed halls of Hillcrest twice, in rapid succession.

"I'm a friend of Veronica's mother and my business is with Veronica."

"Look, buddy . . ." The shadow took a step forward, but Veronica put out her hand to restrain him.

"But how did you know where to find me, Archy?" A note of apprehension crept into her voice.

"Melva told me you would be here."

"My mother?" Veronica cried. "My mother sent you here, Archy?"

"She did."

"Why? What's happened?"

She came toward me and the young man was wise enough to stand his ground. I touched her bare elbow and said, "Let's go outside, Veronica. I'll explain everything."

"Something's happened to my mother. Please, Archy, what is it?" Apprehension was fast giving way to hysteria.

Taking a firm grip on her arm, I began to lead her from the room. Before her young swain could follow, I looked over my shoulder and told him to stay put. "It's a family matter, and I'm taking Veronica home. No need to see us out."

Veronica cut his protest short. "I'm going with Archy," she said. "Please don't interfere. I'll be fine." If he had a name she never spoke it, and it occurred to me that she might know him as well as I did.

As we passed through the doorway I caught the scent of her perfume. Its aroma was very exotic, very arousing, and, surely, very expensive. Walking side by side, I was aware of her height—the top of her blond hair, parted on the left, came well past my shoulder and I doubted that she was wearing high heels. Melva's little girl had truly grown up.

As we went from the dark passage into the somewhat better illuminated entrance foyer, I could see that she was wearing a sleeveless ice-blue sheath, knee length, with a scoop neckline and no jewelry. She didn't need any. Her flawless complexion, blue eyes, and sensuous lips would have dimmed the Hope Diamond. A brief year had transformed Melva's darling from a cute teenager to a ravishing woman.

When I recovered and was sure I could speak with some semblance of authority, I pointed to her smart Judith Leiber minaudière, suspended from her shoulder by a gold chain. "Your car keys in there?"

"Yes. Why?"

"Let me have them."

She stopped short and shook her hand free of my arm. "I will not. And I won't take another step until you tell me what this is all about."

Actually, I couldn't blame her for drawing a line on my intrusion into her life. I had invaded this den of iniquity, interrupted her one-on-one with the shadow, and now I demanded the keys to her car. I owed her an explanation and decided to give it to her without preamble or apology. Knowing that it was impossible to be overheard, I blurted, "Geoff is dead. Your mother shot him."

She froze. Her eyes held mine like two blue agates. I feared she had stopped breathing and hoped I wouldn't have to slap her face, as they do in the movies, to bring her back to the land of the living. I was relieved when she finally mumbled incredulously, "Tell me this is a nightmare, Archy."

"I wish I could, my dear, but it isn't. I'm here, you're here, and Geoff is very dead." If I sounded a bit glib, it was only because I didn't know how else to sound. Telling a young woman that her mother had just committed *murder* was an all-time first for Archy McNally, and may it never happen again.

"I want to go home," Veronica stated.

"Not tonight, Veronica. There's no one there except a team of policemen doing their job." And poor Hattie, I didn't add, with her fist in her mouth.

"Where's my mother, Archy?"

"By now, in custody, I'm sure."

"I want to be with her," she insisted.

"You can't. At least not now. You're spending the night with me." Under any other circumstances the statement would have been embarrassingly suggestive. Here it came off as a declaration of fact, nothing less and surely nothing more.

"Tell me what happened, Archy."

"I will, on the way home. Now please give me your car keys."

"Why?"

"I have a friend here. He'll drive your car home. You, as I said, will come with me."

She obeyed meekly. "What are you driving, Veronica?"

"Mercedes convertible."

Knowing the young set of Palm Beach, I imagined there was more than one Mercedes convertible parked at Hillcrest. "Color?"

"Silver with a blue canvas top."

She handed me the keys and, certain she couldn't leave without me, I told her to wait for me outside the front door. I elbowed my way into the room I had seen Binky emerge from and found him wandering about, still unattached. Poor Binky.

"Did you find her?" he shouted.

"I did. And I need a favor, Binky."

"That's what I'm here for, Archy."

I didn't remind him of his earlier reason for being here and figured he must have given up all hope in that direction. As luck would have it, he had come with a friend, so he could drive Veronica's car to my place while his friend followed in Binky's car. I told him what I wanted him to do, but not why, and gave him Veronica's car keys and a description of her wheels.

"Neat," Binky commented.

"Mercedes-Benz thinks so, too, Binky."

"Is this a case, Archy?" he asked again, hopefully. Binky enjoys playing Watson to my Sherlock.

"The game is afoot, my boy."

With that, I headed for the door, wondering if Veronica Manning would ever express sympathy at the demise of her stepfather.

5

I TOLD VERONICA Manning everything I knew of the events that had taken place in her home after she had left for the evening. She listened with a stony silence that remained for a long time as we drove north. The A1A was now even emptier of cars than on my trip down. Sitting in the passenger seat, my jacket draped over her shoulders and her eyes fixed on the road, the sophisticated lady of impeccable dress and one-on-one encounters now looked more like a bewildered child in need of a champion but not a handkerchief. No one could accuse the Manning women of overreacting.

When I had led her to my car she was shivering, and I suspected the condition was due to shock and the brevity of her dress. Archy the gallant had immediately offered his jacket. Now, driving in my shirt sleeves, I realized her condition could also have been due to the early morning temperature, but being a loyal Floridian I refused to turn on the Miata's heater.

"Do you have a cigarette?" These were the first words she spoke since my disclosure.

"No. But you do."

Without hesitation she dug into my jacket pockets until she found what she was looking for. "What are these?"

"English Ovals," I informed her. "You'll like them."

"Do you want one?"

"Please."

She put two cigarettes between her lips, struck a match, lighted both, and passed one to me. "I saw a man do this in a movie on the late, late show," Veronica said.

"The man was Paul Henreid and the woman he handed the lit cigarette to was Bette Davis."

"I didn't like him," Veronica announced.

"Paul Henreid?"

"Don't be arch, Archy."

I don't think "arch" was the word she wanted, but rather than put a damper on her clever rebuttal I kept my opinion to myself. Besides, there was an edge to her voice that told me this was not the time to engage in verbal sparring with Veronica Manning.

"If you mean Geoff, one shouldn't speak ill of the dead, my dear."

"Why not?" She smoked, I noticed, without inhaling. The cigarette was merely a prop. Was her stiff upper lip also more show than substance? There was a lot to be learned about this young lady and I imagined the lessons would be sheer delight.

"I don't know why not. It just isn't done," I told her.

"My stepfather did many things that just aren't done."

"Your mother never complained."

"My mother was a fool. Did she ever give you that line about not frightening the horses on Main Street?"

"As a matter of fact, she did."

"Don't rock the boat. Don't rattle the beads. Leave well enough alone. Less said, soonest mended. Those are some other tenets my mother swore by. She knew what he was up to, but instead of tossing him out on his behind, she pretended it didn't matter as long as he didn't frighten the horses on Main Street. When her own eyes blew the cover on her denial, the volcano finally erupted."

Melva's daughter sounded like a cross between a page out of a Psychology 101 text and a lawyer summing up the defense's case.

"Maybe she loved him. Did that ever occur to you?"

"If you're referring to his prowess in the bedroom, Archy, just say so."

"I would, if that's what I was referring to."

She rolled down the window and discarded her cigarette. Waste not, want not was a tenet I lived by, but didn't say so. The cigarette's glow carved a red line in the early morning breeze, and I recalled the red line extending from the hole in Geoff's chest down to his navel—his body as cold as his stepdaughter's feelings for him.

"I'm sorry," she said, raising the window. "I'm just rambling."

"I understand."

She turned her head toward me. "There was a time when I thought mother would marry you."

"And would that have pleased you?" My heart gave a tiny leap in anticipation of her answer. Archy the fool.

"I liked you and you made me laugh a lot. But the way you dressed! I was afraid of what the girls at school would say if they saw you in one of your silk berets. I think I was going to try to palm you off as an artist."

"Con artist, no doubt."

"Well, you must admit your style is not exactly conventional."

"I'm an individual."

"You're cute, Archy."

Finally, a statement we both agreed upon.

After this brief respite from our more weighty conversation, she lapsed into silence once again, and I did nothing to discourage it until we neared home. Then, quite casually, I asked, "Did you turn on the alarm at the front gate when you went out this evening?"

She was either nodding out or in a trance. "Did I do what?"

"Your mother told me tonight that the first person to leave the house in the evening turned on the security system at the front gate. She said it was a house rule."

"It is. And yes, I usually turn it on."

"And did you tonight? Or should I say last night?"

She shook her head. "I honestly don't remember. Why? Is it important?"

"It wasn't on when I arrived at your place."

"If I turned it on—and my guess is that I did, out of pure habit—Geoff must have turned it off when he came in."

"Why would he do that?"

"Because we don't keep it armed during the day. It's not necessary and a nuisance with all our coming and going."

"But no one would turn it off when they came in," I argued. "That would leave it unarmed for the remainder of the night."

"Archy, I have a headache and I don't understand what this is about. Maybe I didn't turn it on when I left. I can't remember. But what does it have to do with my mother . . ." And here, Veronica Manning finally broke down and cried.

Hobo came out to greet us, rather reluctantly I thought, and took an immediate shine to Veronica's ankles. No fool, Hobo. I took her to the guest room on the second floor, which, thanks to Ursi, was always at the ready.

"It was my sister's room," I said, "and when she visits with her family she still occupies it. I'm sure you'll find something suitably feminine to sleep in. There are fresh towels in the bath and perhaps even a jar of night cream to make you feel right at home."

"Thank you, but I'm a soap-and-water girl." She allowed my jacket to slide off her shoulders with the graceful ease of an exotic dancer. Archy the optimist. "I'm going to look a sight in this dress at breakfast."

"A very lovely sight, night or day," I said. "But I think my sister has left some casual wear about. Mostly things that she's grown out of, but you didn't hear that from me. Jeans and sweatshirts abounded, as I recall, and I'm sure you'll find some that will fit."

"Jeans, a sweatshirt, and Manolo Blahnik pumps. How chic."

"Hey, I told your mother I'd put you up for the night, not outfit you. But with any luck there should be a pair or two of Dora's sneakers about."

"Dora? Of course, your father's passion for Dickens. You see, I haven't forgotten.

Where's Dora now?" Veronica removed her Blahnik pumps as we talked. Perhaps if we talked long enough . . .

"Arizona. Scottsdale, actually."

"And she has a family?"

"Indeed. A husband and three children. Or is it three point two children? Well, you can be sure Dora has whatever the national average boasts. They are a very average family, but nice in spite of that."

"I'm sure," she said with little enthusiasm. She walked to a window at the far end of the room and pretended to look out, but I was sure all she could see was the dark reflection of her own face in the glass. Then she turned to face me once again and cried, "What's going to happen to us, Archy?"

"Do you want me to say everything is going to be just fine?"

"Don't you dare."

"Okay. Then I'll tell you. It's going to be a three-ring circus with you and your mother jumping through the hoops and the press cracking the whip. I was able to protect you tonight because we're one short step ahead of the media, but when your mother was booked—I would say about two hours ago—the news hit the wire services. My guess is that the local boys are already charging your unarmed security gate and the New York boys are cabbing it to La Guardia and Kennedy. Unless you choose to disappear, it's going to be hell, kid."

"I won't leave my mother," she protested. "When will she be released?"

"If, not when, the judge allows her out on bail. There could be a hearing as soon as tomorrow, or today, actually. She'll have called her lawyers in New York, but the earliest they can get here is late tonight."

"Can you represent her until they arrive?"

"Unfortunately, no. A disagreement between myself and Yale Law makes that impossible. But I will ask my father to arrange to have someone from the office speak to Melva first thing this morning."

"Thank you, Archy."

"Now let's try to get some sleep. We'll need it, believe me."

"What are her chances, Archy?"

"Very good, I would say. Her offense, I'm sure, will be tried as a crime of passion. Seeing Geoff and that women having sex in her home rendered your mother temporarily insane, making her not responsible for her actions. It wasn't premeditated murder.

Hence, they'll most likely go easy on her. Of course, a lot depends on the corroborating evidence of your stepfather's playmate."

"Is that necessary?" She seemed naïvely surprised.

"Necessary? My dear Veronica, it's imperative. Without her testimony, Melva's word is pure hearsay."

She shook her head and grimaced. "But it's so sordid. So cheap. The kind of thing people like us don't talk about."

How pathetic, I thought. "If it's the kind of thing people like you don't talk about, then it's the kind of thing people like you shouldn't indulge in. But you did. Or your stepfather did, and the volcano erupted, unquote."

"I'm sorry, Archy." She buried her face in her hands and bowed her head, causing her hair to cascade like a golden veil. "How many times have I said that tonight?"

"Who's counting?"

"I didn't mean it the way it sounded," she said, picking up where she had left off. "But suppose they can't find this woman?"

"It's not a thought conducive to a good night's sleep, so let's concentrate on something more cheerful, like World War Three."

She smiled and came to me, kissing my cheek. I was once again aware of her particular scent and—not helping my role as benevolent and benign benefactor—the feel of her breasts against my chest. Veronica Manning wasn't wearing a bra.

"Thank you, Archy. I'm grateful for your help and this elegant port in a storm."

I wondered what would have happened if I took her in my arms and kissed those sensuous lips. I was ashamed of my thoughts, but that didn't make them any less potent.

In my third-floor nest I undressed, splashed cold water on my face, and got into bed. Sleep did not come when my head touched the pillow—or for some time thereafter. My mind throbbed with thoughts both prurient and academic. The former I know how to quiet, but refrained; the latter I struggled with until dawn.

Why was the alarm at the front gate of the Williamses' house turned off?

Did Veronica always give her mother the address of where she could be found when she went out in the evening?

When Melva heard a car return she said she thought it was Geoff. Why didn't she think it could have been Veronica, who was also out that evening?

And something Hattie said had struck me as odd at the time, but the thought had vanished before taking root. What was it?

When I did fall asleep, I dreamed I heard Hobo barking.

6

THE PIERCING RING of my telephone jolted me out of a sound sleep at ten A.M. I awoke thinking Quasimodo had lost it in the campanile and immediately pulled the covers over my head. This did nothing to discourage the caller. I rose and moved toward the dastardly object like Boris Karloff in *The Mummy.* The telephone, it is my belief, is the underlying cause of modern man's inhumanity to man. Its jarring summons on this gray morning did nothing to dispel that learned thesis.

"Archy here."

"Archy's father here."

This mummy was instantly wide awake, if not raring to go.

"Yes, sir?"

"Did I wake you?"

"I was about, sir."

"About what?"

"About to get up, actually."

"Late night, Archy?"

"Late morning would be nearer the mark."

"I take it the young lady Ursi told me was asleep in the guest room is the Manning child?"

"She's not a child," I quickly corrected, in defense of my lascivious longings. My few hours' rest had done nothing to alleviate my untoward desires. "She's twenty-one, at least."

"The child's age is of no consequence, Archy."

"If you say so, sir."

"And I take it, once again, that the rather showy vehicle blocking our garage, and making me late for an early morning client meeting, belongs to Miss Manning?"

Hanging by the thumbs was too kind a punishment for Binky Watrous. Chinese water torture? Iron mask? "It is. I had to . . ."

"No need to explain, Archy. Regarding our bid for poor Melva's case, you've obviously held up your end very well indeed, and I've been doing my share here at the office."

Bid? I thought I was helping a friend, not selling the services of McNally & Son. The sire's approach to things material never ceased to amaze me when it didn't amuse me. And judging from his hale and hearty tone, father was in a jubilant state this morning, which I attributed to the sound of cash registers ringing on Royal Palm Way.

"I spoke to Melva's lawyers in New York," he continued. "They do have a good man qualified to practice in Florida, and he, with a team, are on their way here as we speak. I've offered them office space at McNally & Son as well as *carte blanche* use of telephones, fax machines, etc. They have wisely accepted. We'll also give them input from our perspective as Florida-based counsel."

When they see the *carte blanche* tab, they'll think they've rented space in Buckingham Palace. Of course, I didn't say that. What I did say was, "I was going to ask you to send one of your attorneys to the courthouse to see what they could do for Melva before her lawyers get here."

Our operation is a legal supermarket, sans the pushcarts and double coupons. Estate planning, taxes, revocable and charitable trusts are our mainstay, but we also employ associates skilled in litigation, real estate, copyrights, trademarks, patents, divorce, malpractice, personal and product liability, and, on a retainer basis, a man qualified to practice criminal law. This last was surely the man father would dispatch to represent Melva.

"Naturally, I sent a most qualified attorney to consult with Melva first thing this morning."

Naturally. "How is Melva doing?"

"Remarkably well," father said. "Class will tell, my boy. We're trying to get a bail hearing as soon as this afternoon, but I doubt that will happen. However, I'd rather have her lawyers here when we go before a judge."

So, if she's not let out on bail, McNally & Son won't be held accountable. Shrewdness, like class, will also tell. "Very good, sir. I thought I would stick with Veronica, Miss Manning, that is, and help her get back to her home without being bamboozled by the press."

"Very noble, Archy, I'm sure. However, I need you here at precisely twelve noon."

"Nothing that could be postponed?" I asked hopefully.

"Afraid not, Archy. We have an appointment with John Fairhurst the Third."

Well! No wonder *mon père* was jubilant. McNally & Son suddenly held Malva Ashton Manning Williams and John Fairhurst III in tandem, so to speak, and all in one day. John the First was a mogul on par with the Messrs. Morgan, Gould, Carnegie, Mellon, and Frick. I could see my father twirling his mustache as he spoke the name. John Fairhurst III was Palm Beach's most distinguished citizen and its richest, although to Prescott McNally those attributes would seem redundant.

"*We* have an appointment, sir? Surely you don't mean Discreet Inquiries."

"I think I do. Mr. Fairhurst was a bit vague on the phone, which, from past experience, makes me believe that he's in an embarrassing situation."

"Surely not like Vance Tremaine," I protested, perhaps too ardently.

"We won't jump to conclusions until we hear the man out. Now leave the girl in your mother's care and get here as quickly as you can. And Archy, do dress properly for this meeting."

I was rudely awakened to run to the aid of a rich man caught with his pants down and instead of a thank-you I was served a backhanded slur on the appropriateness of my choice of apparel. If I didn't need the job I would have gone back to bed; however, my bed went with the job, or, put more bluntly, if my job went so would my bed—and board.

I showered, shaved, and stood in my T-shirt and briefs—the ones depicting rabbits in pursuit of rabbits—contemplating my wardrobe when the phone rang again. Before I could say, "Archy here," Lolly Spindrift assaulted me with "Is she still with you?"

"Who's she, Lol?"

"Don't get cute with me, Archy. You owe me. Remember Vance Tremaine?"

"I also remember *The Alamo* and *The Sands of Iwo Jima*. Both starring John Wayne."

"You're holding Veronica Manning," Lolly insisted.

Geoff's murder couldn't have made the early editions, but Lolly's editors must have called him as soon as the news hit the wire services. Lolly, after all, was their society editor, and Melva Ashton Manning Williams was society with a capital S.

"Holding her under lock and key? Never."

"You're at your worst when you try to be clever, Archy. Veronica is with you, I know."

"Flattery will get you noplace, Lol, and how, pray tell, do you know Veronica is here?"

"I talked to Binky Watrous."

"Since when is Binky Watrous a prime source for your gossip sheet?"

"Since one of my spies among the young set told me he saw Binky and Veronica at some ghastly party last night. I know Melva is in custody and I can't get to her yet, so I tried to contact Veronica but couldn't get through. I think the phone at the Williams' manse is off the hook. I called my informer on the off chance that he knew something and struck pay dirt."

The Palm Beach grapevine was in overdrive and only luck had prevented Lolly's spy from seeing me at that ghastly party, but thanks to Binky this didn't prevent me from being fingered as Veronica's guardian.

"Binky, by the by, is in a foul mood," Lolly added. "He says he's in need of a rabies shot, thanks to you."

Rabies? Was I to be spared nothing this wretched morning? A glance at my desk clock forced me to put Binky, rabies, and child spies on a back burner. Wishing to do the same with Lolly Spindrift, I ceded, "Okay, she's here, but I'm on my way out and can't talk now. Later, Lol, I promise."

"I want an exclusive, Archy."

Why not? Lolly Spindrift was a friend to the rich and famous of Palm Beach. He would be kind, if nothing else, and give the proper slant to his interview with Veronica— kind mother, wicked stepfather—it could go a long way in shaping the coverage the press would give the story, all to Melva's advantage.

I remembered that Lolly Spindrift was one of the last people to see Geoff alive. Lolly drove Geoff to Phil Meecham's party, where, most likely, Geoff picked up his playmate. Lolly, whose job it was to note and record such facts, could certainly identify the woman. I'm sure the details of the murder were not yet public knowledge, so Lolly had no idea that he would be a pivotal figure in Melva's defense. But his role in this passion play deemed it even more practical to give him the exclusive interview with Veronica Manning he so craved.

"What's it like at Melva's place?" I questioned, stalling for time.

"Pure havoc. The front gate looks like a mob scene for a DeMille epic. A couple of cops behind the gate are keeping them from storming the castle. The police station and the courthouse are also under siege."

"All bases covered," I said. Just as well Veronica stays here for now. "I'll call you later this afternoon, Lol, and arrange something."

"Promise?"

"On my word, Lol."

"You'll have to do better than that, Archy."

Employing a smart Anglo-Saxon expletive, I told Lolly Spindrift that he could go do unto himself as he would have others do unto him, and hung up.

I selected the blue suit and rep tie I had worn to lure Ginny, but substituted a pair of sensible brogues for the Allen-Edmonds kilties. On the second floor, I paused at the guest-room door, which was closed, hoping to catch a glimpse of Veronica—or did I want Veronica to catch a glimpse of me in my corporate attire? Either way, it proved a futile maneuver.

"Don't you look nice," Ursi greeted as I entered the kitchen. Did this imply that I don't always look nice?

"Coffee, Ursi, please. Black and strong," I answered, without so much as a good morning. Ursi was at the stove, as usual, and Jamie was seated with a cup of coffee and the morning paper before him.

"I'll brew a fresh pot, Mr. Archy. Won't take a minute."

"Father had a problem getting his Lexus out of the garage this morning?" I directed this at Jamie. He nodded without taking his eyes from his newspaper. So taciturn is Jamie that in his presence a clam appears verbose.

"Miss Veronica is still asleep," Ursi was saying as she plugged in the electric perc.

"How do you know who's in the guest room?" I directed this at Ursi.

"Mrs. Marsden, of course," Ursi replied, as if I should have known better than to ask.

"Mrs. Marsden?" I cried. Mrs. Marsden was Lady Horowitz's housekeeper.

"Yes, Mr. Archy. Mrs. Marsden went to the Williamses' house this morning to take Hattie a tonic for her change of climate malaise. She makes it herself, and it's the only thing that helps poor Hattie. Well, when she got there she thought the place had been burgled, what with the reporters and the police and . . ."

"How did she get into the house?" I asked incredulously.

"The tonic, Mr. Archy. She told the men at the gate she had to deliver the tonic."

"And they let her through?"

"But of course, and not a moment too soon. Poor Hattie was in desperate need . . ."

"Is the coffee ready, Ursi?" I broke in, needing it more than poor Hattie needed Mrs. Marsden's tonic.

"Almost, Mr. Archy."

"So Hattie told Mrs. Marsden what transpired at the house last night and Mrs. Marsden has passed it along, house to house, on her way back to the Horowitz place." I spoke as one who knows.

"Isn't it terrible, Mr. Archy. Poor Mrs. Williams."

No one had yet said "Poor Mr. Williams," I noted.

"When I went in to air the guest room, like I do every morning, I saw we had company and told Mr. McNally." Ursi spoke as she poured my coffee. "That was before Mrs. Marsden's visit, when we only suspected who the guest might be. We didn't know you had gone to fetch Mrs. Williams's child until Mrs. Marsden told us—she having got that news from poor Hattie."

My head was spinning, but not too fast for me to protest "She's not a child, Ursi. Twenty-one, at least." I accepted the steaming cup of java with thanks and joined Jamie at the table.

"Can I get you a proper breakfast, Mr. Archy?" Ursi offered.

"No time, but I could hang around long enough for a toasted muffin."

Father knew, but obviously had not told them, who occupied our guest room. If he had, he would have had to tell them about the murder before he knew all the facts, which was not Prescott McNally's style. Also, I'm sure, he didn't want to upset mother with the news sooner than was necessary. "So why," I thought aloud, "did you suspect it was Veronica before Mrs. Marsden played Paul Revere?"

"Because of Hobo." It was Jamie who answered.

"Hobo?" My stomach quivered, threatening to eject the hot coffee I was pouring into it.

"When Hobo attacked your friend parking the Mercedes . . ."

Thanks to Lolly's mention of Binky being in need of a rabies shot, I didn't have to hear the rest of Jamie's story.

"What a ruckus!" Ursi exclaimed, serving my muffin, which I doubted I could get down, let alone keep down.

"When I heard the racket," Jamie continued, "I went down to see what was going on. Hobo had him by the ankle and I had all to do to shake him loose." I wanted to ask Jamie if it was Hobo or Binky who got shook, but refrained.

"What a sight," Ursi said. "I watched from the window, ready to call the police if need be, but then I recognized your friend, Mr. Archy, and told Jamie it was okay."

"Wasn't there someone with Binky?"

"Yes," Jamie said. "There was a car behind the Mercedes, but the boy in it wouldn't get out to help the other lad."

"He was afraid of Hobo biting him, too," Ursi said. "I offered to wash and bandage the boy's leg, but he refused my help. Just drove off with his friend."

I had the disquieting feeling that I was trapped inside an Olsen and Johnson movie.

"This Binky said the car belonged to Veronica Manning and he was delivering it on your orders, Mr. Archy. Then he limped off to the other car. That's why we suspected it was her in the guest room," Ursi finished.

I didn't think I could take much more, but I had to know—"Why was father late this morning? Why couldn't you just move the Mercedes so he could get the Lexus out of the garage?"

"No key," Jamie said and went no further. I wondered if he had spoken his alloted number of words for the day and whether I would have to wait until tomorrow for the rest of the story.

"The key wasn't in the ignition?" I prompted.

Jamie shook his head.

"Did you try the glove compartment?"

Jamie nodded.

"And?"

"It was locked," Ursi said. "We had to jimmy the lock."

"I figure," Jamie began, coming to life, "that the boy opened the glove compartment with the ignition key, but didn't actually unlock it, if you get what I mean—then he put the key in the compartment, and when he closed the door, he locked the key inside."

I silently sentenced Binky Watrous to a year in the pen with Hobo as his cellmate.

Mother was in the greenhouse surrounded by her beloved begonias. She wore a printed dress and gardening gloves and sported a dark smudge on her forehead. In this verdant setting, she looked as calm, serene, and happy as this lovely lady had every right to be. I had foolishly, and perhaps naïvely, hoped to keep mother from learning about the murder, but Mrs. Marsden's visit had brought about the inevitable sooner rather than later.

"Why, how nice you look, Archy," she stated as I entered the greenhouse, which was warm even on this sunless morning.

I kissed her flushed cheek and took her gloved hand in mine. "You've heard about Melva Williams?"

"I have, Archy. Mrs. Marsden was here earlier, as I suppose Ursi has already told you."

"Melva's daughter spent the night with us, mother."

"We thought it was Veronica," she said, putting down her trowel. "Is she very upset, Archy?"

"Yes, mother, but the young are resilient. It's Melva I'm worried about."

"That's kind of you, Archy. But I thought Melva's husband fell off a horse and died a long time ago."

"He did, mother. He was Veronica's father. The dead man is Geoffrey Williams, Melva's second husband."

Mother shook her head. "How things have changed, Archy. Time was when everyone had just one husband."

"I know, mother."

"And something like this happening among people we know—why, it was unheard of. I don't understand it, Archy."

"No one can understand something like this, mother, so don't dwell on it. Concen-

trate on your flowers. They are so beautiful."

"Yes, Archy, aren't they?" She nodded
and smiled, happy to focus on something
other than the vulgarities of modern life.

"I must go to the office, as father is
expecting me. When Veronica gets up and
has had her breakfast, I was wondering if
you would show her your garden and perhaps let her assist you in the greenhouse."

"Oh, Archy. What a lovely idea. I would be
delighted. Shall I say how sorry I am that her
father fell off his horse?"

"No, mother. I don't think that will be necessary. But you might tell her the name of
every variety of begonia you so ardently
raise and nurture."

"Of course. She would like that, wouldn't
she, Archy?"

"Yes, mother, she would like that very
much."

7

"ARCHY? MY, MY, don't you look nice."

First Ursi, then mother, and now Mrs. Trelawney, my father's secretary. Not exactly an authoritative triumvirate of male fashion, but even so, this diverse threesome had me regretting that I had not had a chance to show myself off to the lovely Veronica this morning. Would she have turned my female admirers into a quartet?

I acknowledged Mrs. Trelawney's compliment with a humble bow of the head, a gesture denoting modesty and the self-chastising employee who was ten minutes late for a meeting with the boss.

"I didn't have time to put together my expense account, Mrs. Trelawney, so it will have to wait until tomorrow."

"Fine, Archy. It's been a busy morning and, truth be told, I'm not in the mood for lyrical fiction."

"I'll pretend I didn't hear that, Mrs. Trelawney."

"And I'll pretend I didn't say it. Do you want to go out, come in, and start all over again?"

"I can't spare the time."

"I'll say you can't." Extending her arm, she waved her wristwatch at my face.

"Lovely, my dear. Is it a Rolex or a Timex?"

"Whatever it is, *my dear,* it says it's twelve minutes after twelve. You are late."

"Better late than never, Mrs. Trelawney."

"Around here, better never late, Mr. McNally."

"Is the great one here?" I nodded toward the closed door of father's inner sanctum.

"Which one?" Mrs. Trelawney questioned.

"How many are we expecting?"

"Well, there's the one in residence, and the other who arrived on the stroke of twelve. Had you not stopped to chat with

Herb you would have been here before him."

Herb is the security person who keeps us safe from his post inside a glass booth in our underground garage. "How do you know I passed the time of day with Herb?"

"He called me as soon as you pulled into the garage. You should have walked in here three minutes later, not ten."

"You are a remarkable woman, Mrs. Trelawney. The KGB's loss is McNally and Son's gain."

"Get in there, Archy. I'm to bring tea at half past noon."

"Sneak in two aspirin on my saucer and earn my undying gratitude," I pleaded.

"I don't want your undying gratitude. I want your honest expense account."

Offer the improbable and they demand the impossible. I squared my shoulders and marched into the lion's den.

John Fairhust III was a handsome man—noticeably tall even seated—slim, with a full head of white hair and blue eyes that looked guardedly at everything that came into their view, including Archy McNally. His handshake was firm and his smile more inviting than his stare.

"Sorry I'm late, but my morning appointment ran over and the traffic on Worth Avenue is a harbinger of the approaching season."

Father raised one eyebrow at my opening salvo, but noticing the slight widening of his lips beneath his mustache, I knew I had passed muster.

"No problem," Mr. Fairhurst assured me. "I was enjoying your father's company. He was up at Yale, too. After my time, to be sure," he added with a sigh of resignation.

"I was right behind you, John," father gallantly replied.

John! Well, already on a first-name basis. How cozy. But then, Prescott McNally was a fakir par excellence who knew how to charm cobras, especially rich and famous ones.

As Yale was not a subject I wished to dwell upon, I scrutinized John Fairhurst III while he and pater replayed a Yale/Harvard football game whose participants were now either great-grandfathers or dead. Dressed in gray flannels, a double-breasted blazer, and school tie, all Fairhurst needed was a patch over one of those blue eyes to be mistaken for a Hathaway model awaiting his cue. But don't let that mislead you. Fairhurst's white shirt was more Turnbull & Asser than Macy's mezzanine. His even tan and flowing white mane cried out for a glass of tonic water in one hand as the other rested gently on the steering wheel of a cabin cruiser, and—presto!—we had the man from Schweppes. The guy was a living manufacturer's logo.

When my grandfather Frederick McNally was a mere boy practicing pratfalls for his future career as Freddy McNally—a bulbous-nosed burlesque comic on the old Minsky circuit—Fairhurst's grandfather was helping women and children into lifeboats before taking his place beside men of good breeding and little sense, all hell bent on going down with the ship, thereby ensuring Hollywood an endless supply of oceanic disaster films.

"And now," Fairhurst was saying, "the reason for my visit." He removed an envelope from the inside breast pocket of his blazer, handling it as if it were either scalding hot or contaminated. He passed it on to father, who read it with his glasses perched on the tip of his nose while a look of unbridled horror crossed his face.

"Well," Prescott McNally exclaimed to the piece of paper in his hand, "what a vile piece of hogwash."

I was bursting with curiosity, but father, making the most of the moment, read the vile piece of hogwash a second time before letting out yet another, "Well!"

"May I?" I leaned forward in my chair and reached across father's desk, my interest piqued beyond endurance. He was about to pass it over when there was a quiet knock on the door followed by the entrance of Mrs. Trelawney behind a tea trolley. We all smiled sheepishly, and father, dropping the letter like a hot potato, said, "How nice, Mrs. Trelawney. Just what we needed, yes, John?"

Fairhurst readily agreed as Mrs. Trelawney played mother. We could have been in the middle of a garden club confab, delighting one another with tales of rose blight and the pros and cons of forcing late bloomers to strut their stuff before their time. Palm Beach society could make the British stiff upper lippers look like wimps, and the head of McNally & Son reveled in this charade like a ham playing to the balcony. And, alas, so did I—proving once again that bird dip does not fall far from the carrier pigeon.

Two white dots decorated the saucer given me by our tea lady. Bless her. I vowed to remove my lunch with Connie (appearing as "Sgt. Al Rogoff PBPD") from this week's expense account.

Our collective smiles departed along with Mrs. Trelawney. We were left holding steaming cups and saucers, our eyes looking at everything in the office but one another and the sheet of paper resting benignly before father.

Placing my tea on the desk, I inched my fingers further along and tried once more to get my hot hands on the epistle that had brought us together.

"May I?" I repeated.

Father nodded. Fairhurst sipped rather noisily for one of genteel birth. I retrieved the letter and my tea, quickly downed the two aspirin while my cohorts examined the ceiling, and leaned back in my chair to read. Typewritten on a sheet of very ordinary white paper was the following:

John Fairhurst III

The Fairhurst Foundation states with each grant, "Given in memory of John Fairhurst who died April 15, 1912. A passenger on the ill fated Titanic, *John Fairhurst courageously assisted women, including his wife, and children into lifeboats, giving them hope when, for him and his peers, all hope was gone."*

This is a lie. Your grandfather, dressed in one of his wife's gowns and hat, was himself assisted into a lifeboat and ultimately returned to the safety and comfort of his home.

In return for $25,000 your secret will remain a secret. I will contact you again with instructions for delivery of the money. If you do not agree to these terms, I will provide the press with proof of my allegation.

There was no signature.

The account of a man fleeing the *Titanic* in drag was not a new one. It has long been alluded to in books and films—the latter dramatically portrayed in Fox's 1953 *Titanic,* starring Barbara Stanwyck and Clifton Webb. In this, the best *Titanic* film ever made, it is the versatile character actress Thelma Ritter who unmasks the skirted pretender.

I put the letter back on father's desk and asked to see the envelope it came in. As I thought, it was posted in Miami, the biggest city within an easy drive from Palm Beach. I waited a respectable minute for the head of McNally & Son to speak, but when our silence segued from a meditative pause into gross embarrassment, I began to suspect that father refused to even think what had to be said. I had no such compunction.

"Is this true, Mr. Fairhurst?"

John Fairhurst lowered his teacup and dabbed at his lips with the linen napkin supplied by Mrs. Trelawney. "May I speak in complete confidence, Mr. McNally?"

"Our name is discreet, sir, and please call me Archy."

Fairhurst once again applied the linen to his lips. "It's true," he stated.

Father looked as if John Fairhurst III had just shouted, "No, Virginia, there is no Santa Claus, now shut up and deal."

"I don't understand how . . ."

"How we got away with it?" Fairhurst finished for me. "I'll explain." He returned his cup to the trolley and proceeded to let us in on the Fairhurst family secret.

"As the letter says, grandfather got off the *Titanic* dressed as a woman, with grandmother's help I'm sure. Naturally, no one asked for names or identification of the people transferred from the lifeboats to the rescuing ship. Remember, confusion reigned ashore as well as at sea and the world was horrified, or perhaps mesmerized, by the disaster. When the surviving passengers sailed into New York harbor, the newspapers had already assumed that John Fairhurst had done the noble thing and reported him dead.

"My grandparents went directly to their home in Hyde Park in upstate New York. They were neighbors of the Roosevelts, don't-you-know. The Roosevelt Democrats, that is. They spoke, of course, only neighborly thing to do, but I never heard it said that they had broken bread with them."

Father was nodding as if he knew the consequence of breaking bread with the wrong Roosevelts.

"I've always assumed my grandparents thought the situation over and decided it would be easier, and less humiliating, for poor grandfather to play dead rather than to confess to what he had done. Why end a celebrated life on a less than venerable note?"

Unable to contain the thought, I exclaimed, "How did your grandfather manage to keep the fact that he was not dead a secret?"

"Not as difficult as one would suppose," Fairhurst answered. "Grandfather was far from young when he married, and sired a son at the end of his natural life. He lived only a few years after the *Titanic* went down. His widow, with her infant son, observed a long period of mourning in complete seclusion, which was not unheard of in those days. They were attended by an English couple who had been with them for years. When grandfather died, in return for their silence, the couple were pensioned off and returned to England, where they lived rather lavishly in a charming home in Kent. Grandfather was never very social and I think he enjoyed his life as a recluse, surrounded by his books, pursuing his love of ancient Greek lore, and watching his son grow.

"I also think grandfather was ashamed of

his cowardly act and perhaps thought of his confinement as penance," Fairhurst explained.

Father and I listened attentively but made no comment. John Fairhurst went on to extol his grandfather's extraordinary business acumen as if to make up for the man's shortcomings.

"Grandfather was once a partner of Andrew Carnegie, don't-you-know. Broke with him early on and started up a few smelteries of his own and turned the heat up on old Andy, he did. Ha, ha."

Like Andy Carnegie, I was not amused.

"So he lived out his life in quiet comfort and seclusion, and when grandfather died a second time, he was the first Fairhurst to be cremated. Interment, don't-you-know, would have been a bit awkward," Fairhurst concluded.

John Fairhurst III knew how to turn a phrase, I'll say that for him. I didn't ask how they managed to get a death certificate for the old boy because I knew money could buy anything, including death certificates and love. Or should that be *especially* death certificates and love?

"Mr. Fairhurst," I began, "by coming to us I assume you have no intention of paying to keep this a secret."

"Correct, Archy. For several reasons. The first is that I am certain this person would not stop at the requested amount. It would be the beginning of a lifetime annuity."

"I'm glad you are aware of that, sir."

"Also, in compensation for grandfather's moment of weakness, the Fairhurst Foundation was founded as a charity devoted exclusively to the care and education of needy children. For three quarters of a century our foundation has given millions to orphanages, endowed children's hospitals, provided scholarships, funded medical programs, and much, much more. We have paid, many times over, for the seat on a lifeboat grandfather may have taken from a poor boy or girl. I wish neither to make a mockery of this largesse nor see it become an embarrassment that might make it necessary to terminate the foundation. I want you to find the culprit and stop him before he brings down the Fairhurst Foundation."

I thought *mon père* was going to stand up and applaud. To his credit, he didn't.

Quickly assaying the situation, I concluded that the letter was a useless clue as to the blackmailer. Typewritten on what appeared to be copy-machine paper, it could lead to the villain only in a television police procedural. Besides, Fairhurst had made it very clear that the letter could be shown to no one, including an expert who might tell us the make and model of the typewriter used and not much more. This was a case for a bloodhound, and it seemed the best place to start sniffing was in Fairhurst's own backyard.

"Mr. Fairhurst, who besides yourself knows about this?"

"The letter, or my grandfather's indiscretion?"

"Both, please."

"Only my wife and I know about both the letter and grandfather's escapade."

"Your children?" I asked.

"No, Archy. I thought it best to let the story die with me. Saw no reason to pass it on to my heirs, and my wife agreed."

"I think you should keep the letter, Mr. Fairhurst. It's of no use to me, and I don't want to be responsible for its safe keeping."

"Very sensible," father said, relieved.

"And," I continued, "I don't think we can do very much until you receive the letter instructing you where and when to deliver the money. They will have to give us a contact point, and that can lead directly to them—which they know—so how we play it from there will win us, or lose us, the day. I can guarantee nothing, Mr. Fairhurst, but our sincere effort to foil the scheme." This was my standard close.

"I understand, Archy, and I appreciate your help." Fairhurst returned the letter to the inside pocket of his blazer.

"Mr. Fairhurst, do you have any idea how a family secret known only to you and Mrs. Fairhurst came to be known to a common blackmailer?"

"I honestly do not, Archy."

"And one more thing, sir. How many are on your household staff?"

"There are a butler and a housekeeper, and a secretary who assists both me and Mrs. Fairhurst. Cleaning people and gardeners come daily and are overseen by Peterson, our butler, and the housekeeper who happens to be Mrs. Peterson."

Not a large crew for a house often compared to Mar-A-Lago, the former home of Post Toasties heiress Marjorie Merriweather Post. Mar-A-Lago is now owned by a New York realtor. I imagine the "dailies" who come in to round out the Fairhurst staff constitute a small army.

"Do you trust them, Mr. Fairhurst?"

"Implicitly, Archy. The Petersons have been with us for over twenty years, and Arnold, our secretary, for a dozen years at least."

"I see . . ."

"Oh, I almost forgot my chauffeur, Seth Walker. He's part-time, as my wife and I don't gad about as much as we used to. I took him on about a month ago, but he came highly recommended by Geoff Williams—you know, Melva's husband."

My flabber- was gasted, but this didn't throw me off the scent. Sooner or later I would have to check out Fairhurst's staff and I decided that sooner would be better than later. "I would like to visit your home and have a look around. Naturally, I'll come on some pretense so as not to arouse suspicion among your staff."

"Call me and I'll arrange it," Fairhurst agreed.

John Fairhurst III had hired a chauffeur recommended by Geoff Williams, who was dead, thanks to Geoff's wife whose daughter had moved in below me, which led to Binky being bitten by Hobo, thereby precipitating a rabies alert.

I should have ordered two Quaaludes.

8

FATHER HAD MADE lunch reservations at Ta-Boo', known for its delicious green linguine, which I declined in favor of hurrying back to the delicious Veronica. I left father, explaining Melva's situation to Fairhurst, who kept shaking his head while muttering the inevitable "Poor Melva." Perhaps a gratuitous lament in retaliation for Melva's ancestors crossing the Atlantic on the *Mayflower* and settling in Plymouth, where their good Yankee sense told them not to push their luck and traverse it again on the *Titanic*.

Palm Beach society is a relatively small tribe. Most evenings, members in good standing are obliged to mix and mingle over cocktails, dinner, and charity events. Afternoons, they cross on another's paths on golf courses and tennis courts or toot at on another from deluxe watercrafts. Mornings, they sleep in. I have long felt that life here is nothing more than a conjurer's trick performed with a dozen talking heads and a thousand mirrors.

Ergo, it was no surprise that while schmoozing with his betters over a martini or across a table, Geoff had recommended a driver to Fairhurst; it was the driver who was the enigma. Had Geoff tried to palm off an upstairs maid who knew her way around a gentleman's bedroom, I would have given the matter a sly wink and a yawn. Seth Walker was the reason I wanted to pay a call on Fairhurst. I hadn't tipped my hand at the meeting because I like to play my cards close to the vest—preferably my green and blue tattersall.

I was still astounded over the number-one Fairhurst's indiscretion, as number three had labeled it, but as I sped along in my red Miata, I changed gears, literally and figuratively, and shifted into a Melva Williams mode. At Discreet Inquiries, when it rains it pours, although you couldn't prove this by the weather. When I drove out of our underground garage, small patches of blue were poking holes in the gray ceiling. A good omen for what I had in mind for this afternoon's adventure.

I was going to attempt to K two B's with one S. Not an easy kill, especially if the birds are capricious and the stone small. Unlike David, I didn't own a catapult, but I did have a few strings I could pull to my advantage. Archy the puppeteer.

I found Veronica in the kitchen, where Ursi was readying lunch. Daylight did nothing to diminish my charge's ethereal evening beauty, and Dora's jeans and sweatshirt, both a tad too small, helped to accentuate the positive. My only surprise was that her elegant evening purse had obviously contained a pair of horn-rimmed reading glasses, which Veronica now wore to pore over the afternoon paper. Melva's face, staring out from the front page, was the only disquieting note in a room redolent with an aroma that promised grilled cheese and bacon sandwiches.

"Any word of my mother?" Veronica asked as I came into the kitchen.

"One of our lawyers is with her and her legal people are on their way here. My father has been in contact with them since early this morning." Being aware that I wasn't going to be complimented on my attire, I turned to Ursi and pleaded for a beer.

Veronica pushed the newspaper aside and questioned me further as I took the chair opposite her. "When can I see her, Archy?"

"We tried for a bail hearing this afternoon, but I don't think we're going to get it. Tomorrow, I imagine. When bail is set, she will be free to come home."

"Why can't I go to her now?"

"Because they won't let you see her and I don't think you want to fight your way through the reporters waiting outside the police station and the courthouse. Not to mention the picture you would make in those jeans and that sweatshirt. We want to play down lust, Veronica, and play up family values."

She smiled reluctantly, annoyed with herself for not being able to resist the compliment. Had I found the path to her heart? Did I want to find the path to her heart? A dilemma, but one I might enjoy sparring with.

"Would you like a drink, Miss Veronica?" Ursi asked as she served my beer. "Lunch will be ready in a few minutes."

"If you bring another glass, I'll share Archy's beer."

"Perhaps you ought to bring another beer, Ursi," I advised. "Archy is thirsty."

Veronica's hand rested on the newspaper, one finger stroking the image of her mother's cheek. "It's horrible, Archy." She dug into the pocket of Dora's jeans and came up with a crumpled handkerchief that looked as if it had been put to use all morning. I reached out to cover her hand with mine, but Ursi returned with another beer and another glass, so instead of holding Veronica's hand I poured her beer.

I hate watching a woman cry, especially when it's not in my power to stem the flow. "Drink," I ordered. "It'll do you good."

She sipped the brew and used her handkerchief to blot the foam from her upper lip. "It's awful," she repeated.

"The beer?"

This got me a grimace rather than a smile. "No, silly. This." She tapped the newspaper with her forefinger.

"Last night I asked you if you wanted me to tell you that everything was going to be just fine, remember?" She nodded. "You still want the truth?" She nodded again, her fingers clutching the handkerchief. "This," I gestured with my glass to denote the newspaper, "is just the local press. The story will draw national attention, and when the tabloids get into it, the facts will give way to fiction, pandering to the voyeur in all of us."

"It's been on television, too," she said. "Not only the local and Miami stations, but even CNN aired it with footage of the mob at our front gate and aerial shots of the house."

"I'm sure they bought the footage from one of our networks, just as they did when a local California station provided them with the sight and sound of O. J. Simpson playing the Pied Piper to the Los Angeles police department. But never fear, they'll have their own crew down here by tomorrow, as will the other cable and commercial networks. Like I said, kid, it's just day one. Our job is to think about what we can do to help your mother."

"Later," Ursi said, putting down a tray of sandwiches between us. "First, think about lunch. Grilled cheese and bacon, and I've got pickles and homemade slaw. Your mother, Mr. Archy, won't be joining us, as she's resting."

Ursi's tone, not an unfamiliar one, told me I was being reprimanded for forgetting mother and I deserved the censure. However, I had a lot on my plate, what with the Fairhurst indiscretion, the Williams murder, Veronica's tearful blue eyes, Binky's rabies, and now a thick-cut grilled cheese and bacon sandwich on crusty sourdough replete with a pile of kettle potato chips. But still, I was ashamed of my errant behavior. "Is she not feeling well?" I said, my concern sincere.

"She's fine," Veronica broke in. "I'm afraid I tired her. She gave me a tour of her garden and then—and then . . ."

"Yes?"

"I'm afraid I wasn't a very attentive guest. I insisted on seeing the afternoon paper. Jamie went for it. Later I wanted to watch the news on television, and I . . ."

"And this upset mother. Is that what you want to say?"

"I'm so sorry, Archy. She's a dear, she really is. You're right, I think the news upset her." She shook her head, her blond hair careening in a manner peculiar to expert snipping and shaping. "I know it upset her," she amended.

"My fault, really. You had enough to worry about without being concerned with mother, too. She'll be fine after her nap. Now eat your lunch."

"What a way to repay your kindness."

Now I did place my hand over hers. The fair skin was smooth and cool to my touch. I felt a tingling in a part of my anatomy that had nothing to do with gastronomic expectations.

Ursi joined us at table, nibbling at her efforts while we devoured them with gusto. She and Jamie often joined us for breakfast and lunch but never for dinner, which, thanks to the Master, was a very formal affair. Jamie, Ursi explained, was off in mother's station wagon with Hobo, which explained why neither had greeted me upon my return. I told Veronica about Binky's encounter with our canine and got the laugh I had been trying to elicit from her since my arrival.

"I know it's not funny," she defended herself, "but what a sight it must have been. Poor Binky."

I was ready to throw Binky to the lions for another Veronica Manning smile.

The repast put some color into her cheeks and courage into her heart. "You've been very kind, Archy. You've all been very kind," she repeated with a nod to Ursi. "But now I want to go home. Poor Hattie is alone and must be beside herself."

"No need to worry about Hattie. She has her tonic, thanks to Mrs. Marsden, and she's only been alone for a little more than half a day."

"It seems like ages," Veronica answered.

"I told your mother I would watch over you, and I intend to do just that. Put up with us for another night, Veronica, and when your mother comes home tomorrow, you can join her."

"I don't want Hattie to spend another day and night alone in the house without some reassurance, and I can't get her on the phone. I think she's got them all unplugged." She looked about anxiously. "Do you have a cigarette?"

I surrendered one of my English Ovals and, after lighting hers, helped myself to one. Ursi reluctantly brought us an ashtray before clearing the table.

Puffing, but not inhaling, Veronica continued to rally me to her cause. "I must have clean clothes, Archy, especially if we're to pick up mother tomorrow and take her home. You said it will be a photo op for the press, and I should be dressed more somberly than this." She spoke with a flutter of her hands. "And last night's dress is even less appropriate."

"I know," I told her. "I've thought about all that. You can't be seen shopping on Worth Avenue, either. That would be worse than appearing in Dora's jeans."

"If Mrs. Marsden got through, why can't we?" she concluded.

"Oh, the police would let us in. You live there, remember? But we'd have to plow through the press at five miles an hour with them all over the car like camera-toting leeches."

"I don't care," she cried, stubbing out her cigarette. I made a mental note to buy a generic brand to feed her extravagant smoking habit. "If you want me to spend the night here, I will. But today I'm going home to get the clothes I'll need for tonight and tomorrow and to let Hattie know we haven't abandoned her. We'll drive in and out, and to hell with the press, Archy. If you won't come, I'll do it alone."

"When we drive out, Veronica, they'll follow us right here, learn where you're staying, and set up shop outside my front door. We won't have police protection as does the murder scene, and Hobo has extracted his pound of flesh for the season."

"Follow us?" She shuddered as she spoke.

"What is it?" I asked. "Are you ill?"

She shook her head. "You said they would follow us and I thought of her—the Princess of Wales—being chased by the *paparazzi.*"

The poor kid. She was terrified. "Put it out of your head, Veronica. No one is going to follow us." Now I was more determined than ever to go through with the plan I had worked out earlier. Operation K two B's with one S. "Archy is going to get you in and out of your home without anyone knowing you've been and gone."

"How?"

I held up my hand. "First, you have to agree to granting Lolly Spindrift an interview."

"What?" she shouted.

"An interview with Lolly. Do you know him?"

"Know him? Last season," she confided, "we both had our eye on the same young man. I won."

"I wonder why?" I pondered, looking at her perfect face, even lovelier when animated as it was now. Then I explained, slowly and carefully, all the advantages of giving Lolly the interview.

"You want me to nail Geoff to the wall," she stated rather than asked.

The young certainly don't mince words. "Not so anyone sees the hammer in your hand—restraint is the key word. Also, I think Lolly's questions will tend to encourage you to subtly compose the picture of a long-suffering wife and her roving husband. Lol likes Melva."

"And he didn't like Geoff?"

"Oh, he liked Geoff all right, but Geoff didn't reciprocate."

"Then it was the first carnal offer my step-father turned down."

As I said, this crowd tells it like it is. "There's another reason we have to be kind to Lolly, Veronica."

"And what's that?"

"Your mother told me he picked up Geoff last night and drove him to Phil Meecham's party. It was there that Geoff must have met his lady friend. Lolly is a keen observer of the human mating game and is probably the only person who was at Meecham's bash who can identify her—the others being too preoccupied with their own lascivious pursuits. In fact, he might even know who she is and where we can find her."

She stared at me for a few moments, her eyes unseeing, before asking, "Is that really necessary?"

This was the second time she had balked at the mention of Geoff's last partner in copulation. Why? Was it someone she knew? Someone Geoff had seen since his arrival in Palm Beach less than two weeks ago? But then Geoff was a fast worker. Melva had said the girl was young. As young as Veronica? Could she be a friend of Veronica's? Is this why Geoff felt safe inviting the girl into the house? If Melva was awake when they arrived, he could have said that Veronica's friend had given him a ride home. If Melva was asleep and Veronica still out, he could make his pitch. Risky, but then, Geoff

Williams always bet on the long shots and usually won—until last night.

It made sense, but these were still early days, and Veronica was testy enough without any further probing into what was turning out to be a sensitive topic.

"My God, Veronica, I told you last night that it was not only necessary, but vital to your mother's defense."

"Suppose he didn't meet her at Phil's party?"

"If she doesn't come forward on her own, we'll have to beat the bushes until she comes out screaming. Right now, let's hope Lolly will make that unnecessary."

She lapsed back into her own private world again until I coached, "Then you'll do the interview?"

She gave me a weary smile. "Only if you get me home and back, as promised."

"That's the beauty part of my plan, Veronica. You can do the interview on your way to and from your home."

"Are you for real, Archy?"

"*Cogito ergo sum.* Look that up in your Latin primer, young lady, while I slip into something comfortable."

* * *

I climbed the steps to my aerie, where the first thing I did, after doffing my suit jacket, was dial Lolly Spindrift.

"It's about time," he greeted.

"I'm not a scribe, Lol. I work for a living, and right now my hopper runneth over."

"You're not the only one, Archy. Our community is alive with the sound of malicious gossip. Everyone's telephone line is busy, above and below stairs. We are being invaded by the fourth estate, including, I hear, *The New York Times,* and some fool called me and asked if it were true that Ted Turner had already snapped up the movie rights to Melva's story. This town hasn't had so much publicity since Lady Mendl declared Palm Beach no more exclusive than Coney Island—and that was sixty years ago."

"You know, Lol, I've always thought Lady Mendl was right on target."

"Thanks to the likes of you, she was."

"If I weren't a gentleman I would respond in kind."

"Respond by telling me where and when I get to pow-wow with the Manning child."

"She's not a child."

"Temper, temper. Did I cause your lecherous libido to turn scarlet with shame?"

"Need I remind you what people living in glass houses shouldn't do?"

"A truce, *mon ami*—now, was the young lady receptive?"

"Not when she remembered you were last year's competition. However, she relented when I told her how kind you were going to be to her mother."

"Okay, Archy. I get the drift. I will sacrifice integrity to partisanship."

"There's more, Lol."

"With you there always is."

"It's a give-and-take world we live in," I preached. "The trick is to take as much as you can get your hands on and give as little as possible."

"And what do you want to get your hands on, Archy?"

"Phil Meecham's yacht."

"You're kidding?"

"I'm not."

"But why?"

"First, it would be an ideal venue for your meeting with Veronica, and second . . ."

When I explained my plan I gained a willing ally.

"The interview plus this caper will get me a Pulitzer, Archy." Lolly was delighted.

"Will Phil agree?"

"Don't worry, he owes me," Lolly assured me.

Kindly, he did not expand on the nature of Phil Meecham's obligation.

"By the by, Archy, you've heard the reason for my competing with Veronica Manning?"

"Yes."

"Well, he's reappeared this season as, of all things, Phil Meecham's first mate."

9

I RESURRECTED MY bell-bottom jeans with the button fly, purchased during my stay in New Haven at an Army/Navy surplus store. At the time, this outlet was giving fierce competition to J. Press and Chipp for the Eli trade. I topped a blue and white boat-neck pullover with a yachting cap and shod my feet in a pair of Topsiders. My role model for this outfit was Cary Grant aboard the *True Love,* in the film *The Philadelphia Story,* but my mirror told me I had somehow managed to clone a cross between Gene Kelly and Rudy Vallee.

"Anchors Aweigh," Veronica said.

"How did you ever guess?"

"Archy, we're not—"

"Never anticipate," I broke in. "All that's required is that you put your trust in Captain Courageous."

She stepped back and surveyed her leader. "Captain Gorgeous, I would say."

I blushed, but not enough to be noticed. To countermand my maidenly response to her compliment, I barked, "We'll take your car, but I'll drive." I had decided upon this to give our excursion as low a profile as possible. There are, you see, a thousand Mercedes convertibles in Palm Beach but only one red Mazda Miata. This being the only town in the world where conspicuous consumption is the rule rather than the exception.

"If we're taking my car, I'll drive, but only if I know where we're going."

"To meet Lolly Spindrift aboard Phil Meecham's yacht."

Her blue eyes opened wide and a moment later she let out a squeal of delight, jumping up and down and clapping her hands like a child learning that chocolate had replaced spinach on the school lunch menu. "I can give Lolly his interview on my way home," she cried. "You're a genius, Archy."

"Or a fool," I countered.

"No. A genius. And I love you." She ran into my arms and kissed me on the cheek.

I was once again aware of her scent and the feel of her breasts—incongruously firm and pliant—against my chest. My response was instant and impossible to hide, but with her fingers playing with the nape of my neck, she either didn't notice, which was impossible, or was enjoying it, which was wishful thinking.

Whatever the case, I broke the embrace a moment before it reached the point of no return—or was this, too, wishful thinking?

"Can we do it?" she asked, unaware of the coyness of the question in light of what had just passed between us.

"I don't know, but we're certainly going to try. Now let's move it." I was about to punctuate the order with a slap on her posterior but grasped her elbow instead.

She tossed back her head and laughed. "I feel like the heroine in a James Bond movie."

And, I thought, you look like the heroine in a James Bond movie.

At the garage we met Jamie and Hobo, who were just returning from their outing. Hobo leaped out of mother's wood-paneled Ford station wagon and once again set upon Veronica's ankles—licking, not biting. Does this dog know his priorities?

"The vet checked him over and he's fine," Jamie said as if we knew what he was talking about.

"Why the vet?" I wanted to know.

"The boy Binky was worried about rabies, so I thought we should be sure the dog was healthy, which he is, so tell your friend rabies shots are not necessary."

"He's adorable." This from Veronica, who was now on her knees, stroking Hobo's ears.

"Do me a favor, Jamie. You call and tell him. The name is Watrous and he's in the book. And tell him I'll be in touch."

Hobo tried to follow Veronica into the Mercedes, but I forcefully reminded him that this was a two-seater vehicle.

Lolly and Phil Meecham welcomed us aboard the *Sans Souci*. Both men warmly embraced Veronica and expressed their sympathies. I took this as a sign that those who counted were closing ranks around Melva, and devil take the hindmost in the form of Geoffrey Williams.

Meecham, who had to be three score at least, was still in good shape, with a leathery complexion, thanks to years spent on the deck of his yacht under the Florida sun, and only a few threads of gray visible among his thinning, sand-colored hair.

In contrast, Lolly Spindrift guarded his complexion with the diligence of a southern belle. Lolly was a firm believer in Helena Rubinstein's admonition that "a woman should never allow a ray of sun to touch her naked skin." Along with Count Dracula, Lolly and Helena kept the faith. Today, Lolly wore a white, wide-brimmed creation that had him looking like an extra in *Panama Hattie.*

Behind the welcoming committee stood the first mate, and damned if *he* didn't look like Cary Grant aboard the *True Love.* He greeted Veronica with a peck on the cheek which I thought a bit forward for the hired help, but on the *Sans Souci* such lapses in etiquette were not only tolerated, but encouraged. Phil beamed at the beautiful youngsters, his predilection being boys and girls together. The mate's name, by the way, was Buzz. (Give me a break!) What a caper this was turning out to be.

As Buzz prepared to hoist anchor, Phil led us into the grand salon which was larger than my entire third-floor suite, and offered us drinks. He mixed a batch of Bloody Marys for which we were all thankful, except Veronica, who insisted on a Virgin Mary. Was she trying to tell us something?

I suggested Lolly and Veronica remain in the salon for their chit chat and excused myself, taking Meecham with me. As we stepped on deck the big craft lurched away from the dock, and I grabbed the railing for support.

"How are your sea legs?" Meecham asked, and grinned, hoping for the worst, I'm sure.

"They would be happier resting in a deck chair."

"Let's go to the fore, Archy, so we can see where we're going rather than where we've been. It'll keep your mind off the ship's roll."

"Does pretty boy know how to drive this tub?"

"I may be a sucker for the young and the bad, Archy, but I'm not a fool when it comes to my safety. Buzz is a qualified yachtsman, both sail- and engine-powered. He got his training in Newport with the best of 'em."

Of course. Young men like Buzz were a staple in places like Newport, the Hamptons, both East and South, Martha's Vineyard, and other fancy watering holes around the world. Their appeal was to both men and women who could afford to pander to their more base desires, and Buzz and his ilk could respond to either sex because the loot, not the gender, was the attraction.

I would say that our Buzz was twenty-somethingish, giving him a few more years to catch the brass ring. If he didn't, and few do, he would join the roster of some seedy escort service along with his has-been female counterparts until the advancing years once again forced him to move on— forever downward. But right now Buzz's star was on the ascendant. As Meecham's first mate, he was performing Veronica Manning a unique service in her hour of need, and hoping one or the other would return the favor in kind. Don't count on it,

Buzz. Meecham goes through pretty boys like nobody's business, and Veronica's guardian is Archy McNally, who might have his own plans for the young lady.

"Does Buzz know where we're going?" I asked.

"Certainly. When Lolly called and told me the plan, Buzz checked the location of the house and mapped out a water route. Don't worry, we're in capable hands."

We eased into deck chairs, and I was content not to have spilled a drop of my drink on the way fore, which turned out to be the front of the ship.

"We're moving north on the Intracoastal Waterway, which runs through Lake Worth. Straight ahead you can just make out the shoreline of Peanut Island at the mouth of Lake Worth Inlet," Meecham explained. "There, we'll go east and enter the inlet flanked by Palm Beach and Singer Island— then straight into the Atlantic."

The fact that I was James Bond had not yet reached my stomach, which churned in counterpoint to our diesel engine. Knowing that Buzz was in the cabin above us, steering, kept me steady as we went. I hoped Lolly and the heroine were faring better than Double-O-Seven. But Lolly, I knew, was in his glory. He was hot on the trail of a breaking story and seven leagues ahead of the competition. Lolly always wanted to be the Cholly Knickerbocker of Palm Beach, and here, finally, was his chance at national recognition.

For the young, or those whose reading habits are a notch above newspapers of yore, Cholly Knickerbocker was the logo for the Hearst syndicate's society gossip columnist—most prominently featured in the now-defunct *New York Journal American.* There were several Chollys, the second none other than Igor Cassini, brother of the guy who put Jackie in those pillbox hats and smart suits. One of Igor's wives (he had four at last count) was Charlene Wrightsman, daughter of the oil baron billionaire Charles Wrightsman.

Wrightsman, long a pillar of Palm Beach society, owned an oceanfront mansion near the more modest home of Joseph Kennedy. The Wrightsman house, furnished with priceless French eighteenth-century antiques and paintings, served as the "White House" on at least two occasions. President Kennedy rested at Wrightsman's after his return from his historic meeting with Khrushchev and after his even more publicized trip to Paris with Jackie.

Wrightsman's annual New Year's Eve Ball was the most sought after invitation for many a season. The party came to a climactic ending the year the Kennedy brothers and brothers-in-law got up a touch football game in the ballroom and bumped into several of those French antiques.

Palm Beachites never cared much for the rather caustic prose Igor employed to chronicle their antics, and when, in his heyday, Igor and his brother were the winning doubles team at the Bath and Tennis Club Tournament, the Palm Beachites liked him even less. Igor will go down in history as the guy who coined the term "Jet Set."

But it was the first Cholly Knickerbocker, Murray Paul, who was Lolly's mentor. Paul, a misogynist who lived with his mother, once rolled up his trouser legs on Fifth Avenue to show off his gold-plated garters, coined the phrase "Café Society," and told a young lady who complained of having to sleep with producers to get ahead, "Nobody gives a damn who you sleep with. In this world, it's who you're seen dining with that counts."

Poor Lolly. There were no phrases left to coin and nobody gave a damn who you dined with in the closing years of our century. It's who you slept with that counted. Lolly could report on Lady Horowitz's dinner parties, which no one wanted to know about, but scooping Meecham's yacht parties, which everyone wanted to know about, would be imprudent if not downright libelous. This keen observation led me to casually remind my chairmate, "Your party last night will go down in Palm Beach lore as the last gala attended by Geoff Williams."

Meecham sipped his drink thoughtfully. Then, with a shrug, he stated, "Really? You couldn't prove it by me."

My stomach gave a lurch, which had nothing to do with the *Sans Souci.* "What do you mean?"

"I mean," he said, "that you couldn't prove it by me. I didn't see Geoff or Melva last night."

"You couldn't have seen Melva—she stayed home. But Geoff came."

Another shrug. "Could be. Look, Archy, I don't always get to socialize with all my guests." He raised his glass and explained,

"A few too many, too early, and the parade sometimes passes me by."

"Who was on board last night?"

"The usual suspects."

"How many?" I probed.

"I think I invited about thirty, so I assume sixty showed up."

A big group, plus a few too many libations, and a host couldn't be chided for neglecting a guest or two. Things were looking up. "Did you notice Lolly in the crowd?"

"Of course," Meecham answered.

"Well, Lolly came with Geoff Williams," I exclaimed.

That, finally, got Phil Meecham's undivided attention. "Lolly and Geoff together? Really? Is that why Melva shot him?"

Peanut Island loomed ahead of us and I figured the boat was making more progress than I was. "No, Phil. She shot him because he couldn't remember who was at your party."

My words went either unheard or unheeded as we sailed through the Lake Worth Inlet before plowing into the Atlantic with a thrust of the prow that bespoke the apocalyptic clash between irresistible force and immovable object. While the Atlantic was indeed an irresistible force, Meecham's expensive tub was far from immovable. In fact, the yacht's motions were rather like the undulations of the Minsky chorus girls who added the oomph to Grandfather McNally's act that kept the paying customers begging for more.

"We'll calm down once we get our stride," Meecham reported.

I deposited my glass in a hole in the arm of my deck chair made especially for this purpose. I had hardly touched my tomato and vodka but noticed that the only thing left in Meecham's glass was the swizzle stick, which, incidently, was a plastic rendition of a celery stalk. "How close to the shore can we get?" I asked, hoping my stomach would focus in on the S word and give me some peace. It didn't.

"Buzz said the tide is with us, so I suppose we can get within a hundred yards of the beach."

I would hate to see the tide when it was agin' us.

Meecham took a deep breath and ran his fingers through his hair in a futile attempt to keep it off his forehead, where the wind insisted it belonged. "I love the ocean," he called, competing with the roar of the surf and the drone of our diesel engine.

"So do I," I yelled back. "I swim every day, weather permitting."

"I use the pool at the Bath and Tennis," Meecham said.

"I prefer the ocean," I answered, then added, "for swimming."

"At the Bath and Tennis the pool water is piped in from the Atlantic," Meecham informed me.

If I swam offshore of the Bath and Tennis, might I get pulled into one of their pipes and end up doing laps with chartered members? In my cerise Speedos? Perhaps I had better rethink my bathing attire.

We were moving south now under a partly cloudy sky and a sun playing peekaboo with the Atlantic Ocean. Buzz had us close enough to the shore so that I might easily pick out the elegant Breakers—the Palm Beach Country Club—and the Bath and Tennis Club, which I now knew was sucking in the water beneath us. A few minutes later First Mate Buzz turned off our engine, allowing the *Sans Souci* to rock in the surf like an oversize sitting duck.

"This must be the place," Meecham announced, rising from his deck chair.

As we approached the salon, Veronica and Lolly stepped out onto the deck, where Buzz was already waiting. The scribe resembled a cat who had just enjoyed a bowl of cream, so I assumed all went well with the interview. Veronica had tied back her hair with what appeared to be a simple piece of string and looked more enticing than ever. Buzz, as previously stated, looked like Cary Grant from the neck up and an ad for an exercise machine from that point down. Archy looked a bit green around the gills for more reasons than I care to elaborate on.

"There's the house," Buzz said, pointing toward shore. He was rewarded with a touch of Veronica's hand on his muscled arm.

"I'll stay with the ship," Meecham informed us. "The rest of you get into the speedboat. Buzz'll pilot you onto the beach."

I hadn't counted on either Buzz or Lolly coming ashore with us. Just how I had imagined getting Veronica and me to the house and back to the ship, I couldn't for the life of me remember. On film a quick cut would get us to the house and another would have us back on the *Sans Souci.* Sorry, Oscar, but life does not imitate art. And having brought Lolly this far into our confidence, there was no closing the door in his face at this juncture. The next time I decided to play James Bond, I would have a closer look at the script.

Buzz opened the gate cut into the ship's railing and stepped onto the small, square platform, to which was attached a flight of stairs. These led to a smart speedboat that bobbed in the surf like a baby duck alongside its mama.

"I'll lead," Buzz told us, full of the confidence of youth, beauty, and a master's degree in nautical protocol. "You next, Veronica, than Lolly—Archy can bring up the rear."

I doubted if Buzz had the brains for astringent humor, so credited that last command to ensure that two strong, young men formed protective bookends for our expedition.

"And," Buzz advised, "I suggest you take off your shoes and socks and roll up your pant legs, but bring your shoes with you. You'll need 'em ashore." He might be first mate on the *Sans Souci,* but he was captain of that speedboat.

I have often heard that one should never look down during a precarious descent, so I looked up and saw a chopper heading straight for our little party.

"Smile, kids," I shouted down the line, "we're on *Candid Camera.*"

10

HATTIE WAS WAITING for us on the beach. Veronica fell into the faithful housekeeper's arms and the two had a long cry before a word was spoken. The men hung back: Buzz sticking with the speedboat; Lolly mentally inscribing the scene; me, feeling a little like Moses having delivered his people safely across the Red Sea, breathing a sigh of relief.

"First, I saw the big boat," Hattie began, sounding as if she had spotted the Loch Ness monster on our shores. "Then the little boat. Then the helicopter." We all looked up at the chopper that had escorted us from ship to shore. It was still circling, the din of its engine carried by a strong offshore breeze. Buzz, wouldn't you know it, was smiling and waving at the pilot and crew. "I didn't know what was happening, Miss Veronica."

Veronica put her arm around the old lady's shoulders and gently began to propel her toward the house. Lolly and I followed, and Buzz, who had to stay with the speedboat, was content to smile for the cameras. I hoped a stiff neck would be the end result of his vanity.

"When I saw the blond hair, Miss Veronica, I knew it was you. I thought you were bringing Missy home. Where is Missy? The policemen in the house tell me nothing and I don't ask."

"I'll explain everything to you as soon as we get inside, Hattie," Veronica promised. "We haven't much time. First I want to go to my room and pack . . ."

"Pack?" Hattie moaned. "Why pack? Where are you going? Where's Missy?"

"Hattie, please." Veronica spoke more sternly now, like one accustomed to giving orders and having them obeyed. "I said I would explain everything and I will. You brew a pot of coffee for Mr. Archy and Mr. Spindrift and then come to my room—and bring me a cup."

"Did you say the police are still in the house, Hattie?" I asked as we approached the pool.

"Yes, Mr. Archy. Two. In the solarium, where the accident happened."

Accident? Was Melva's housekeeper doing a little missionary work? If so, no fool Hattie. And there it was again, like a pinprick to my brain. The thought that Hattie had said something last night that I should have questioned on the spot—but didn't. What was it?

"What's happening out front?" Lolly wanted assurance that his colleagues were still waiting, in vain, at the gate.

Hattie, leading our procession, stopped abruptly, and we all followed suit. Marching behind Mother Hattie in her black dress with white collar and cuffs while clutching our shoes, we must have resembled a group of worshipers walking barefoot to the shrine of Our Lady of Guadalupe.

"Out there?" Hattie cried. "At the front gate? A mob like Grand Central Station at the rush hour. Cameras, walkie-talkies, telephones without cords, spyglasses, and even a truck selling coffee and sandwiches but the police got rid of it, thank God.

"Mrs. Marsden came with my tonic this morning, bless her, and the policeman said there's a crazy lady out there saying she's delivering medicine. Only crazy one around here, mister, is you, I told him. Let her through or I'll call the police."

So, to avoid redundancy, Mrs. Marsden made it through, and Hattie, fortified by her tonic, was feeling her oats.

"I tried calling," Veronica began, hoping to stem the tide, but this only brought about another verbal deluge from Hattie.

"After they took Missy away, and the house still full of policemen, I couldn't sleep. Then I did finally nod off, four or five in the morning, but then the calls started coming in and never stopped. The policeman told me to pull the plugs. I say, 'No, Missy might want me.' He says, 'Missy can't call.' I didn't believe him but the phones don't stop and none of the calls were from Missy. Everyone wanted a statement. 'I have nothing to say,' I told them. After, I just pick up and hang up, don't even put it to my ear. Then I give up waiting for Missy but I don't know how to pull the plugs, so I ask the policeman and he does it."

"Poor Hattie," Veronica said. "Is there food in the house? Do you have everything you need?"

"Plenty of food, Miss Veronica. But I have no appetite. My change of climate sickness and then the . . ." Hattie once again burst into tears. Veronica, attempting to comfort her, joined in.

"Come," Veronica urged once again. "Let's get inside. I need that coffee."

We were nearing the solarium, where I noticed that all the blinds were tightly drawn. Lolly gave me a poke in the ribs and pointed, mouthing a silent "In there?" Before I could confirm or deny, Hattie exploded once more.

"We can't go through there," she announced, like a Historic House Tour guide telling her group the private quarters were off limits. "They were in there until it got light. Taking pictures, I think. Then the ambulance came and they took . . ."

Veronica saved us from another round of crying and comforting by taking the lead and marching toward an unobtrusive back door. "We'll go in through the kitchen," she stated.

"Shake off the sand and put on your shoes," Hattie commanded. "I mopped the floor twice today. What else was there to do?"

The kitchen was huge, all white tile and chrome. There were enough professional-grade appliances to make any restaurant chef jealous. The fact that it was used to serve three people who ate out four nights out of seven boggled my mind—but then my mind is easy to boggle.

Hattie went straight for the electric perk, and Veronica told us to wait in the drawing room before disappearing upstairs. Lolly followed me, taking in every detail of the rental mansion. "Do you know who this place belongs to, Archy?"

"No. Do you?"

"An old couple who went into hock to get their daughter married to an English title. Now they have to rent the place every winter and go live with their daughter and son-in-law in his family castle. No central heat, sixty bedrooms, one loo, and if you want to take a bath you have to order the hot water a week in advance."

"You're kidding."

"Would I lie to you, Archy?"

"Yes."

Melva once told me that the New York apartment and the East Hampton house were all the real estate she wanted to own. One of the advantages of being very rich was having the means to rent, at exorbitant rates, a mansion in Palm Beach or a castle in Ireland, and walk away when the season ended.

The drawing room brought back memories of last night, and I wondered if Melva had dressed before the police arrived, or greeted them in her peignoir. Strange the things you think about at times like this. Melva had wondered if Geoff's date drove off naked a minute before she pulled the trigger. And there it was again—what did Hattie tell me?

"You know the way to the solarium?" Lolly asked.

"You heard Hattie. It's a no-no and the police are still in there."

"One peek, Archy. You want to see it as much as I do."

I did, but only because I thought a look at the room might start the little gray cells meshing and endow me with total recall of all that Melva and Hattie had told me last night. It always worked for Mr. Poirot. "Quick," I said, "before Hattie brings the coffee. She'll think we're ghouls."

"Well, aren't we?"

I retraced the route I had taken last night. Then, I had found the solarium door open, and did again. But instead of Geoff, dead, I was greeted with the sight of Sergeant Al Rogoff and one of his men who looked young enough to be Al's son—both alive. As is our custom in company, Al and I exchanged a brief nod but said nothing. The room looked as serene as a picture out of a glossy magazine. All traces of last night's "accident" were gone. The photographers and print men must have done their thing hours ago, so why the no trespassing order with the police still there to enforce it? I would have to ask Al, but not in front of Lolly and the rookie. I foresaw lunch at the Pelican, and so did Al.

"You can't come in here," Al told his unwelcome visitors.

"I know," Lolly answered, "we just wanted to look in. We're here with . . ."

"I know who you're here with," Al said. "I saw you coming."

"One if by land, two if by sea," I recited. The rookie looked at me askance (impudent pup) and Al shook his head. "The yacht was my idea," I proudly told them.

"It figures," Al commented. I wanted to tell him to forget lunch at the Pelican but remembered that silence was golden. If I was going to be of any use to Melva Williams and John Fairhurst III, I would need all the help I could get and Al Rogoff was my *numero uno* contact on the PBPD.

"Would you please tell the young lady I'd like to see her as soon as possible," Al ordered.

"Can I know why?" I asked.

"No," he said, "but I'm sure she'll tell you why as soon as I'm finished with her."

I gave Al our covert nod but he didn't nod back, so I gently pulled Lolly out of the doorway and saluted the boys in blue. "Ta, ta, lads."

The rookie raised his hand to wave, but Al shot him a look that froze the hand in midair, rendering the kid an indoor traffic cop. I looked at the boy suspiciously before retreating.

I learned after returning from the scene of the crime that I was not Monsieur Poirot.

We made it back to the drawing room just as Hattie entered from the other door, tray in hand. Coffee, cream, sugar, and a plate of jumbo macadamia chocolate-chip cookies. The cookies reminded me of after-school treats and I would have liked to ask for a glass of milk, but didn't dare.

"When will Missy be back," Hattie demanded as she set down her burden.

"Miss Veronica will fill you in on what's happening," I assured her. "And if all goes well, Missy will be here by this time tomorrow."

"Thank you, Mr. Archy. You always bring good news." From your lips to God's ear, I thought. "When Mrs. Marsden asked me where Veronica was, I told her Mr. Archy is taking care of her." She beamed at me and Lolly giggled.

"Pour the coffee, Lol," I said.

Hattie was showing me her hand and it took me a moment to focus in on what she was saying. ". . . They pressed my fingers on a pad and took my prints like on the TV. See, they're still dirty. I washed but it doesn't all come off. The policeman said it takes a little time." With that she left us to our repast.

Now I thought I knew why Al wanted to see Veronica, but still wasn't sure why the room was off limits after the police had been and gone. Lolly served our coffee, and one taste of my cookie told me it wasn't out of a box or the freezer. When Lolly planted himself in the chair Melva had sat in last night, my taste buds deserted me. She had looked so small and fragile. I couldn't imagine what she looked like in a jail cell and didn't even try. Instead, I munched my chocolate chip.

"How did the interview go, Lol?"

"Splendid. She's very articulate and, in case you haven't noticed, very pretty."

"I noticed, but I'm surprised you did."

"Sticks and stones . . ." Lolly retorted and sipped from the fine bone china cup.

"Did she give you any details of what happened here last night?"

"No, because she wasn't here when it happened and said she thought a statement from the police or Melva's lawyers would be forthcoming."

Veronica was not only very pretty and very sexy, but also very smart. A rare combination indeed. If she had to choose between Buzz and me, whom would she pick? Handsome Buzz or cute Archy? Robert Taylor was handsome and Mickey Rooney was cute—and I wish I hadn't made that comparison.

"Where was the body, Archy?" Lolly was still mentally filing his story.

"What makes you think I know?"

"Because Veronica told me Melva called you last night and you came right here. I know you couldn't resist going into that room and having a look."

I had to get some information out of Lolly, and keeping to my creed of give-and-take, I knew I had to give before taking. "On the floor, just parallel to the couch."

"Faceup or -down?"

"You're the ghoul, Lol."

"No, Archy, I'm the reporter."

"There are those who would say the labels are interchangeable."

"I'm not one of them. Faceup or -down?"

"On his back."

Lolly was making hieroglyphic marks on a small notepad. Good grief, he knew shorthand. Was Lolly a graduate of Katherine Gibbs? In that hat, why not?

"What was he wearing?"

I stopped munching. "Don't you remember?"

Lolly stopped jotting and looked up at me, seated just across from him. "Me? Remember what?"

"What Geoff was wearing last night, that's what."

"Archy, are you daft? How would I know what Geoff Williams was wearing last night?"

I thought I was back on the *Sans Souci,* trying to get some information out of Phil Meecham. So did my stomach.

"Didn't you see Geoff last night?"

"Archy, we're going in circles here. What are you saying? Out with it, now."

"You picked up Geoff last night and drove him to Phil Meecham's party."

If I had sent my coffee cup flying into his face, he couldn't have looked more surprised. Lolly was a competent actor. In fact, I think he did a few unremarkable seasons so far off-Broadway they called it Bucks County, PA. He was also a competent liar. Had he been carved out of wood by a sentimental Italian in need of a son, Lolly would be able to sniff out gossip in Hollywood

without leaving Florida. But no one, Barry-
more or Pinocchio, could pull a face like that
and not mean it.

"Why would I pick up Geoff and drive him
to Phil's yacht?"

"Because he called you and asked you
to do just that?" It was a question, not a
statement, and I knew what I was going to
hear before Lolly spoke the words.

First he laughed, the sound more cynical
than joyous. "One, I've been trying to get
that lug to call me for ten years. Two, he
never did. Three, he wouldn't get in the
same car with me, alone, if he needed a ride
to the hospital. Four, what the hell is this all
about?"

I calculated my options, which didn't take
long, because I had none. Geoff had lied to
Melva, and now I had to tell Lolly Spindrift
the truth. And did it matter? The tawdry
scene played out in the room presently
guarded by Al Rogoff would be public
knowledge by tomorrow morning if it hadn't
already been leaked to the media. Besides
all that, maybe Lolly could still tell me something that would help us identify Geoff's last
piece of forbidden fruit. Lolly knew more
gossip than any servant, lawyer, or mar-

riage counselor in Palm Beach. Most important, what Lolly didn't know, he would go to great lengths to learn.

"He was nude," I stated, as blandly as if I were asking Lolly to pour me another cup of java.

I should have waited until Lolly had downed his last sip from the expensive piece of Limoges. One mustn't gasp and swallow at the same time. It makes breathing difficult. After he finished gargling with Hattie's fine brew, he began making wheezing sounds that had me wondering if I should administer the Heimlich maneuver. By the time it occurred to me that I didn't know how to perform the Heimlich maneuver, Lolly came up for air.

"Flat on his back and naked!" he cried. His face was as red as a stoplight.

"And dead," I added.

"What happened here last night?" Lolly leaped out of his chair, spilling a few drops of coffee on the poor old couple's carpet. If the spots remained, Melva would have to pay for the cleanup, which, I'll admit, was the least of her worries at the moment.

With Lolly standing over me, I told the story just as I had heard it from Melva. No embellishing, no editorializing—just the facts.

"Who's the girl?" he eagerly asked.

"Funny, Lol, but that's what I wanted you to tell me."

Lolly began pacing, shaking his arm in the air like Dr. Frankenstein trying to figure out where he went wrong. "You know what I learned in the gossip business, Archy? I learned that if you don't ask the right questions, you'll never learn what you want to know."

"The girl's identity is what we want to know. Melva's defense will depend on it."

"The *crime passionnel*." Lolly rolled the words around on his tongue as if he were savoring a fine wine. I would lay heavy odds on what the headline would scream from the front page of his rag.

"The girl appears in the final scene, Archy. We have to start from where the curtain rises and take it scene by scene until we get to the finale." He walked to the table where Hattie had placed the tray, and helped himself to a cookie. "So, scene one. Geoff had no intention of going to Phil's party. He had a date. Why didn't he pick up the girl like any gentleman would?"

"Because Geoff Williams was no gentleman. Also, Melva said he didn't want to leave her without transportation, should she decide to go out," I told him.

"I never knew Geoff to be considerate, especially to his wife and more especially when he was hot to trot, so to speak. And Melva is not poor. If she wanted transportation she could call a taxi, or more likely a limo service, and go where she liked, when she pleased. He didn't pick up his date because he couldn't."

"And I think I know why," I joined in, warming to the game. "Melva said she was young. Suppose she was a friend of Veronica's, living at home and not wanting her parents to know that her date was a married man. That could also be the reason why he took her back here. They couldn't go to her place, and she wasn't the motel type."

Lolly pointed at me with half a chocolate-chip cookie. "Very good, Archy. See how far we've gotten already. A young girl, living at home, of respectable lineage. So, she's one of us."

I never knew "one of us" to be either overtly respectable or shy of motels. "Why did Geoff use you as a beard?"

"Simple. Let's say that he knew the lady knew me. She has to pick up Geoff. If Melva happens to see her, the girl says she's filling in for poor Lolly who's laid low with the gout."

Not bad. It was the same reasoning I used to figure out why Geoff had taken her back to the house. If Melva was awake, he could say the girl drove him home because Lolly couldn't, and if she were a friend of Veronica's, that would make it even more plausible.

I summed up our hypothesis. "So we have a young girl, living at home, who may or may not be a friend of Veronica's. She's anti-motel, knows you, and likes married men. How many girls do you know, Lol, who fit the mold?"

"I'm thinking, Archy. There are, I know, exactly four boys who live at home and like married men. But girls . . ."

"Think hard, Lol. A lot depends on it."

"Oh, I will. And I'll make an appeal in my story and column. But if Melva's story is quoted verbatim, and it will be, the shy young lady will be labeled 'The Rider' and be asked to pose in jodhpurs for *Town and*

Country magazine. Do you really think she'll come running to Melva's defense?"

"We have to try, Lol. If we can't produce her in the flesh, we have to conjure up her presence in the mind of a jury. The hunt for the mystery woman will do just that."

I could hear Veronica and Hattie chatting as they came down the stairs. Before we had to restrict our deliberations, I quickly mentioned something to Lolly that had been bothering me since we left the yacht.

"Strange how that chopper knew exactly where and when we would be landing."

"Yes, isn't it," Lolly answered, fingering but not taking another cookie.

"How much do you think one of the major television networks would pay for information like that?"

"A lot, Archy. And sometimes more than money can be used for bait if the circumstances are just right."

"Meaning?"

"Meaning I gave a little and I'm going to get back a lot."

In the game of give and take, Lolly Spindrift was a doyen par excellence.

11

DINNER THAT EVENING was exceptionally splendid, if rather low-key given the circumstances that brought Veronica Manning to our table. The linen tablecloth and napkins were standard for our evening meal, but the silver candelabra complete with ivory tapers were, I'm sure, the Master's idea. The floral centerpiece came from mother's garden, and she beamed with delight when our guest commented on its perfection.

Mother, as I had predicted, was completely recovered from the afternoon's unpleasantness and looked enchanting in a simple beige dress adorned with a single strand of pearls. Tennessee Williams wrote that blue is the color of distance and royalty. Having attended scores of weddings, my sister's included, I can say with some authority that beige is the color of mothers attending their offspring's nuptials. Was Madelaine's choice of dress, like a politician's necktie, sending a message? If it was, her favorite son was not dismissing the idea out of hand.

Veronica did not pack a portmanteau for her overnight stay, but neither did she stuff a backpack for camping out. She wore a lightweight merino wool dress that was Givenchy's genuine article—Ginny, eat your heart out—and, consistent with the previous evening's attire, no jewelry, costume or otherwise.

Mother, in her golden years, and Veronica, in the full bloom of youth, were the quintessence of the alpha and omega manifestations of the *femme fatale.* Sunrise, sunset—expectation and remembrance of things past.

Dare I assume that Veronica Manning would be amiable were I to press my suit?—and I don't mean the one I'm wearing. I dared, all right, but did I want to? A union between the McNally and Ashton-Manning clans would render father delirious with joy even as the Ashtons and Mannings revolved in their graves. Mother would be happy if I married Little Orphan Annie, and Lolly Spindrift could report on the May-December wedding with all the rancor of his chosen profession. In short, everyone would be pleased except, perhaps, the groom. But did that matter? To the groom, it most certainly did.

Ursi outdid herself with a crown roast, each little chop so succulent one envied Hobo the joy of sucking each bone dry while we poor humans were not allowed to touch these treats with anything other than knife and fork. Alongside the roast were potatoes Anna and sugar snap peas with lemon zest and cracked black pepper. For the accompanying wine, I passed up the traditional Burgundy in favor of a sturdier côtes du Rhône to impress our company. If she noticed, she did not comment on the wine steward's expertise.

Conversation was polite and guarded, but to completely avoid Melva's predicament would only serve to draw attention to it. Father told Veronica that her mother's lawyers had arrived in Palm Beach. "A team of three," he said, "and two, I am happy to say, are admitted to practice in Florida."

I silently questioned father's joy at that bit of news.

"I expect more will be coming down if needed," he went on. "I booked them into the Chesterfield Hotel on Cocoanut Row. Do you know it?"

"I know the Leopard Bar there," Veronica admitted.

"Of course," father said, "I'm sure it's a favorite with your set."

The Chesterfield! Score one for McNally & Son. The Chesterfield was a deluxe hostelry without the notoriety and pomp of The Breakers. Had Melva's crew been put up at the latter it would have evoked the image of wealth and privilege. Jurisprudence frowns upon the world seeing Ms. Justice winking behind her blindfold as her scales are being tipped with pieces of eight.

With the likes of Veronica Manning in our midst, I feared *mon père* would drag me off to the den for a cigar and port, leaving the ladies behind to gossip over their coffee and puff pastry. In fact, father and I often did go into the den after dinner for a nip and a smoke while mother joined Ursi and Jamie in the kitchen for coffee and an exhilarating hour at the TV, watching Ursi's favorite sit-coms. Mother could name all the members of these coaxial cable couples just as a previous generation knew all members of the celluloid Hardy, Aldridge, and Bumstead broods.

I roused the group out of the lethargy that often follows a sumptuous meal by reminding them that we had a nine o'clock date with the Cable News Network.

"I don't enjoy watching the news on television," father said as we filed into the den. "I prefer a good newspaper with an intelligent editorial staff."

"I think you'll find this the exception to your rule, sir," I answered.

"And I think I know why," Veronica joined in, taking her place in the comfortable leather chair I usually occupy when conferring with father. "You're going to see how Archy averted the press and the curious in getting me to my home and out again."

"Archy on television?" mother asked, sitting next to father on the settee. "Should we call in Ursi and Jamie?"

"I dare say they'll be watching in the kitchen," father told her. "And I know all about my son's escapades, Veronica. In fact, all of Palm Beach knows, thanks to Clara."

"Clara?" Veronica questioned. "Should I know who she is?"

"She's the upstairs maid of your nearest neighbors on Ocean Boulevard," father explained. "Clara watched your arrival and departure through binoculars—"

"From an upstairs window," I couldn't help injecting.

After paying tribute to my wit with an icy glance, my sire continued his tale. "And then she called Mrs. Marsden . . ."

When he strokes his mustache, as he was now doing, father takes on the air and verbosity of Disraeli addressing Parliament.

"Well," Veronica said, "I think Archy was very clever to come up with the idea, and very resourceful to put it into motion and make it work."

"My son is smarter than he likes people to know," father bragged, as if I were something he had just plunked down on the auction block—and perhaps I was.

"Yes," mother agreed, with a beatific smile directed at me.

Without missing a word I pretended to hear none of this as I opened the doors of the mahogany credenza that hid the television screen from pater's disapproving view. "We'll see our afternoon cruise on the *Sans Souci* and more," I told them.

"More?" Veronica asked, looking apprehensive.

"Promise," I said.

"But how do you know the network will carry it at exactly nine o'clock?" Veronica insisted on knowing, and not for the first time since I had made the announcement.

"Trust Archy," mother said.

After tuning in to the news channel, I kissed mother's rosy cheek before taking my own seat.

"More on the Palm Beach society murder," was the anchor's lead-in, immediately followed by the predicted aerial shot of us climbing out of Meecham's yacht and into the speedboat, the camera staying on us until Veronica fell into Hattie's arms. The voice-over explained what we were doing and why, intercutting shots of the melee in front of the Williams' house to stress the point. Some wag at the network decided on the bouncy air known as "I'm Popeye the Sailor Man" to accompany our caper.

Most prominent from the air was Veronica's blond hair and Lolly's panama hat. When the zoom lens moved in on us it focused on Veronica, whose beauty surrendered nothing to the small screen, and on Buzz at the helm of the speedboat. Our pilot, I noted grimly, looked more like James Bond than the guy in the yachting cap and boat-neck striped shirt. Yes, it hurt.

"And now, standing by in his office is the man who accompanied Veronica Manning on her watery trail to the safety and comfort of her home: Palm Beach society columnist Leonard Spindrift."

I almost fell out of my chair. Leonard? I knew "Lolly" was a byline dreamed up by Lolly's editors, who believed that a woman society columnist would prove more appealing than a man. However, we were all so used to calling him Lolly we had forgotten he had a real name. But Leonard? I would have put my money on Bruce.

Veronica squealed, then covered her mouth with her hand as she glanced over at me. Father nodded his approval. "The name

Lolly always reminded me of a child's candy," he said with conviction. Strange, it always reminded me of a jowly woman in Hollywood proclaiming, ". . . and here is my first exclusive."

Well, her namesake, if indeed that's what our Lolly was, did have an exclusive that quickly overshadowed our brief moment of comic relief. All eyes were on the screen and all ears attuned to Leonard Spindrift's words.

First he discussed his interview with Veronica Manning aboard Meecham's yacht, making the cruise sound as purposeful and as hazardous as Bogart and Hepburn's ride on the *African Queen*. He stressed Veronica's devotion to her mother and alluded to her stepfather's imperfections. The philandering stepfather number was implied rather than stated. No one likes to hear ill of the dead—especially the murdered dead. Good work, Lolly. Or should the credit go to Veronica?

I looked at Melva's daughter as she listened to Lolly. Poised, alert, and clear-eyed—Veronica Manning was young in years but not in experience. She would prove a crutch, not a worry, to Melva.

"And now," Lolly said in a tone that heralded the arrival of his purpose on national television, "with Veronica Manning's permission, I am going to reveal a fact regarding this tragedy that, as of today, is known only to the police. Prior to the confrontation between Melva Williams and her husband, Geoffrey, Mrs. Williams came upon her husband in a compromising situation with a young woman unknown to Melva Williams.

"That woman fled the scene before the shooting occurred and is not, in the legal sense, a witness to the crime. However, she is vital to the case as a corroborating witness to Mrs. Williams's account of the incident. The police will be seeking her; Mrs. Williams's lawyers will be seeking her; and now, on behalf of Mrs. Williams's daughter, I am asking the Mystery Woman to contact the Palm Beach police immediately.

"To the Mystery Woman I say—neither I nor Melva Williams nor the police can guarantee you anonymity. We can only appeal to your conscience to provide a ray of hope to a woman who is perhaps a victim of circumstance rather than an architect of premeditated malice.

"You have just heard a dramatic appeal to . . ."

I used the remote to turn off the television. The silence we had managed to escape at the dinner table now infiltrated the den. I looked at Veronica and nodded my encouragement. She answered with a brave smile that gave me goose bumps. It was mother who broke the spell of Lolly's telecast. "If you will excuse me," she said, "I think it's past my bedtime."

Father helped her to her feet and she took his arm, anxious to escape from a scene I'm sure she didn't quite understand. "Please stay, Archy—and you, too, Veronica," father said, "I'll be back before I retire and I should like a word with both of you."

Veronica wished her hostess a good night, and I kissed mother before father escorted her from the room. When the door closed behind them, brave Veronica broke down in tears. I went to her and put my hand on her bent head. Her hair was silky smooth. "Lolly did a great job," I said.

"The Mystery Woman," she sobbed. "How humiliating for mother."

"But necessary," I told her. I removed a tissue from the box on father's desk and handed it to her. "In the movies the guy always has a handkerchief, but I seem to be fresh out."

She blotted her eyes and managed a smile. "Poor Archy. I've been an albatross around your neck since last night. How can I ever repay you?"

I could have mentioned a few ways but bowed to the solemnity of the moment. "I don't want to be repaid. I promised your mother I would watch over you, and that's just what I'm doing."

She looked up at me and took my hand. "Is that the only reason, Archy. Because you promised mother . . ."

"Thank you for waiting," father said as he opened the door and entered the den. Seeing Veronica's hand in mine, he turned to close it, giving us time to separate. "Mother is settled in," he announced as he took the chair behind his desk, a signal that the class was being called to order and teacher would preside.

"Archy, why don't you pour us a drink. Veronica, what can we offer you?"

"Is a kir possible?"

"Of course," father assured her. "Brandy for me, Archy."

I mixed Veronica's kir and poured two Rémys into brandy snifters. After serving the drinks, I pulled a chair alongside Veronica's, and reached into my suit pocket for an English Oval. "Does anyone mind?" I asked politely, sitting.

"Not if I can have one," Veronica answered.

Father produced an ashtray from a desk drawer and placed it in front of us with a show of impatience. I have seen the Master enjoy a good cigar in the company of gentlemen but never in the presence of a lady.

"The bail hearing is set for tomorrow at eleven," he began. "Your mother's people will meet in my office at nine to be briefed by our man who has been acting on your mother's behalf since this morning. He will also guide them through the maze of the Florida judicial system."

"Will they grant bail?" Veronica nervously tapped a bit of ash from her English Oval into the ashtray.

"I would like to answer positively and without conditions," father said, "but one can never be a hundred percent sure of anything when standing before a judge."

"Let's say it's a silly little millimeter less than certain," I added to ease her anxiety— and to save my English Oval from being extinguished before its time.

Father nodded in agreement. "One could say that."

"I would like to be at the hearing," Veronica stated.

"And your mother's lawyers want you there," father told her. "A show of family unity is very important during the early stages of a case like this. I'll be leaving for the office at eight tomorrow morning, and I suggest you come with me, Veronica. I'm sure they will want to confer with you before the hearing. From there, you can accompany your legal people to the court-house. I've arranged a car and driver for them. The driver, I think, will be necessary until they get to know their way around the area. Your car can remain here and Archy will see that it gets back to your home later in the day."

Well, Archy was *persona non grata* at Melva's bail hearing. Why?

"Mr. McNally, I want to thank you for your help and hospitality." She put out her English Oval and deposited her drink on the desk. Both had a long way to go before they could be considered consumed. "I know you want to talk to Archy, and unless you have more to tell me or want me to stay, I would like to go to my room. It's been a long day."

"No, there's nothing more I have to say," father told her, "and I think a good night's rest is a most sensible idea."

She rose and father and I did the same. "I'll show you up," I offered.

She shook her head. "I don't want to lose my status as preferred guest, so I'll find my own way. Good night, Archy, and Mr. McNally, I'll see you at seven."

"Half past six if you want breakfast," father reminded her.

"Oh dear." And with a toss of her blond head she left us to our brandy and masculine parlance.

"I expected to accompany Veronica to the hearing," I said as soon as the door closed behind her.

"It's what I wanted to discuss with you, Archy." He reached into a drawer and came up with a box of cigars. Taking one, he used an instrument made for the express purpose of snipping off one end before lighting up. "She's taken quite a shine to you, Archy." He exhaled the words along with a cloud of smoke.

"A port in a storm, sir."

"I think there may be more to it than that."

"She's very young," I said.

"She'll be twenty-two next month."

"You know, sir?"

"I thought it prudent to know. A fifteen-year difference is not unheard of."

I stopped sniffing my brandy and took a generous slug. "It's early days, sir, and I think Melva is top priority at the moment."

"Indeed. I was just speculating, Archy. Just speculating. The counsel I assigned to Melva told me about this so-called Mystery Woman. What have you learned, Archy?"

I brought him up to date and when I finished he said, "You're something of a fop, Archy, but you're not a fool."

I didn't know if I should be flattered or insulted. "I'm your son, sir." Now he didn't know if he should be pleased or indignant.

"Do you know what I'm thinking, Archy?"

"Yes, sir. We're all assuming that Geoff lied to Melva about where he was going last evening. One could also assume that Melva was lying when she told her story."

"Exactly. And Geoff isn't here to counter anything she says. Whom do you believe?"

"Melva is an old and dear friend, sir."

"I know that, Archy. What's said here is said in complete confidence, you know that."

"I do, sir. I think Melva is telling only a part of the story. I mean, I think she knows who the Mystery Woman is, and is protecting her."

"A friend of Veronica's," he quickly stated. Father is a quick study, and Geoff's reputation is no secret in Palm Beach.

"Yes, sir."

He enjoyed a few more puffs on his cigar while engaged in thoughtful meditation. When he had worked it all out, he said, "There are too many variables here, and, as you've just said, it's early days for any decision making. For that reason, Archy, I'd like you to back off until Melva has consulted with her attorneys and we know exactly the stance they will take in her defense. Any assumption on our part that is contrary to the defense and leaked to the wrong people could be disastrous for Melva."

I agreed with what he said, although I was a little chagrined at what he might be implying. "Do you think Lolly's appeal on national television was ill-timed, sir?"

"No, no," he quickly responded, waving his cigar to make the point. "It was just a matter of time before this Mystery Woman became public property. Lolly's presentation was very sensitive, very dramatic. I take it you used Lolly to commandeer Phil Meecham's yacht, and he alerted the network in return for his fifteen minutes of fame."

"Yes, sir."

"But you take my point, Archy. While attempting to help Melva, or Veronica, you called on Lolly, but you had no way of knowing that Lolly would carry the plot one step further for his own purpose. As it turned out his purpose suited ours. But, for argument's sake, suppose it had not. Then the disaster I mentioned would have become a reality. Something to avoid at all costs."

Nothing I hadn't thought of, but I've learned the better part of valor is not to bring such things to father's attention. It caused a chill to run through the castle, and I would hate to find the moat raised just as my Miata was pulling in for the night."

"I agree, sir, but I want to poke about a bit and see what I can come up with."

"Do, but keep your own counsel and a low profile."

"Like keep out of the courthouse tomorrow morning?"

"Correct. Let's keep Discreet Inquiries discreet, and while we're on that subject, is there any progress on the Fairhurst case?"

"Nothing to report, but there is something I would like to follow up on. Once Melva comes home tomorrow, as I'm sure she will, and Veronica is back in the nest, I'll have time for the Fairhurst case."

"Don't abandon the girl, Archy."

"I won't, sir."

12

IT WAS MIDNIGHT when I finally reached my third-floor retreat, a mere twenty-four hours since Melva's call. I hummed a few bars of "What a Difference a Day Makes." In that sentimental song of yore, the day went from cloudy to sunny, thanks to the appearance of the object of the singer's affection. My day had gone from murder to blackmail to high jinks on the high seas in less time than it took Peter Piper to pick a peck of pickled peppers. The only thing resembling the sun in Melva's case was her daughter's lovely tresses, which were beginning to become an obsession with me. Another oldie but goodie advised, "Beware My Foolish Heart."

I undressed and washed, thinking that until father mentioned the Fairhurst business I hadn't given it a moment's thought since John Fairhurst III passed his unwanted epistle around the Master's private office. I would have liked to tell Fairhurst to fess up to granddaddy's folly, but that would put Discreet Inquiries out of business and Archy out of a job and, most likely, a home—and I liked my digs on the third floor, be they ever so humble.

The brandy had spoiled my taste for a small marc, but an English Oval was certainly called for to bring closure to this day of infamy. Too tired to update my journal, I wrapped myself in a paisley silk dressing gown, lit up, and stretched out on my bed.

The only lead, if you could call it that, in the Fairhurst case was the chauffeur, Seth Walker, who got his job through Geoff Williams, recently deceased. Coincidence? Probably. Geoff doing a good turn for the son or brother or boyfriend of one of his lady friends or a bookmaker to whom he owed a favor. Geoff's love of things fast ran the gamut from greyhounds to women. But

Walker was the only unknown quantity in the Fairhurst household, making him the logical suspect. Circumstantial evidence, I know, but for the present it would have to do.

The only person who could enlighten me regarding the life and times of Seth Walker was Geoff Williams, and, for obvious reasons, he wasn't talking. Mrs. Marsden, CEO of the Palm Beach Broadcasting System, might be able to tell me something about Seth as she was also the unofficial delegate to the union of domestic engineers. That, however, would entail a visit to the home of Lady Cynthia Horowitz, where I could not show my face without appearing before Connie of the black tresses.

If Connie had not broken our date last evening, I would not have been at home to receive Melva's call. Had I not received Melva's call, I would not have been cast in the role of guardian to Melva's daughter. Connie, then, was entirely responsible for my involvement with Veronica Manning. My conscience was clear.

I heard a sound that I would attribute to mice in the wainscotting, were I residing in a tale of mystery and imagination by Mr. Edgar Allan Poe. But I was in our three-story dwelling on five acres in Palm Beach, where the mice seldom found it necessary to come in out of the cold. I might imagine it was a raven tapping on my chamber door, but instead of "Nevermore" my visitor stage-whispered, "Archy?"

"It's open," I called, sitting up and adjusting my robe to receive company. I regretted not wearing an ascot. Noel Coward never appeared in a robe without an ascot adorning his neck. I hurried, barefoot, from bedroom to sitting room just in time to see the door open and Veronica poke her head into my sanctuary. "I can't sleep, Archy."

"Me, neither. Come on in and we'll declare this our private chat room."

She wore a blue cotton robe over a pair of crisp white pajamas. Her blond hair was braided into two pigtails. The only things lacking were cheeks shiny with cold cream and a book of obscure verse bound in moroccan leather. How delightfully unglamorous. Why, she could have been visiting her next-door neighbor at the Tri-Delt sorority house. "Did I catch you in your pajamas?" she said, closing the door behind her.

"Real men don't wear pajamas, Veronica, but they do eat quiche."

"So this is where you hang out," she said, looking around. "It's like a pied-à-terre."

"More a toe-à-terre," I said modestly.

"Silly, it's just a figure of speech." She looked longingly at my English Oval, and I was forced to sacrifice another to four puffs and sudden death.

After giving her a light, we kept our eyes on each other, avoiding, I think, looking into the next room, which she had to know was my bedroom. I offered her the only comfortable chair in the room and pulled out the desk chair for myself. "Did you try counting sheep?" I asked.

"Can't you ever be serious?" she accused.

I thought I was being serious, but who am I to disagree with a lovely visitor garbed in PJ's? "No, I cannot," I told her.

Having been nurtured on threats of global warming, ozone depletion, invasion by swarming killer bees, and universal extinction via nuclear war and cholesterol, I decided a long time ago that the only way to cope was to follow the advice of Mr. Pagliacci and *Vesti la giubba.* No, I don't intend to add a clown's collar to my already esoteric wardrobe—it's just a figure of speech, like pied-à-terre. Do my glad rags hide a broken heart? I'll never tell.

I'm not impervious to Melva's predicament, I just deal with it in my own way. But being a soft touch for blue eyes about to brim over, I quickly added, "But then I'm not serious about never being serious."

"Archy, I'm so scared," she suddenly confided.

"You have a right to be, and I don't mean to sound glib."

"I know. You're sweet, Archy."

"Your mother has the best legal team money can buy, and I think she has a good chance of beating this thing."

"Do you really think so?"

"I do, and so does my father, but he would never admit it. Lawyers don't offer opinions because they don't want to be told they were wrong."

"Why did you get bounced out of Yale Law, Archy?"

"If I said that during a concert of the New York Philharmonic I streaked naked across the stage wearing a Richard M. Nixon mask, would you believe me?"

"No."

"Then consider the subject closed." I put out my cigarette and passed the ashtray. I thought about Melva and wondered if she had really gone back to two packs a day. My hunch was, she had—and with good reason. Veronica returned the ashtray, which now contained two dead soldiers—one having succumbed to old age and the other snuffed out in infancy.

"I wish you were coming with me tomorrow, Archy. I could use the support."

"You'll be in good hands. Being seen with your mother's lawyers and not a gentleman friend, especially one known to be a private snoop, will help Melva's cause, believe me."

"Appearances," she exclaimed. "From now on it's all that matters. Mother and I will be scrutinized like germs under a microscope—and judged accordingly. I want to run and hide, Archy. Would you come with me?"

"I'd be tempted. But, no, I'll stick around and see this thing through with Melva."

"So will I. I was just . . ."

"I know you were." Then, seizing the moment, I asked what had been on my mind since I broke the sad news to Veronica. "Tell me something. How did you feel about your stepfather? Yesterday you said you didn't like him. Did you mean it, or were you in such a state of shock that you didn't know what you were saying? And this is not for print. I'm not Lolly Spindrift."

She looked at me with those blue eyes wide open and seemed to give the matter a great deal of thought. When she did speak it was as if she were reciting a mantra that had been echoing in her pretty head longer than her tender years warranted. "I didn't feel anything. Neither like nor dislike. All my girlfriends had crushes on him, and I thought they were silly. When I grew up and began seeing what my mother refused to acknowledge, I simply blocked him out. Can you understand that? To hate him would be to validate him, and I wasn't ready to concede even that. Between mother and me, Geoff had it made in the shade, as they say."

"You told Lolly that your stepfather treated you more like his sister than a daughter."

"That might have been an exaggeration, but not a big one. Geoff was certainly more interested in his tailors and barbers and how often he could get his name in the society columns than in looking after me. But then I didn't need him, did I? I had mother and school."

"I wouldn't make an issue out of those schoolgirl crushes unless you think one of your friends . . ."

She shook her head adamantly. "No, I don't think any such thing. Besides, none of my school friends are here, in Palm Beach. The Mystery Woman is someone Geoff picked up at Phil Meecham's party."

And that seemed to lay to rest my theory that the Mystery Woman was a friend of Veronica's. However, I now had to resurrect a painful fact to my late-night caller. "Veronica, Geoff never went to Meecham's party."

She looked stunned, as if I had tossed a glass of cold water in her face. "But . . ."

"Lolly didn't pick Geoff up and drive him to Meecham's boat, and neither Lolly or Meecham remember seeing Geoff at the party."

"He lied to mother," she cried.

Of course, I didn't counter with the fact that mother could be lying to us. The poor girl had enough to think about without putting that bee in her bonnet. "He did," I agreed.

"But who did pick him up? You said the Rolls never left the garage and I had my Mercedes."

"The girl, we presume. Who else?"

Again she seemed to mull over this new development as she was apt to do before making a statement. Veronica Manning did not rush in where angels fear to tread. Then, very slowly, the bee found her bonnet without my help. "But that conflicts with mother's story. I mean, without Lolly's and Phil Meecham's backing, it's only her word against Geoff's."

"And she fired the gun and Geoff is dead. Sorry, but them are the facts, as my friend Al Rogoff would say."

"Then we must find this Mystery Woman, Archy—we must." She was now wide-awake and animated—arms and pigtails in motion.

"I've told you how important that was more than once, young lady."

"A reward," she almost shouted. "We'll offer a reward and Lolly can announce it on the television. One million dollars. Who wouldn't trade their reputation for a million dollars?"

"Who? Why, someone who doesn't need a million dollars, that's who. On the other hand, those who do need a million bucks and couldn't care less about reputations— and their number is legion—will come out of the woodwork in droves to say they are the Mystery Woman. Don't forget the Hollywood starlet or two in need of publicity, as well as several transgenders who want to show off their new ball gowns. It would become a joke, Veronica. Melva's tale will go from suspect to broad farce."

"But they would have to give the police particulars," she argued. "Time, place, describe our house, things like that. Details only the real Mystery Woman could know."

I hated to burst Pollyanna's bubble, but the sooner her feet touched the ground, the better it would be for all concerned. "The prosecution could say she had been briefed by Melva's lawyers, or by Melva herself. In short, the witness was bribed a million bucks to say what the defense needed saying."

She hit the ground so hard I thought I heard the thud. "Sorry, kid. The Mystery Woman will have to come forward of her own accord. Of course, a newspaper or one of the networks might offer a reward, less than a million, I'm sure, but the burden of proof would be on them, not on your mother and her lawyers."

I wanted to go to her and take her in my arms. For the sake of propriety as well as my blood pressure, I kept my seat. "I thought Lolly's pitch was right on target, and it *could* work. In fact, I'm thinking the Mystery Woman might even give herself up to Lolly."

Veronica was shaking her head, putting the pigtails in motion once more. Clearly, she had more faith in the power of a million bucks than in Lolly Spindrift's powers of persuasion. So did I.

"Now," she whispered, "all we can do is wait and see."

"There were posters displayed during the last big war that were intended to boost the morale of wives and mothers. They stated, 'Those who wait, also serve.' "

"I'm glad you're waiting with me, Archy."

Her confidence was unfounded, but only I was privy to that. "Might you answer one more question before I toss you out of my toe-à-terre?"

"Of course. As long as it's not too personal."

"What's *too* personal?"

"I'll let you know when I hear it."

"Do you always give your mother the address of where you can be reached when you go out in the evening?"

"Of course not. Whatever gave you that idea?"

"Your mother gave me the idea when she handed me the address of Hillcrest House as if she were handing out business cards."

She cocked her head and began tugging on one of her pigtails. The gesture, coupled with her outfit, made her look more like twelve than twenty-two. I wished I would stop thinking about age. Hers and mine.

"I remember!" The shout was accompanied by a clapping of her hands. "Fitz. Fitz."

"What?" I thought she was demanding a carbonated soft drink.

"Fitz," she exploded again. "Elizabeth Fitzwilliams. Fitz and I were going to a movie last night but she called in the afternoon and said she was stuck at a dinner party her parents were giving. She couldn't get out of it because one of the invited couples was bringing their son—a plebe at Annapolis—and Fitz had to balance the table, if you know what I mean. Not that Fitz didn't want to hang around. Show Fitz a plebe from Annapolis and I'll show you a woman—"

"Veronica, just the facts. I am not interested in Fitz's sex life."

"You wouldn't say that if you saw Fitz."

"Prettier than you, is she?"

She gave me a demure smile.

"I take it the piece of paper your mother gave me was intended for Fitz."

"Exactly. Fitz said that if the plebe was a nerd she would plead a headache after dessert and call me. I got invited to the party at Hillcrest, so I left the address with mother in case Fitz did call and wanted to join me."

And there it was. A most logical explanation to a perplexing question. I hoped Melva, too, had logical explanations for the questions she was going to be asked. "Who invited you to the party at Hillcrest?"

"Too personal," came the reply, quick as a speeding bullet. She stood. "If I'm going to look bright-eyed and bushy-tailed in the morning, I'd best go to bed."

"You said that to my father two hours ago, and then you came straight here." I stood.

"But now I have no one left to visit."

"There's Hobo."

"That animal has an ankle fetish."

I closed the three-foot gap between us. (A toe-à-terre says it all.) "Like Master, like dog."

"Oh, Archy!" She threw her arms around my neck, and for the third time (who's counting?) I was made uncomfortably aware of the swell of her breasts. This was becoming a habit—one that could prove as addictive as nicotine, and just as lethal.

We kissed. The gesture was neither passionate nor platonic. I would call it warm, tender, and a promise of things to come. When we parted, she rested her cheek against my chest.

"That was dreadfully naughty," she whispered.

"Yes, it was."

"I'm to blame. Don't feel guilty."

"What I'm feeling is not guilt," I answered, twirling one of her pigtails between my fingers. "But if you don't get out of here right now that's just what I'll be feeling—after the fact."

She broke away, laughing, and vacated my quarters.

My bachelor digs, once as sacrosanct as a monk's cell, had been invaded by Veronica Manning. A harbinger? Like Nathan Detroit's big song from my favorite show, *Guys and Dolls,* was it time to "give up the cards and dice and go for shoes and rice"? Nathan was portrayed by ol' Blue Eyes in the film version of that Broadway hit, and I knew that tomorrow I would be humming one of Frank's favorites—"I Couldn't Sleep a Wink Last Night."

13

NOT WANTING TO encounter Veronica, I slept in until I was certain she and father had left for the McNally Building. After taking a cool shower—since Veronica's arrival, cool showers have become *de rigueur* around here for more than sanitary reasons—I shaved with the help of a mirror that reflected a face twice as big as the one God had given me, then splashed on a bit of witch hazel to help soothe the razor burn.

I never use an aftershave because its five-and-dime odor overpowers the very expensive and irresistible cologne I dab, ever so modestly, on the back of my neck. I will not tell you its name because I do not want to share my scent with every school-boy, caddie, jock, and Wall Street yuppie who can afford its hefty price. I will reveal all when, in my old age, I write a *Histoire de ma vie* to rival Casanova. (Of course, Casanova would never have let Veronica out of his clutches last night.)

I donned silk briefs depicting neither T-Rex nor rabbits on the run, but the sign of the goat in tribute to the Capricornian Veronica. These were followed by boot-cut jeans, a T-shirt with the logo IF MUSIC BE THE FOOD OF LOVE, PLAY ON, which was designed especially for the Pelican Club Sextet and penned, I think, by The Bard, and my size-ten-and-a-half white bucks, because this was Palm Beach on a sunny day. Feeling preppyish, I topped it all with a porkpie hat.

I was ready to face a hearty breakfast fol-lowed by Connie Garcia, when the phone rang. Having not learned my lesson, I picked up the dastardly instrument.

"Archy here."

"Hi, Archy. It's Binky."

"Binky, my boy, did you hear the good news? Hobo is as healthy as you."

"I'm not so healthy, Archy."

This did not bode well. "What ails you, Binky?"

"Well, I'm having trouble getting around."

"This would have nothing to do with Hobo's nip at your ankle, I hope?"

"Nip? He dug his teeth in, Archy."

"He's a small dog, Binky."

"Even small dogs can exert two hundred pounds of pressure with their jaws."

This was far too scientific for Binky Watrous. "Who told you that, Binky?"

"The Duchess."

I might have known. The Duchess, for those existing in blissful ignorance, is neither a lady of rank nor Binky's mother—but his aunt. You see, Binky was rendered an orphan of the storm at an early age and was taken in by auntie, who thought that one day she would be repaid by a grateful nephew. Having long given up the hope of financial reimbursement, the Duchess has been reduced to settling for Binky's getting a job and moving out of her home, board, and life. But to date, Binky has not been able to find gainful employment and remains a ward of Auntie Dearest.

"Did Hobo draw blood, Binky?"

"Well, it's red . . ."

"I repeat. Did Hobo draw blood?"

"The ankle is swollen, Archy. The Duchess had me soak it in warm water and Epsom salts, then she bandaged it, but I can't put pressure on it and it's hard to walk."

"Is it, Binky? Or did the Duchess tell you you couldn't walk?"

"Well . . ." Binky hesitated. "We had to get an ambulance to take me to the emergency room at the hospital."

This was too much. "I hope you're kidding. Why did you go to the emergency room for a scratch on your ankle?" I asked, as if I didn't know.

"The Duchess said everything should be documented."

Just as I thought. The Duchess was looking to make back twenty-five years of expenditures on Binky Watrous in one raid on McNally & Son's insurance brokers.

"You're suing?"

"Nothing personal, Archy. The Duchess said your father must be insured for millions."

"And how many millions are you looking for, Binky?"

"We don't know yet. I have to get a lawyer. Do you think your father would represent me?"

"My father can't represent you in a suit against himself. That would be carrying conflict of interest to obscene heights. And just what are you claiming you suffered, thanks to little Hobo?"

"Hobo caused me to be shocked, hurt, and indignant."

Good lord, the Duchess must have been burning the midnight oil, poring over legal texts. "Tell the Duchess you don't have a case, Binky."

This struck a chord. "I was working on a case," Binky reminded me. "I'm entitled to workers' compensation, too."

The Duchess had left no stone unturned in her lifelong quest for solvency. "Did you ever hear of Sam Spade collecting workers' compensation?"

"No, Archy."

"Did you ever hear of Philip Marlowe collecting workers' compensation?"

"No, Archy."

"The Green Hornet?"

"No, Archy."

"Only sissies collect workers' compensation."

"I've never even been to San Francisco, Archy."

Spare me, God. "Binky, I am working on a case, and so I must leave you to soak your ankle and examine your conscience. I'll get back to you regarding your suit."

"We saw you on television. Great maneuver, Archy. A murder case! How's Veronica doing?"

"Nice of you to ask, I'm sure. She's doing better than others I could name and, you may as well know now as later—Hobo broke a tooth on your ankle. We have to puree all his food. We are shocked, hurt, and indignant, and we're countersuing. See you in court, Binky."

"We who are about to be sued salute you," I greeted Ursi in our kitchen.

"What now?" she sighed.

"Binky Watrous is suing us."

"Because of Hobo?"

"None other."

"Binky is a good boy," Ursi stated.

"If you mean his aunt put him up to it, you're right, Ursi."

"He'll get over it, Archy. The boy adores you."

"But the Duchess obviously doesn't."

Ursi poured me a large, freshly squeezed, and chilled glass of orange juice, which I accepted with a heartfelt thank-you. After draining the glass, I poured myself a coffee from the electric perk.

"What can I get you, Archy?" she asked.

"Thanks to Binky, I'm feeling a bit delicate. Just some scrambled eggs and bacon would be nice."

"Toast or muffin?"

"Toast, please. Is mother in the garden?"

"No. She and Jamie are scouting the nurseries in search of new and exotic begonias." Ursi spoke as she broke eggs into a bowl after lining a frying pan with bacon strips, then sliced two hearty slices from a fresh loaf of marbled rye. In minutes, the aroma in the kitchen would get the juices going and my delicate stomach would make a remarkable recovery.

What, I wondered, did an exotic begonia look like? And between Jamie's tight lips and mother's forgetfulness, I also wondered what the conversation was like in the wood-paneled Ford as it headed for unsuspecting nurseries. But knowing our Jamie, I was assured that mother would chatter, Jamie would listen, and they would return with the station wagon filled with exotic begonias.

"How did it go this morning, Ursi, everyone get off on time?"

"Of course, Archy. Your father wouldn't have it any other way."

"How did Veronica look?"

"Lovely, as I'm sure you know. But she hardly touched her breakfast. Just coffee and dry toast. Poor little waif."

"If all goes well, her mother will be home this afternoon, and that will make her feel better, I'm sure."

"But look what's still before them. A murder trial. What a scandal." Ursi shook her head as she scrambled my eggs.

"What's the gossip, Ursi?"

"Oh, it's a bit early in the day yet, but judging from the few calls I've gotten all the talk is of the boat ride and the Mystery Woman. Clara, who spotted Mr. Meecham's boat and never left the window until Miss Veronica was in Hattie's arms, says it was like Dunkirk. And, Archy, there's a pool been started to guess the Mystery Woman. One hundred dollars to enter and winner takes all."

"Are you entering, Ursi?"

"I'm not sure. A hundred dollars isn't easy to come by."

"But you think you know who the Mystery Woman is, don't you?"

"Do you?" came the instant reply.

"If I did, Ursi my love, I'd tell you her name and you could claim the pool."

"I think everyone, up- and downstairs, has their suspicions, Archy."

"I'm afraid you're right, but suspicions based on fancy, not fact, can be dangerous for both the suspector and the suspected."

"Then I'll keep my thoughts to myself and my hundred dollars in the bank." Ursi finished putting together my breakfast plate and not a moment too soon. I was starved.

"Miss Veronica asked me what time you usually came down to breakfast."

"And what did you tell her?"

"Your father told her you usually do paperwork in your room before coming down. What's paperwork, Archy?"

"Beats me. I think he was trying to impress the young lady."

"Well, she's certainly obsessed with you, Archy."

"You think so?"

"I know so. She missed not seeing you at breakfast."

"I'm just a port in a storm for Veronica," I told her, hoping she would disagree.

"I've heard of people putting into a port in a storm and falling in love with the place."

Subtlety was not one of Ursi's virtues. "Right after breakfast I'm off to see Connie," I announced.

Ursi put my plate of bacon, eggs, and rye toast before me and lamented, "Nothing is ever easy, Archy, is it?"

Hobo, tail wagging, came running to say hello while yapping happily, displaying a fine set of teeth. I didn't have the heart to tell him we might have to pull a few for his court appearance. When I saw Veronica's car, I remembered that I had been assigned to drive it to her home before the day was over. I had intended to use Binky for this chore, either having him drive the Mercedes or following me in my Miata, giving us return transportation. Until I talked him out of suing—if I could—it would be best to keep Binky and the Duchess out of my hair.

Binky, I knew, thought I was working on Melva's case, which I most certainly was not. Aside from sheltering Veronica, Melva had not sought my help, and there was really nothing I could do for her except, perhaps, keep my eyes and ears open regarding the Mystery Woman. The Fairhurst affair was my only case, and the less Binky, or anyone, knew about that, the better.

There is no alarm at the entrance to the Horowitz house on Ocean Boulevard because there is no gate. So social is Lady Cynthia that, aside from a revolving gate, a no-gate policy best serves the almost steady stream of traffic between the Boulevard and Lady C.'s oak front door. But don't let that fool you. This architecturally correct copy of an antebellum southern plantation, transported to Florida's Gold Coast, was encompassed by a high wall of coral blocks surrounding the estate, as well as the large patio and swimming pool area at the rear of the main house.

Each time I approached the place, I could hear Max Steiner's unforgettable theme music and fully expected to see, in gigantic letters, the words "Gone with the Wind" floating across the mansion's facade.

What I saw on this perfect Palm Beach day were the six flags Lady C. has hoisted each morning around her pool. Each represents the native land of her ex-husbands. It is a tribute to those responsible for Lady C.'s huge fortune. "Our only regret," they seem to whisper, while snapping smartly in the ocean breeze, "is that we didn't demand a prenuptial marriage contract."

Mrs. Marsden answered the front door chimes. "I saw you on television," were her opening words. Well, I could think of worse places to be seen—but not many.

"I hope you enjoyed the show, Mrs. Marsden."

"I've seen worse. Lady Cynthia is out, but Connie is in the office," she informed me. "You know the way."

Mrs. Marsden is a regal black woman with the posture and deportment of a marine sergeant. Widowed early in life, she had, I know for a fact, put two children through college while maintaining her sanity in the employ of Lady Cynthia Horowitz. Neither an easy feat.

I say this to correct any misinterpretation of my previous remarks regarding her character. Gossip in Palm Beach, up- and downstairs as Ursi would have it, is a way of life. It relieves the boredom of existing in a close-knit society and gives us an excuse to touch base with our peers on a day-to-day basis. Mrs. Marsden and her fellow domestics, with few exceptions, never indulge in malicious gossip. One wishes the same could be said for those who employ them.

"In fact, Mrs. Marsden, I would like a word with you before I go in to see Connie," I said as I entered the entrance foyer which could accommodate the entire Boston Pops, instruments and all.

She paused momentarily and turned to me. "The Mystery Woman?" she intoned, eyes unblinking.

With those two words, Lolly had started a snowball rolling down a hill that was taking on the proportions of an avalanche. And never mind that it never snowed in Palm Beach. "No," I said. "I think that's something best left to the police. I'm interested in the new chauffeur at the Fairhurst house. Do you know him?"

She drew back her head and eyed me head to foot before answering. "Is he in trouble?"

As Melva's friends were closing ranks, so would the domestics should one of their own be the accused. "Not that I know of, Mrs. Marsden," I quickly assured her. "It's a personal matter and I ask in confidence and hope you will afford me the same courtesy."

She gave that a moment's thought, and then remembering that as Connie's fiancé I was more "them" than "they," she shrugged and said, "He's new on the job, but I've seen him around."

"How does he strike you?"

"Uppity, is my opinion, but don't quote me, Archy."

"I won't, but in what way is he uppity?"

"Well," she began, "when we have a large reception, which is almost every day lately, I always invite the drivers into my kitchen for light refreshment and to pass the time. The last big do we had, about three or four days ago—it was for a children's hospital, although I never saw a child in Palm Beach that needed charity—this Seth shows up with Mr. and Mrs. Fairhurst. Good looker, I'll say that for him. Well, he isn't in my kitchen two minutes when he's passing up my coffee and asking for a proper drink. Imagine that!" This was delivered as if even the thought of serving proper drinks in her kitchen was appalling.

" 'Drivers are not supposed to drink,' I told him. And when my back was turned he took a can of beer from the refrigerator. Nervy, I call it."

"But not uppity," I reminded her.

"Oh, that." Mrs. Marsden was worked up and going full steam ahead. "Next thing I knew he was no longer in the kitchen, and then I spotted him mingling with the guests. Took off his cap, he did, and made his way in like he was invited."

"No one said anything?" I asked.

"In that crush, no one noticed."

"Did he cop a proper drink?"

Mrs. Marsden shook her head. "I wouldn't know that so I'm not saying. I would have told him to leave except he was talking to poor Mrs. Williams's daughter, Veronica, and I didn't want to make a fuss over nothing."

I pricked up my ears without flexing a muscle or batting an eye. If Mrs. Marsden didn't want to make a fuss over nothing, neither did I—if indeed it was nothing. Geoff knew Seth Walker. Why hadn't it occurred to me to ask Veronica if she knew Seth Walker? Or had Seth singled out Veronica because she was the prettiest girl in the room? Either way, Veronica now knew Seth. That was obvious.

14

CONNIE WAS ON the telephone trying to explain why Lady Cynthia Horowitz would not allow a tent city to be erected on her ten acres as a publicity stunt to aid Florida's homeless. Waving me to a chair, she admonished the caller with "No! No, no, no. Not for a week, not for a weekend, not for a day and not for an hour." With the press of a button she banished the intruder.

The "telephone" in Connie's office was a keyboard upon which red and green lights twinkled like Christmas-tree baubles. The gizmo resembled a prop from an old Buck

Rogers serial film of a bygone era. With the tip of one finger, Connie can connect and disconnect calls or redirect them to other persons in Lady C.'s household. She can hold a conversation, hands free, from any part of the room. She is equipped with voice mail, caller ID, call waiting, and call forwarding. The inimitable Ira Gershwin had it right when he penned, "Let's Call the Whole Thing Off."

"Well, if it isn't Popeye the Sailor Man," was Connie's open.

"You caught my act."

"Thanks to Lolly Spindrift, everyone in Palm Beach caught your act."

"So, Lolly alerted the troops to our little caper."

"The way I heard it," Connie said, "Lolly called a dozen people with the news and then asked each of them to call two people, who would then call—"

"The old pyramid game," I cut in. "And it worked. What did you think of it?"

"I think the guy driving the speedboat should have his own show. So does Lady C."

"Tell Lady C. the guy belongs to Phil Meecham."

"That won't discourage her, Archy. It will just pose a challenge and make her more determined."

"Good lord, Connie, she's a hundred years old."

"Not quite, but still waters run deep."

In Lady C.'s case, I would call it a flood tide. "What does she think about her ex-tennis maven being aced by his wife?"

"She said Geoff died the way he lived—in the saddle, as the saying goes."

"I hate to put a wet blanket on the lurid rumors, but he was quite alone when the end came."

"Recently alone, according to Lolly." The phone rang and Connie once again pressed a button, sending the call into the next century, which, come to think of it, wasn't that far off. "And Lady C. wants it made perfectly clear that she is not the Mystery Woman."

"Which means she wants everyone to believe she is. Well, tell Lady C. she has nothing to fear. Young, is how Melva described her nemesis."

"You tell her, Archy. I have my job to consider." Remembering her manners, she then asked, "How is Melva doing?"

"The bail hearing is going on as we speak, and I expect she'll be back home before long. The worst is yet to come for poor Melva."

"Why did she do it, Archy?"

"You heard Lolly. She caught him in the act and lost her head. Oh, that's what her lawyers will plead. Temporary insanity. Murder without malicious intent or forethought. It's worked before and it can work again."

"I never liked Geoff Williams," Connie admitted.

"You're at the end of a long line composed mostly of women he wronged. But don't tell me you were never caught under his spell, Connie."

"Not me," she stated. "The driver of that speedboat is more my type."

"Buzz?" I exclaimed.

"Cute name," Connie said as if she meant it. There's no accounting for taste.

"He's a child, Connie."

"So is Ms. Lolita Manning."

That got me right where I live, as intended, I'm sure. "What's that supposed to mean?"

"What's what supposed to mean?" She feigned surprise.

"Lolita, that's what."

"You've been baby-sitting the girl for two consecutive nights, is what I heard."

"She's twenty-two, Connie, not twelve, and I was helping Melva. She asked me to look after Veronica until things quieted down."

"Lolita Manning never needed looking after, is the way I heard it."

"Her name is Veronica."

"Archy and Veronica. Just like in the comics and twice as funny. Is it true Veronica spent both nights at your place?"

"You're overreacting, Connie."

"I don't think so. I'm just curious. I hear she's become quite enamored of 'Uncle' Archy."

"This, no doubt, from Lolly Spindrift. Have you been on the phone with him all day?"

"As a matter of fact, he was here," Connie said. "Summoned by Lady C. She wants to give a ball, Archy, a masked ball. All the ladies will be masked, as I understand it. A Mystery Woman's Ball is the theme. Get it?"

"That's macabre," I said. "I don't put it past Lady C., but Lolly would never be a part of such a thing."

"Oh, no? He almost swooned over the idea. Lolly sees it as bigger than Truman Capote's Black and White Ball. I think he's already talking to the national television networks. All the women unmask at midnight except the Mystery Woman, who refuses to be identified. They're hoping the real Mystery Woman will show up—hence the television coverage. Lolly is beside himself with ideas."

"Lolly is bonkers. This is macabre, Connie. Nothing less."

"You're overreacting, Archy. And it isn't macabre, it's Palm Beach, remember?"

"It's the worse possible thing for Melva's case. She needs sympathy, not a bunch of rich people making fools of themselves. The identity of the Mystery Woman—and I wish Lolly had never dreamed up that phrase— is crucial to Melva's case. All this will do is force the Mystery Woman to stay in hiding."

"I agree, Archy, and I'm not gloating. I like Melva as much as you do. All I'm doing is giving you the facts so you'll know what the tide might be dragging in." She took a deep breath and went right on. "And speaking of rich people making fools of themselves, delivering Lolita—excuse me, Veronica—to her back door by yacht is not going to have the crowd in the bleachers cheering for Melva."

"I was doing a good turn, and it worked. How was I to know Lolly would turn it into a publicity stunt for himself? And now that he's had a taste of fame, his appetite is ravenous. I've got to talk him out of this masked ball."

"It's Lady C.'s ball. Not Lolly's," Connie stated, and rightly so. "She'll do it with or without Lolly's advice and consent."

Lady C. has always been sweet on me, even after our run-in over my father's virtue. "I'll talk to her. She might listen."

"Maybe you could offer her a trade-off?" Connie suggested.

"Such as?"

"Deliver Buzz in exchange for her dropping the masked ball idea."

"All she has to do is open her checkbook and Buzz will come running."

"Madam is loath to write checks. Penurious is the word for Lady Cynthia Horowitz. She got millions from her first five marriages, but all her last husband left her was his title. Hence, the Lady is feeling a bit pinched."

"I take it the late Leopold Horowitz was really knighted by Her Majesty."

"Yes, for a lifetime devoted to the mating habits of beetles. His book on the subject is considered the definitive source."

"If he had researched the mating habits of Cynthia before he married her, he might still be alive today."

"Don't be silly, Archy. Leo fell out of a tree in pursuit of a beetle on his honeymoon."

"She pushed him."

"That's not kind, Archy."

"Lady Cynthia is not kind. I've got to talk her out of this madness, Connie."

The telephone rang once again and Connie once again zapped the call with a touch of her fingertip. Turning back to me, she asked, "Do you know who the Mystery Woman is, Archy?"

I shook my head. "No. Cross my heart. Why? Do you?"

"No. But rumors are flying up and down the A1A faster than the traffic. Ever hear of a gal named Elizabeth Fitzwilliams?"

I nodded, but didn't divulge my source.

"She's a fast package, as we used to say, and she was seen having a drink with Geoff the night before the murder."

Fitz could have been in one of our local pubs when Geoff walked in, and seeing a friend of Veronica's, he stopped to say hello. An encounter that would never have been remembered if Melva hadn't lost her head. This kind of gossip and conjecture was inevitable. People were suddenly going to remember every female Geoff Williams had ever said hello to, from waitresses to *grandes dames.*

Veronica said her stepfather was not smitten with any of her friends, and I believed her because, as some Roman said, *cui bono?*—who benefits from the lie? In this case, no one—hence, no lie. Veronica wouldn't sacrifice her mother to spare a friend a bit of embarrassment. And what Geoff was up to the night before his death was a moot question. Whom he was with the night he died is what mattered.

Here, I recalled the purpose of my visit to Lady C.'s commodious residence. "Remember the guy Lolly was interested in a few days back? The one he spotted at Lady C.'s reception."

Connie cocked her head in the way she does when she's trying to recall something. "The one I saw talking to Veronica Manning?"

She couldn't get Veronica out of her mind, and my question didn't help the cause. "One and the same," I ceded. "He's John Fairhurst's new chauffeur."

"Who told you that, Veronica?"

"Connie, I wish you would stop saying that name. It's boorish."

"Did she get a peek at your third-floor lodgings?"

"No!" I lied.

Cui bono? Archy, I'm ashamed to admit. But I'll think about that tomorrow.

"And we were well chaperoned," I continued. For effect, I raised my right hand, and in lieu of a Bible, I placed my left hand on Lady C.'s Palm Beach telephone directory. "Nothing—I repeat—nothing inappropriate passed between Veronica Manning and *moi.*" Surely a kiss or two could not be construed as inappropriate? Besides, how binding was the Palm Beach telephone directory?

"Oh." Relieved, she waved a hand at me. "I was just teasing you, Archy. That was a very clever trick you pulled, getting her home by boat, and the top of your hat was quite fetching. I've never seen you the way birds do."

Consuela was backing off. I had won our little game, which just goes to prove what car and insurance salesmen have long known: First you lie, then you swear to it, and then you make the sale.

"Thank you, Connie. And I know you were kidding when you said Buzz was your type."

"I wouldn't go that far, Archy."

She laughed. I laughed. And disaster, once again, was averted. But for how long? I had a lot to think about tomorrow.

"So tell me, how did a chauffeur crash the reception?"

"It wasn't the first time and, I'm sure, it won't be the last time that's happened. The way people dress these days, you need a scorecard to tell the guests from the caterers."

"I trust that was not a slur on my wardrobe, Ms. Garcia."

"I love your wardrobe, Archy. Especially the top of your hats."

"Are you busy tonight, Connie?"

"I was going to stay home and wash my hair, maybe rent a film, and just hang out, as Veronica might say."

"Veronica goes home to Mommy today, and Uncle Archy will make you dinner while you wash your hair. Rice and beans?"

"How'd you ever guess? Shall we say seven?"

"And I'll rent the film. You have lousy taste in films, Connie."

"I'd like to see something made in the last twenty years, Archy."

"Like I said, you have lousy taste in films." I rose to go. "Would you punch out a number for me before I leave?"

"Let's have it," she answered.

I gave her the number for the "palace," as Al Rogoff calls the police station, on County Road.

"Sergeant Rogoff," the familiar voice boomed across Connie's office.

"Archy here," I boomed right back.

"Yes, sir. How may we help you?"

This meant someone was in hearing distance of Al's desk. "I'm heading for the Pelican. I'll stand you a burger and a bottle of suds."

"A break-in? You say the window is broken?"

"And the rain she's coming in . . ."

"Where are you located, sir?"

"The bar of the Pelican in half an hour."

"Very good. I'll be there ASAP, sir."

"I'm starved, Al. And thirsty."

"I feel the same way, sir. About break-ins, that is."

"Ta-ta, Sergeant."

Connie pressed her magic button. "You're both nuts," she said.

"That reminds me. I'll bring the nuts for our cocktails."

"Was that dirty, Archy?"

"Why, Connie . . ." I blushed.

15

"HOW'S THE MARKET today, Mr. Pettibone?"

"Fair to middling, Archy. Fair to middling."

"Much like myself," I said to our bartender and factotum, Simon Pettibone, as he placed before me a hand-drawn glass of ale topped with a head of foam. It looked too perfect to consume, but that didn't stop me from hoisting the brew to my parched lips.

"I would stay clear of utilities and investigate corn futures," he advised. "It was a dry summer and corn will be at a premium."

"I'll remember that, Mr. Pettibone," I said politely, although I could not for the life of me figure out why anyone but pigs and cereal manufacturers would be interested in the future of corn.

Mr. Pettibone keeps his eyes on Wall Street as well as on the Pelican Club, and excels in both venues. Six months after the club was founded it went bankrupt, thanks to gross mismanagement on the part of its founders. The Pettibones were taken on to run the club, which they did, and do, with military efficiency if not always with a great deal of style. But who's complaining? Since the Pettibones moved into the second floor of the two-storied clapboard house that is the Pelican Club, our bottom line has gone from red to black, the amenities vastly improved rather than diminished. One of those amenities was son Leroy's cooking, an essential reason why the club was usually overflowing at lunch and dinner.

And if Simon Pettibone took his own market tips as seriously as those who followed his advice, he might very well be the richest man, or woman, in our lodge.

"We watched you on the television last night, Archy," Mr. Pettibone said, with a nod toward the big screen hovering over the far end of the bar. I wondered if those who appear regularly on television are subjected to the same disclosure by everyone they meet. If his statement meant that Mr. Pettibone had watched it on the bar screen, everyone in the club must have gathered around for the boat ride and Lolly's announcement. Knowing the Pelican boys, I guessed all of them thought he knew, perhaps intimately, the identity of our Mystery Woman.

Mr. Pettibone served gin and tonics to a couple at the bar before returning to me. "Poor Mrs. Williams," he intoned. Somewhere between New York and Palm Beach, there must be someone saying, "Poor Mr. Williams." Perhaps a waiter Geoff once overtipped?

"I remember her and the girl coming here with you in the old days, Archy. Pretty little thing, that girl, and what a stunner she's become, if the camera doesn't lie."

"Indeed it doesn't, Mr. Pettibone. Her name is Veronica, as you may recall, and what you saw on the television screen is what you get in person. Maybe even more so." Veronica somehow managed to insinuate herself into every conversation I had

had in the past two days. But then, she was that kind of girl.

After filling a bar order for Priscilla, who looked ravishing in a miniskirt and halter, her father returned to say, "Terrible tragedy, this affair. The kind of thing you read about that isn't supposed to happen to people we know. How is the child taking it?"

"Stoically, Mr. Pettibone. And we're hoping her mother will be out on bail today."

"How will she plead?"

"Oh, she's already admitted to the crime. The trial will decide cause, not guilt."

"The bail will be a million at least," Mr. Pettibone stated.

"I think the lady can scrape it together."

Mr. Pettibone leaned across the bar conspiratorially and said in hushed tones, "The boys are getting up a pool to name the Mystery Woman. Five hundred bucks a pop. I thought I'd mention it, as they didn't know if you'd be interested, seeing as how close you are to Mrs. Williams and things in general. They all saw how you smuggled the child in and out of her home, right under the noses of the press, on Mr. Meecham's yacht. You're a hero around here, Archy."

A hero, I thought, who is close enough to Melva and her daughter to know the identity of the Mystery Woman. These sharks wouldn't let me near the pool if I offered them odds and they were using Pettibone to deliver their message.

I was about to tell him that the domestics were also getting up a pool to name the Mystery Woman when I was struck by an idea too wickedly clever to resist.

"You're right, Mr. Pettibone, it would be unethical for me to participate. And in case the boys are thinking of offering bribes, you can tell them I have no idea who the lady might be, but if they're lucky enough to get an invitation to Lady Cynthia Horowitz's masked ball, they just might find themselves dancing a two-step with the Mystery Woman."

Pettibone started as if he'd been poked in the belly. "Masked ball? She'll be there? What's all this about, Archy?"

"Oh, me and my big mouth. Mr. Pettibone, please forget what I just said."

He removed my empty glass and began to wipe the bar with unprecedented vigor. "But, Archy . . ."

Priscilla breezed past and told me she had a corner table for two, if I was interested. "Are you expecting Connie?" she asked.

"No, I'm expecting the guy who just walked in."

"The fuzz," Priscilla announced, staring at Al Rogoff, who looked uncertain as to what he should do now that he had entered our lair. Priscilla's description of our visitor caused several heads to turn.

I motioned for Al to follow me to the corner table and heard Simon Pettibone repeat—"But, Archy . . ." as I drifted away from the bar. If there were more than those two words on his mind, they were lost to the rumble in the room.

"You look like a plainclothes cop in that suit," I chastised Al Rogoff. "Everyone thinks we're being raided."

"You want me to blow my whistle?"

"You'll start a stampede."

"I can't change into a casual jacket and slacks just for lunch. Besides, my attire conforms to the house rules." He pointed to a sign that proclaimed, MEMBERS AND THEIR GUESTS ARE REQUIRED TO WEAR SHOES IN THE DINING ROOM. "I am shod, sir."

In size-twelve police regulation boots, no doubt. Al Rogoff was a big man. A six-foot slab of raw beef with prominent jowls, Clark Gable ears, and unruly sideburns. His personal vehicle was a pickup truck, he used words like "broads" when referring to the fairer sex, and one would suspect that at home he watched the tube in his boxers and T-shirt while popping open cans of Bud in rapid succession.

Al Rogoff was living proof of the old adage "You can't tell a book by its cover." The only time Al Rogoff watched television was when PBS aired a performance by the New York City Ballet or an opera from the Met. Al could listen to the William Tell overture without once thinking, "Hi, ho, Silver, away," and could tell an '82 Médoc from Chianti sold by the gallon. He enjoyed Vivaldi and knew that "La Belle Dame sans Merci" was not a French dominatrix.

I knew all of these Rogoff secrets, which made him slightly uncomfortable in my presence, but beholden to me for my prudence and admiration. We were a team— like Nick and Nora, Perry and Della, Kong and Wray. We were Al and Archy.

Priscilla arrived with two ales and a pair of menus.

"How did you know we wanted malts?" I asked.

"Your date doesn't look like the champagne type," she answered. "The steak tartare is especially good today. I'll be back for your order." Exit Priscilla.

"Steak tartare?" Al raised both eyebrows.

"Have it medium rare. It's delicious."

"That makes it a hamburger," he informed me.

"That's what I invited you for."

"It's pricey, Archy."

"This is a business lunch. To keep us honest, just tell me what's happening at the palace."

Al picked up his glass. "Cheers." He drained half the contents, rid his lips of foam with a napkin, not the back of his hand, and then said, "The ladybird has flown the coop."

"When?"

"As I was leaving to come here."

"How much?"

"One and six zeros. Her people wrote the check like it was one and no zeros."

"For that crowd, Al, it is."

"Your fancy friend is chin deep in you

know what, pal. But she pleaded not guilty at the arraignment."

"No surprise. Did you see her daughter?"

"Only a glimpse. She was surrounded by Mommy's entourage. I got a chance to hold her hand yesterday when I took her prints. My heart skipped a beat, Archy."

"Tell your heart it made a mistake, Al. She's not your type."

"What's my type, Archy?"

"Brünnhilde or Cho-Cho-San. Your pick."

Priscilla returned and we ordered our steak tartare, medium rare. "McDonald's is down the road a way," we were informed. Exit Priscilla.

"Are your men still keeping watch on the Williams house?"

"Just until Mrs. Williams and the girl get back inside with a minimum of hassle, then we'll just patrol the area as usual. We hear she's hired private guards to keep the nasties from her front door."

"A good idea. What was the crowd like at the courthouse?"

"Big and mostly press. And not just Florida newshounds. They're arriving from all over the country. The television crews made the place look like a movie set."

"You might be on tonight's news, Al."

"I caught you last night, pal, and Lolly. He's made the Mystery Woman a national celebrity."

"Any word on the Mystery Woman?" I asked.

"No comment. What can you tell me about her?"

"No comment."

Which meant neither of us knew anything.

Priscilla arrived with our order. Steak tartare disguised as hamburgers and thin, crispy fries to die for. Al squeezed ketchup on his fries and passed the bottle to me. Steak tartare and squeezable plastic ketchup containers—the Pelican is in the midst of an identity crisis.

"Can I ask why you were keeping vigil in the chamber of death yesterday when the boys had called it a wrap?"

"The print boys dusted the room and we got the housekeeper's prints and the perp's prints." I winced inwardly at Melva being referred to as a "perp," but quickly concluded it was better than "broad," although I doubt Melva would agree.

Between bites of his burger and fries, Al continued to explain. "The cleaning people had been in the room earlier in the day and we got their names from the service company who employs them, so we could get their prints, too. That just left the girl, Veronica. I got her prints yesterday when you so thoughtfully brought her home. 'Two if by sea!' Geez, Archy, my rookie thought you were cute."

"What did he think of Veronica?"

Al shook his head. "He didn't say."

"I would be concerned about your rookie, Sergeant." I savored my last morsel of Leroy's culinary delight. "But why the guarded room?"

"The chief wanted to see how many prints he could ID before the room was contaminated, in case we had to go back in for a second dusting."

Two questions answered. Why was Al guarding the murder room long after the police crew had been and gone? Because the chief didn't want the room contaminated before he had put names to the prints his men collected. Why did Melva have the address of her daughter's whereabouts ready to hand me on the night of the murder? Because the information was intended for Veronica's friend Elizabeth Fitzwilliams.

My non- was no longer plussed concerning these two items but it occurred to me that I should make a list of other questions I had and tick them off as I nosed about. It wasn't my case, but I could pass on what I learned to Al, and perhaps a profile of the Mystery Woman would begin to emerge.

"Did they come up with any prints they couldn't identify?" I asked, hopefully.

Al shook his head again, vigorously, and I expected to see his ears flap in the process. "Don't know, Archy."

Except for the reason behind the sealed room, I hadn't learned much from Al Rogoff. Al, however, was about to get a hot tip from me. "Lady Cynthia Horowitz is going to give a ball, Sergeant. A masked ball."

"With my puss I wouldn't need a mask."

"I doubt you'll be invited, Al." Then I explained the reason for Lady C.'s masked extravaganza.

Al made a sound like air escaping from a ballroom. "That's not going to help us find the Mystery Woman, Archy. It'll bring every kook in Palm Beach out of the woodwork that night, not to mention the press. I think I'd better pass this on to the chief. We might have to call out the National Guard. When's the party to take place?"

"No official date yet, but I guess it's ASAP. Lady Cynthia won't want to be usurped by the real Mystery Woman coming forth and making the ball anticlimactic, to say the least. But if I have my way, it'll never happen. I'm going to try to talk her out of it."

"Will she listen to you?"

"I did her a favor once. She owes me." I didn't mention that she had already paid her debt by breaking it off with my father. But for what I did for her I think two for one, in my favor, would just about even the score. However, I was not sanguine. Not at all.

I pulled my wallet out of my back pocket, removed a small envelope and passed it over to Al. "I think you could use this. The firm subscribes as a public-relations gesture but no one at McNally and Son is particularly interested in using it."

He peeked inside the small white envelope and saw a season pass to the Miami City Ballet under the artistic direction of Edward Villella, Al's secret idol. "This wouldn't be a bribe?"

"You know better than that, Al."

He grunted and stuck the envelope in his

shirt pocket. He was too embarrassed to say thank you, but this in no way lessened his appreciation.

"What in tarnation?" Al suddenly exclaimed. "He looks like he's been hit by a truck."

Because my back was toward the door, I had to turn to see what had aroused my lunch partner and saw Binky Watrous coming toward us with the aid of a walker.

Binky approached, slowly, planting the walker firmly in front of him with each hesitant step. "Hi, Archy. Hello, Sergeant."

"What happened to you?" Al asked.

"Tell him, Binky," I urged. "The sergeant could use a laugh."

"Archy's dog bit me," Binky said, and I must say here that even poor Binky looked uncomfortable with the explanation.

"Hobo?" Al exclaimed. "But he's just a little guy."

"Not as little as Binky Watrous," I told Al.

"Archy, can we talk about this?" Binky looked miserable, and for one moment I almost relented before recalling that it was the Duchess, not Binky, I was locking horns with. Looking down I saw that Binky's left foot was clad in what appeared to be a velvet bedroom slipper. A sickly blue velvet slipper.

"And may I remind you that one must wear shoes at all times in the dining room?"

"There are exceptions to all rules," Binky informed me. "That's why seeing-eye dogs are allowed in the post office."

"But the dog must be accompanied by a visually handicapped person. The dog cannot simply wander in, alone, and post a letter."

"I'm handicapped," Binky insisted.

"I hate to be a party pooper," Al said, "but my lunch hour is about up and I'd like to get out of here while my sanity is still more or less intact."

"I'm leaving, too, Sergeant," I announced. "Perhaps this handicapped gentleman would like our table." Al and I rose, and I said to Binky, "I had a job for you this afternoon, but seeing as you're out on workers' comp I'll have to get someone else."

"I can do it, Archy," Binky pleaded with a look that tugged at my heart strings. Those doe eyes will do it all the time. But I had to be strong, or the Duchess might run all over Hobo like a steamroller on a rampage.

"You rest today, Binky." Catching Priscilla's eye, I beckoned her over and said, "Please put Mr. Watrous's lunch tab on my bill."

"Thanks, Archy. I really appreciate that. I know I'll be in better shape tomorrow." Were there tears in those doe eyes?

"One can only hope, Binky. One can only hope."

"You're a heel," Al Rogoff whispered as we made our way out. Or was that the voice of my conscience?

16

THE MYSTERY WOMAN commanded the headlines in all the tabloids, from Key West to Jacksonville and from Maine to the City of Angels. McNally & Son was immersed in a case of national interest, however peripherally, involving a name long synonymous with great wealth and landed gentry. And if that wasn't enough to send the firm's leader into a euphoric seizure, we were privately on the payroll of another name with similar attributes. The entrance to the McNally Building on Royal Palm Way must have looked like the pearly gates to my sire, Prescott McNally. This had to be better than seeing Tiny Tim burn his crutch and dance a jig with the ghost of Christmas Past.

With the words "Mystery Woman," had Lolly Spindrift coined a phrase and thereby earned a place in the gossip columnist's hall of fame?

Would Lady C.'s masked ball indeed become more famous, or infamous, than Capote's Black and White Ball?

Would Binky Watrous and the Duchess receive their unjust deserts from our insurers and live happily ever after?

Everyone suddenly had great expectations, thanks to Melva and the guy reclining on a cold marble slab in the morgue. Did anyone give a hoot for either of them? I cared about my friend Melva Williams, and so did her daughter. How I could best serve Melva was my dilemma. Allow the police and her lawyers to do their job and get on with the Fairhust case, or continue to find answers to the questions that had kept me awake that fateful night. Veronica had solved the mystery of why her mother had the address of Hillcrest House ready and waiting for me, but the other puzzlers kept haunting me like the lingering fragrance of Veronica's perfume.

Why was the alarm turned off at Melva's front gate that night? Did Veronica, on her way out, forget to turn it on, or did someone purposely shut it down after Veronica had driven off? And, if so, who and why?

Why was Melva so sure it was Geoff returning when she heard a car arrive at the house? Why couldn't it have been Veronica, who was also out that night?

What did Hattie say that evening that kept evading me like a disturbing dream the waking mind refuses to surrender or erase?

Would knowing the answers help Melva? I wasn't sure, and I didn't know why I wasn't sure. This was more perturbing than I cared to admit.

I had no trouble getting Jamie to follow me in Veronica's Mercedes convertible as I headed for Melva's place. Even the unromantic Jamie was not immune to the thrill of zipping along the A1A in a luxury vehicle on a balmy day in Palm Beach. Poor Binky. This would have been his shining hour. But the boy had to learn the lesson of that old biblical saying "As you sue, so shall you reap."

Traffic was backed up for a mile as we neared our destination. Rubbernecking, no doubt. Melva must have gotten home hours ago, and one would imagine the gawkers would have dispersed by now. There were, to be sure, the freelance photographers who would practically camp on the highway in hopes of a shot of mother or daughter. Persistence is the attribute, after all, that brings home their bacon.

Melva's front gate looked like the box office of a hit show, but the approach was being kept clear by Melva's security guard. Upon request, I gave him my name and business. He put in a call to the house and a moment later opened the gate for Jamie and me. A few photographers took pictures of the Miata and Mercedes for no other reason than because we had passed muster with the sentry.

Hattie welcomed us with tears of joy, taking Jamie into her kitchen after directing me to the drawing room. I found Melva in the same chair I had left her in two nights ago. She wore a little black dress, but this one had never seen the inside of a shop in South Beach. She looked thinner and paler than on my last visit, but strangely serene. Medication, or the cigarette smoldering between her fingers? I bent to kiss her cheek.

"How can I ever thank you for caring for Veronica?" she said.

"I've never needed to be thanked for spending time with a beautiful woman. And she is both beautiful and a woman, Melva. When did all that happen?"

"When our backs were turned, no doubt. How are you, Archy?"

"As well as can be expected under the circumstances." I sat in the chair I had occupied yesterday, talking to Lolly, which reminded me of the painful facts I had to pass on to Melva.

"That was my line, but you're welcome to it." She waved her cigarette toward me. "As you can see, you're no longer in a smoke-free zone, so light up if it pleases you."

It pleased, so I lit my first English Oval of the day. "Back to two packs a day, Melva?"

"No, Archy. In fact, I've broken my old record, but who's counting? I've also spent two nights in jail and am alive to tell about it."

"How goes it, Melva? No nonsense. Just the facts, ma'am."

She put out her cigarette and adjusted herself more comfortably in the chair. "It was purgatory with a hint of the hell to follow. Does that answer your question?"

I couldn't think of a more eloquent or a more depressing commentary. "You said it all in twenty-five words or less," I told her. "What are your lawyers' prognostications?"

" 'We are cautiously confident, Mrs. Williams.' Does that also say it all in twenty-five words or less?" She reached for another cigarette. If she kept this up, the weed might save the state of Florida the cost of a long-term incarceration or . . . But I would rather not dwell on the alternative. "I think they mean we have a fighting chance," she went on, "and I tend to agree. You know, Archy, I don't even remember doing it, and I'm not practicing for the witness stand. I barely remember calling you that night."

But you do remember, verbatim, *as well as can be expected under the circumstances.* Selective amnesia? I sounded cynical but I've been around long enough to know that he who thinks the worst is seldom disappointed. I took it Melva's lawyers were now writing the script, and like a good little actress she would not ad-lib. Given the circumstances, who could blame her? But I was back to square one: Should I allow the police and her lawyers to do their job and get on with my business? Probably. But before I bowed out, I did have one bit of news to impose upon their cautious confidence.

"Lolly didn't pick up Geoff that night, Melva."

She looked at me for a long time before she answered. The reflexes were too slow for a sharp woman like Melva Williams. She was clearly on medication, and, once again, who could blame her? When she finally did answer it was simply to say, "I know. Veronica told us."

"What did your lawyers say?"

She put out her cigarette. Now I knew where Veronica had picked up the "two puffs and you're dead" habit. Was this the curse of the upper classes or the legacy of Bette Davis? I suspected the latter.

"They think," she said, "what you think. Without Lolly's corroboration I can't prove what took place here two nights ago. People will either believe me or not."

"Could Veronica have heard . . ."

"No, Archy. I'm sorry to say Veronica could not have heard anything. I was in my bedroom when Geoff came and told me he was expecting Lolly Spindrift to call for him. Veronica was in her room, preparing to go out for the evening, which she did before Geoff left. Hattie, as you already know, hadn't left her room all day. We were quite alone when Geoff told me his plans. Or should I say, when Geoff lied to me."

"Veronica had her car and Geoff left the Rolls. Someone picked him up, Melva."

"The girl. Who else?"

"Pretty nervy, wasn't it?"

She laughed or grunted, hard to tell which, and quipped, "Geoff was a pretty nervy guy."

As Lolly and I had speculated, the girl must have been someone known to Lolly. Now I was more convinced of this than ever. It had to be someone who could have said they were calling for Geoff in place of Lolly if Melva was downstairs when the girl arrived. Unfortunately, Melva had been in her room—Hattie in her room—and Veronica had left the house. Blind luck? But who had lucked out? Certainly not Geoffrey Williams.

"We've got to find that girl, Melva. If we don't, it's us against the world."

"Thank you for including yourself in my quest. You're a true friend, Archy. As for the Mystery Woman—I could kill Lolly Spindrift for that infectious label—she will never come forward, and we both know that. I'm going to have to take my chances and go it alone. Lolly was my only hope, and all he's done is literally add to the mystery rather than clear the air. We're thinking of offering a reward for her identity. Not directly from us, of course. Maybe one of the newspapers or television stations. We would guarantee payment."

"Risky. Someone might trace it to you and your lawyers."

"No risk, no gain, isn't that what they say? And we've heard the police have gotten at least a half dozen calls from potential Mystery Woman prospects. Two of them from Hollywood. Will they hold a lineup for me to inspect?"

I pounced on that one. "Can you remember what she looked like? Anything, Melva. Anything at all. Hair color, for starters."

She shrugged and reached for another cigarette. I was beginning to feel like a health nut with my two or three English Ovals a day. "Brown," she said. "And long. It covered her face as she did her thing."

"When she stood and grabbed her clothes . . ."

Melva discounted this with a wave of her hand. "I was looking at Geoff and nowhere else. I can tell you she had a nice figure and, I think, was young."

"Young as opposed to who, Grandma Moses?"

"Under thirty. How's that?"

"Better, but no cigar." Then, because I couldn't help myself, I said, "I know you're drawing blanks about that night, Melva, but you said when you heard a car arrive, you knew, or thought you knew, it was Geoff. Why? Why couldn't it have been Veronica returning home?"

She looked at me as if I were a schoolboy who hadn't done his homework. "You don't have children, Archy, do you?"

"None that I know of."

"Well, if, and when, you do have children that you know of, and they grow to become social creatures, you will learn never to expect them home before midnight. It was eleven or thereabouts when I heard that car.

I never thought for a moment that it could be Veronica."

And another mystery bit the dust. I was getting all the right answers, so I must have been asking all the wrong questions. Back to the drawing board, Archy.

"I'll remember that," I acquiesced without a fight. "And one final word on the Mystery Woman. I have a piece of news on the subject."

"That awful Horowitz's masked ball. The woman should be tarred and feathered."

How stupid of me. Melva probably knew about Lady C.'s plans before I did. Mrs. Marsden must have been on the phone to Hattie even as the plans were being discussed. Now Hattie was giving Jamie an earful, and so on down the line. "I'm going to try to talk her out of it, Melva," I promised.

Veronica, toting a tray that looked suspiciously like the one Hattie had presented Lolly and me with yesterday, entered in a pair of cut-off denims and a polo shirt. "I didn't make the coffee or the cookies," she said. "I am merely the purveyor of Hattie's generosity."

I got up to relieve her of the tray and was rewarded with a peck on the check. "IF MUSIC

BE THE FOOD OF LOVE, PLAY ON," she read my T-shirt. "How romantic."

"It isn't romantic at all," Melva said, rousing herself from her chair. "It's the uniform of that dreadful band he plays with at that dreadful club he frequents." She was at the sideboard where I had placed the tray, pouring three coffees.

"You really know how to hurt a guy, Melva." I bit my tongue, hard, but it was too late. Melva stopped pouring. Veronica stopped chatting. I stopped breathing.

It was Melva who saved the moment. She laughed. Not hysterically, but with genuine humor. "Archy, I love you. I truly do. You are an unpretentious person in a world of pompous asses. I guess I do know how to hurt a guy." She handed me a cup of coffee. "Is this okay, or would you like something stronger?"

"Cyanide would be nice." She gave my hand a gentle squeeze before helping herself to coffee.

The tension passed, and Veronica once again tried to lighten the conversation. "I told mother all about our ride on Phil Meecham's yacht." She had, I noted, legs like Marlene Dietrich in addition to hair reminiscent of her namesake, Veronica Lake. Was there nothing wrong with the creature?

"News of the adventure even reached the jailhouse," Melva said. "A bit showy, Archy, but clever, I'll admit."

"I didn't count on the television coverage. That was Lolly's idea."

Veronica presented me with the cookie tray. "No, thanks. I've got a dinner date and have to save room."

"I thought you might want to stay and have dinner with us," Veronica said, looking disappointed.

"I think we've imposed enough on Archy for a while, Veronica," her mother said. "He deserves a night off from the likes of us."

"I would stay, really, but it's a long-standing engagement I just can't break." Why was I lying?

"Tomorrow night, then?" Veronica asked.

"Veronica, really," Melva reprimanded.

"Tomorrow sounds great," I heard myself say.

Melva looked at us thoughtfully and suggested, "Why don't you two go out for dinner tomorrow? On me. My way of thanking you for all you've done, Archy."

"Then come with us," I insisted.

"I don't want to be seen in public just yet, thank you."

"Mother, please," Veronica pleaded.

"No. Out of the question," Melva stated with a tone that said the conversation was closed.

"Then we'll dine here," I offered.

"You would do me a favor if you took Veronica out, Archy. There's no reason for her to be caged up with me and you're the perfect date for her post-scandal debut."

So, mother thought I was a safe date. Was that good or bad? Either way I had a date with Veronica Manning tomorrow night. And I had a date with Connie Garcia tonight, but I'd think about that tomorrow. I accepted by saying, "I accept."

"Good. Now I'm going to rest." Melva stood up and replaced her coffee cup on the tray. "I'll say thank you one more time, Archy, and look forward to seeing you tomorrow evening."

I rose. "It's good to have you back, Melva, and you have a lot of friends in this town, remember that."

"I'll be up in a minute, mother," Veronica called after her.

"Take your time, dear," Melva answered. "I'm not going anywhere."

When she was out of the room, Veronica turned to me with tears in her eyes. "She sounds brave, but she's really very frightened."

"Is she on medication?"

"Yes. I called Dr. Pearlberg as soon as we arrived home and she called the Lewis Pharmacy. I'm sure the reporters out front noticed the delivery car and will report that we're all on drugs. Dr. Pearlberg said the pills would make mother a little drowsy, but that's fine. She needs to rest."

I knew Dr. Gussie Pearlberg, a psychiatrist, who practiced in Lantana. Al Rogoff had introduced us; he knew her because she had, on several occasions, provided the police with psychological profiles on serial thieves, rapists, and the like. She was also a favorite of Palm Beach society.

"Smart move," I told her. "And I brought your car back."

"Thank you. Not that I'll be going out much. I feel like I'm living under siege."

"You've got to be brave, my dear. Your mother needs someone to lean on. I know she has her lawyers, but they're no substitute for her own flesh and blood."

She nodded and squared her shoulders in a heroic gesture that somehow managed to emphasize her vulnerability. "And can I lean on you, Archy?"

"Do you have to ask?"

And then she was in my arms once again—her cheek resting on my chest and my lips resting on the soft down of her golden head. I exploited the moment for as long as I dared before whispering, "You'd better go upstairs and see if your mother needs anything."

"Are you afraid of being alone with me, Archy?"

"I thought that was evident."

She pulled away, laughing, and touched my lips to hers before heading for the door.

"Tomorrow night," I called.

"Maybe," she teased.

"You see, Archy," Jamie was saying as we drove home, "the way Hattie tells it, she thought they were being robbed at gunpoint. What with the shouting and the fireworks and the car driving off, burning rubber like it was racing in the Indy 500, she was afraid she would find the whole family laid out when she went downstairs. I'm surprised she didn't have a heart attack on the spot. She's got a weak heart, Hattie."

Still under the spell of Veronica's chaste kiss, I wasn't really listening. Call me "bewitched."

I just had time for my swim, a shower, and a change of clothes—white ducks and patchwork madras jacket—before my rendezvous with Connie Garcia.

17

DINNER WITH CONNIE was better than *My Dinner with Andre* but not as hilarious as *Dinner At Eight,* due to the absence of Marie Dressler. I prepared an *arroz avec pollo* which, as you may have guessed, is a basic Cuban dish *avec* Archy's French touch—an '86 Alsatian Traminer, which is more at home accompanying *duck à l'orange,* but Connie didn't know that. As previously mentioned, we are a don't ask, don't tell couple.

It was a delightful evening, as are all my evenings with Consuela Garcia. Like a contented married couple, we knew which buttons to press and which to avoid. We gossiped about everything—from Melva's predicament, to Lolly's television appeal, to Lady C.'s masked ball and Binky's lawsuit—while never once speaking the name of Veronica Manning. Burdened with guilt for sins past, present, and, no doubt, future, I was content to brown, bake, stir, and pour.

The evening offered no surprises, but then, I didn't expect any. There was nothing to bemoan and nothing to shout about. I felt like a cat having his stomach scratched, meowing contentedly while dreaming about the chase. For our after-dinner treat I rented Garbo's *Ninotchka,* but when Connie said she would rather relax on a bed of nails, I put my lady songbirds on the phonograph, lowered the lights, and asked Connie to dance. As I listened to the familiar refrains, I wondered who the poet was thinking about when he penned, "Heard melodies are sweet, but those unheard are sweeter."

I didn't spend the night in Connie's condominium because that would be unseemly. Arriving in my suite, I poured myself a marc, lit an English Oval, and brought my journal up to date. With Connie, I was more content than any man had a right to be. Was

Connie also happy to be alone with whatever peculiar bedtime ministrations struck her fancy? And was this the tie that binds? Our willingness to indulge ourselves when it suited while shunning the responsibilities of a committed relationship?

We were like grandparents, and aunts and uncles, who shower gifts and attention upon other people's offspring without ever dealing with a diaper, a temper tantrum, or a request for a bottle at three A.M. This line of thinking led to the fact that we would soon be ushering in the yuletide season and welcoming my sister and her family into our midst for the holiday season.

Mother was already brimming over with joyous expectation at seeing the grandchildren. So was father, but he tried very hard to hide the fact. Even Jamie and Ursi were gearing up for the arrival of Dora and her clan from Arizona. Jamie would take the children swimming and sightseeing and Ursi would serve them sugared plums and fairy cakes. On Christmas Eve, father would read aloud Dickens's *A Christmas Carol,* and on Christmas morning, Uncle Archy would play Santa. It was all so normal one looked forward to Phil Meecham's

New Year's Eve bacchanal aboard the *Sans Souci.*

As I mentioned earlier, Dora has three children. Twin girls who were named Rebecca and Rowena—Dora being an avid reader of English romance novels—and a boy, who was spared being called Ivanhoe by a three-part television presentation of *Pride and Prejudice,* which ended just as Dora was carried off to the maternity ward to bring Darcy into the world. Everyone said Darcy looked very much like his uncle Archy, and after that observation was noted the next question was inevitably, "Well, Archy, when are you going to have your own Darcy?" To which I always replied, while bouncing the two-year-old on my lap, "One Darcy is more than enough."

But the tone would be set and for two weeks I would be prodded, cajoled, and pressured to "give up the cards and dice and go for shoes and rice." But it wasn't cards and dice I would have to forego, it was my third-floor aerie, my two-mile daily swim, Ursi's cooking, mother's doting, my club, my clothes, my pandering and philandering— my independence. Like Professor 'Enry 'Iggins, "I would rather a new edition of the

Spanish Inquisition than to ever let a woman in my life."

But I knew father expected a scion from his scion to carry on the McNally name, he who would perhaps complete Yale Law and move into the executive suite on Royal Palm Way. I was a few years from the big four-oh mark which I presume is the onset of middle age. While I wasn't pressed with a time limit to reproduce, that might not be the case with my mate, should I choose one. I was sure Connie was still viable in that area, but for how much longer?

Veronica, on the other hand, could produce enough McNallys to equip a courtroom with prosecutor, defense counsel, judge, and jury. And how happy father would be to welcome a "Manning out of an Ashton" into our family.

Veronica was a child. Connie was an adult. Veronica was embarrassed by my haute couture. Connie thought my clothes made a statement—although she never stated the statement. Veronica was the new millennium and I didn't own a computer, a CD, or a touch tone telephone—neither did Connie. Veronica was a spoiled, rich girl who liked attention and would keep me on a short leash—albeit attached to a diamond-studded collar. Connie was as independent as myself and overlooked much for the sake of peace. Connie was good, kind, and stable. Veronica was petulant, rich, and unpredictable. And what had Melva said? No risk, no gain. In either case, I had very little to risk and so much to gain.

But should I pop the question, would either have me? I was certain Connie would say yes, and Veronica was acting like the girl who can't say no. It was Archy whose tongue was tied.

I turned off the lights and got into bed wrestling with yet another quandary of my suddenly bounteous love life. Whom to invite to Christmas dinner. Melva and Veronica would probably be abandoned by their lawyers who would head north for home and hearth, and I was certain neither mother nor daughter would be in the mood to trim a tree or go out for a celebratory dinner. Friends might find the pair a shade too somber for dinner guests, or avoid them on the grounds of not wishing to intrude. I was thinking of asking them here, and including

Hattie who could team up with Jamie and Ursi for the day.

Before Melva's woes, I'd intended to invite Connie, who would otherwise be alone unless she wanted to attend Lady C.'s much publicized Christmas buffet—which was about as jolly as a soup kitchen.

I could have both Connie and Veronica—for dinner, that is.

18

THE FAIRHURST SPREAD was more like Fort Knox than Mar-A-Lago. I called ahead and Mr. Fairhurst told me to ring the house when I arrived at the front gate. I would be directed from there.

The call box was located in a niche in the concrete gatepost. All I had to do was press a button to get a response from the house. A few minutes later, a man riding a motorbike approached the gate, alighted, tipped his hat respectfully, and introduced himself as Hector. "I help out during the day," he told me.

"And who plays gatekeeper at night?" I asked.

"At night, *señor,* they don't get company. It saves on the overtime."

He had the Latino sense of humor and a perfect set of shiny, white movie-star teeth. He opened the gate and I drove the Miata onto the Fairhurst property, idling until Hector locked us in. Tipping his cap again alongside the car door, he said, "What would you like to know, *señor?*"

"The winning numbers in tomorrow's lottery."

"If I knew that, *señor,* I would have my own gate and maybe even a house to go with it."

"What made you think I wanted to ask you anything, Hector?"

"*El Patrón* say we are to answer all of Mr. McNally's questions. You are Mr. McNally?"

"I am."

Fairhurst was certainly cooperating with this investigation. Keeping granddad's secret was top priority around here—which put the pressure on me, since I didn't have a clue to the blackmailer's identity. Hector was an unlikely suspect, but I had to start someplace. Besides, I think he would be disappointed if I left him with nothing to report to *El Patrón* and the rest of the staff.

"Did you ever hear of the *Titanic,* Hector?"

"*Sí, señor.* The big boat that sank a long time ago."

"That's the one. Do you know the name of anybody who was a passenger on the *Titanic* when it went down?"

"*Sí, señor.* I know the name of one person."

"Who's that, Hector?"

"Leonardo DiCaprio."

"Thank you, Hector, I have no more questions."

Grinning happily, Hector mounted his motorbike and preceded me up the curving driveway to the Fairhursts' pink palazzo.

Peterson—I presumed—opened the door to me and announced that Mr. Fairhurst was on the telephone and would join me as soon as he was free. "Would you like to wait in the library, sir?"

Did I have a choice? I followed Peterson, whose undertaker's togs—black suit with tie to match—were about as cheerful as his countenance.

Fairhurst's library was only slightly smaller than the reading room of the Palm

Beach Public Library, but I imagined it contained as many, if not more, books. These were beautifully bound and, I guessed, seldom read. One wall panel of tomes was encased in glass and kept under lock and key. This, of course, immediately drew my attention. More Fairhurst secrets?

"You may smoke, sir," Peterson informed me. "And may I bring you a beverage?"

"No, thank you, Peterson. You are Peterson?"

"Yes, sir. I am. May I be of service, sir."

I pointed to a very impressive oil portrait in an ornate frame that hung over a marble fireplace, flanked by two similar portraits. "Is that the first Mr. Fairhurst, Peterson?"

"It is, sir. By John Singer Sargent." Peterson spoke with pride of ownership, but then butlers often identified, to an alarming degree, with those for whom they buttled. "John the Second is on the left, also by Sargent, and the current Mr. Fairhurst is on the right."

I assumed the current Mr. Fairhurst was not painted by Sargent because the artist would have been dead when John III sat for his portrait. I also assumed the current John's portraitist was not a household name, because Peterson was silent on the subject. I walked to the fireplace and looked up at John I. "The founding father who went down with the *Titanic*," I stated.

"Yes, sir."

Knowing that Fairhurst had prepared the staff for my appearance as the emcee of *Twenty Questions,* I made no excuse when I asked Peterson, "Do you get to Miami often, Peterson?"

"I beg your pardon, sir."

"Miami. Do you go down to Miami often?"

"Never, sir."

"Never? You've never been to Miami, Peterson?"

"No, sir. Nor do I have any desire to go to Miami."

"Do you take vacations, Peterson. You and Mrs. Peterson?"

"We do, sir."

"And where do you go on vacation?"

"Mr. Fairhurst is good enough to put the château in Antibes or the villa at Lake Como at our disposal, if they or the children are not in residence at the time."

I had just put my foot in my mouth while on a fishing expedition. And what did I expect him to say, that he only went to

Miami to post blackmail letters? I was batting zero and Peterson looked as if he knew it. I gave it one more try. "Has anyone, domestics or guests, ever questioned you about the first Mr. Fairhurst's voyage on the *Titanic?*" This was getting dangerously near the purpose of my call but I couldn't go on shadowboxing with the guy.

For the first time Peterson didn't have the answer ready to fire at me like a sheriff with a hair-trigger six-shooter. Was he mulling over the answer or my question? Had I said too much? Did he suspect? Was I out of a job?

"Over the years, sir, surely it has been mentioned," was his carefully considered reply.

"And more recently, Peterson?"

"Not that I recall, sir."

"What do you think of Seth Walker?" I injected like a quick jab to the jaw.

"Not much, sir."

"Really? Why, Peterson?"

"He wears his cap at a rakish angle."

"Is that all?"

"He drives the Rolls as if he'd rather be in the backseat."

Very much Mrs. Marsden's opinion of the lad, I recalled, but this was getting interesting. I wondered if Mrs. Peterson shared her husband's sentiments regarding the new chauffeur. Time would tell. Next I asked, "Mr. Fairhurst's secretary is called Arnold, I believe."

"Yes, sir. Arnold Turnbolt."

"And what does Arnold think of Seth Walker?"

Peterson didn't have to mull this one over. "Arnold rather likes young men who wear their caps on the back of their heads."

Bingo! I had found a chink in the Fairhurst household armor. There was dissension in the ranks, and where there was dissension there was a malcontent. The butler and the secretary were not kissing cousins—and the secretary wished he and the chauffeur were. This wasn't, as John Fairhurst III would have the world believe, one big happy family.

"Meaning what, Peterson?" I probed.

"Meaning Arnold rather likes young men who wear their caps on the back of their heads. I was not editorializing, sir, but stating a fact."

Now where did he learn that? In Antibes or Como? "Did you know that Seth Walker was recommended to Mr. Fairhurst by Geoff Williams? The late Geoff Williams, that is."

Peterson started, his head jerking back almost imperceptibly before he rallied with an exaggerated shrug of his narrow shoulders. "No, I did not, nor is it my business to know such things." Peterson seemed to enjoy adding this aspect of his job description to his answer.

I would have sworn that there wasn't much that went on in this house that escaped Peterson's notice, but didn't press the point. It seemed I had gotten as much out of the butler as I had gotten from Hector. Perhaps Peterson could enlighten me on the mystery of the books behind the locked glass doors.

"I know nothing about them. They are kept locked to protect them from prying eyes. My eyes do not pry, sir."

It's not easy to get two feet into one mouth, but, be that as it may, I had done the trick. For the price of a beer, I would gladly have given this fellow a swift kick in the kimono.

"Will that be all, sir?"

"Yes, for now. But I reserve the right to recall you, Peterson."

"As you wish, sir."

He retreated silently, closing the door with nary a backward glance at his inquisitor. When I spoke to Arnold, I would mention Peterson's comment regarding the secretary's preference in *chapeaus* and see where that led. Fearing that Peterson was looking through the keyhole, I avoided snooping around the tempting glass-enclosed shelves and turned my attention to the portrait of the first John. A brass plate told me he was born February 1, 1862, and died April 15, 1912—surely a night to remember.

Moving to John II, I learned that he was born April 1, 1913, and died March 15, 1988. Seventy-five good years for John II. Born on April Fool's Day and died on the Ides of March. And, I calculated, Grandma Fairhurst was pregnant while crossing on the *Titanic.* Now there was something never reported in the famous Fairhurst fairy tale. On my way to check the current John's visage by a lesser artist, I stopped abruptly and returned for a second look at the second John.

Born April 1, 1913. The *Titanic* went down April 15, 1912, supposedly taking John I with it. Grandma was either impregnated by her husband's ghost or she had carried the second John for twelve months. Could the family have made such a glaring error? Obviously they had. They doctored Grandpa's death date to coincide with the sinking of the *Titanic,* but forgot to adjust his son's birth date accordingly.

Now all I had to find out was who else had read the handwriting on the library wall.

"Sorry to keep you," John Fairhurst said as he came into the room.

"No problem at all, sir," I assured him. "It gave me a chance to talk to Peterson and have a look around."

"Did you come up with anything, Archy?"

"As a matter of fact, Mr. Fairhurst, I have."

"From Peterson?" He looked astonished, but not as astonished as he was going to look when I filed my first report.

"No, not from Peterson, sir, but from using my eyes." I hoped Peterson was listening. "I know how the blackmailer learned what he knows."

"Remarkable," Fairhurst said. "How?"

"When was the last time you had a look at the brass plates on the portraits that record the birth and death dates of your father and grandfather?"

He shrugged and said, "I have no idea. Maybe never. What is all this about?"

It was show-and-tell time, and because he was a quick study, John Fairhurst did not need a pencil and paper to figure the whole thing out. By the time I finished my discourse on higher mathematics, John Fairhurst's healthy tan had taken on a yellowish pall. I led him to a chair, where he sat quietly, staring into space. "But it's not possible," he moaned.

"As you can see, sir, it is indeed possible."

"But how could such a thing happen?"

"As you said, you never bothered looking at those dates, and I doubt if any casual observer ever did. The second brass plate was added to the portrait over seventy years after the first went up. By then, the *Titanic* story was an accepted fact. It would not have occurred to you or Mrs. Fairhurst to fabricate your father's birth date."

"All these years," he said, "and no one ever noticed."

"Oh, but someone did notice, Mr. Fairhurst. Hence, the letter you received and my presence in your home."

Still bewildered, he looked at his grand-father's portrait and asked, "But who?"

Not expecting John I to answer, I jumped right in. "Who has been in this room recently, Mr. Fairhurst?"

"Me. My wife, of course. The children and grandchildren. The servants. Friends. But no one who hasn't been in this room many, many times over as many years, Archy."

"Except for Seth Walker, sir," I reminded him.

"Seth?" Fairhurst shook his head. "Why, I doubt very much if he has ever been in here. He would have no reason to be. We have a cottage on the property which the servants use as a recreation room, or rec room, as my grandchildren call it. It has all the ameni-ties, so why on earth should the boy come in here? Or anyplace in the house, for that matter, except the kitchen, which used to be a gathering place for the help when we employed more staff than we now do."

"You told me Geoff Williams recom-mended the boy, Mr. Fairhurst."

"Yes, he did. Pity what happened. Feel sorry for poor Melva." Then, as if suddenly remembering, he said, "We saw you on television. A bit of a fuss, I would say, Archy. I'd have driven right past those newsmen and run them over if they got in the way."

This I could believe.

"Nice yacht, don't-you-know," he continued, "but I don't approve of that Meecham person."

I doubted if the pronouncement would break Phil's heart.

"Lolly Spindrift was rather overdramatic, I thought. Mystery Woman, indeed. It's a family matter and should be kept in the family, is how I see it."

Given what I now knew about his family, I could appreciate his sentiments. "How did Geoff come to recommend Seth Walker?"

Fairhurst shook his head as if he didn't know, while at the same time answering my question.

"We met at the bar of the club one night— the Bath and Tennis, that is—and I guess I mentioned what with the season approaching, Mrs. Fairhurst and I would need a driver. Part-time, to be sure. We don't get about much, don't-you-know. Town is full of phonies and oddballs. Williams mentioned this Seth boy and a few days later the boy contacted me and I took him on."

"When was this meeting with Geoff Williams, sir?"

"A month ago. Maybe six weeks. I've no idea, and what does it matter?"

Geoff was in Palm Beach a month ago? Why? Melva never said anything about this. But why should she? Or, why shouldn't she? Every time I scratched a surface labeled Seth Walker, I came up with Geoff Williams. Come to think of it, was Geoff Williams ever in the Fairhurst library?

"I don't know that it's important, sir. Before I leave I'd like to speak to Arnold, if I may."

He got up, a little shaky on his pins, and said he'd send Arnold to me. "He's probably with my wife. We received a dinner invitation from that Horowitz woman, the one who calls herself a Lady, and Arnold is helping my wife compose a credible refusal. Do you know the woman, Archy?"

"We've met, sir."

"I'll get Arnold."

"Before you go, sir, would you mind relating what you told your staff about my visit? I mean, how did you explain my coming here for the sole purpose of asking questions?"

"I told them you were coming and to answer any questions you might put to them. That was all. No reason to explain."

And I bet you never have to say you're sorry, either.

"It's been a help, sir. Thank you."

Arnold was a refreshing change from Peterson. He was all designer jeans, cord jacket, sneakers, and a great big smile. "Rumor has it that you're from the FBI, but I think you're Archy McNally of Discreet Inquiries."

He offered his hand and I shook it.

"You think correctly, Mr. Turnbolt."

"Make that Arnie. So what's up? Has the silver gone missing, or is it Mrs. F.'s tiara? It's an heirloom you know. She bought it at auction from the estate of the late Wallis Simpson, and you know where Wally's hubby got it from."

I saw that I was not going to have any trouble getting Arnie to talk but shutting him up might prove difficult. "Nothing as exciting as diamonds or silver, Arnie."

Arnie nodded toward the glass-enclosed shelves. "Don't tell me someone nicked a first edition of *The Memoirs of a Woman of Pleasure?*"

"Is that what's kept under glass? Rare first editions?"

"Rare first editions of what is called erotica in genteel circles and all with the artists' original sketches," Arnie gushed. If Peterson took pride in the Sargents, Arnie associated with the esoteric. "Did you know there was a companion to the *Memoirs* called *The Memoirs of a Man of Pleasure?* Well, it's in there, not to mention *Adventures of a King's Page,* published by Charles White in London in 1829. Mr. F.'s collection is the envy of the Vatican, Archy."

The old geezer. All don't-you-know proper on the outside with Fanny and some king's page literally smoldering under lock and key. John Fairhurst III had better things to read than the brass plates beneath his ancestors' portraits. I wondered if he tucked the blackmailer's letter between the His and Her memoirs.

To prime the pump I offered a casual

remark vis-à-vis the butler: "Peterson said he didn't know what books were kept locked up because he wasn't a snoop."

"And I say a pox on Peterson. What else did Miss Manners report? That I'm Madam's pet? It's his usual song and dance routine. He can't stand the fact that Mrs. F. and I are on a first-name basis."

"As a matter of fact, it was your chumminess with the new chauffeur that seemed to annoy Peterson."

Dear Arnie let go with what is known in genteel circles as an expletive. "Did he also tell you Mrs. P. dotes on Seth? In fact Mrs. P. has a weakness for the masculine gender on the good side of twenty-five. I'd tell you the story of Mrs. P. and the houseboy at the villa in Como but you have to be accompanied by a parent or guardian to hear it."

Good grief! The three live-in servants were as compatible as a stick of dynamite and a match. While I could see them blackmailing one another, I couldn't see them sticking it to the boss. Not for a paltry twenty-five grand. The Petersons were getting near pension time, and Arnie was probably too attached to that tiara as well as his lady boss to take the money and run. The blackmail letter was a weirdo get-rich-quick scheme by someone who thought twenty-five thousand bucks was a million—which brought me back to the guy who didn't like his seat in the family Rolls.

"Between us, Arnie, what do you think of Seth Walker?"

"Between us, Archy, tell me why you want to know."

"I can't do that. Discreet Inquiries is the name of the firm, remember? And I think Mr. Fairhurst told you to cooperate."

Arnie sighed. "What's a working boy to do?" Then he talked and appeared to revel in every word. "Seth has been around, Archy, if you know what I mean. He's young, handsome, not too bright, but top-heavy in the street-smarts department. He wants to get ahead and doesn't care who he steps on while climbing the ladder. He told me he took this job as a way of getting his foot in the door."

"What door?"

"Ask Seth."

"I will. Do you know what his connection is to Geoff Williams?"

"You mean the late Geoff Williams. *Quel*

mess, Archy! I assume Mrs. Williams's religion precludes divorce."

The guy was a stand-up comic with an audience of one. "Do you know Seth's connection to the late Geoff Williams?"

Arnie shook his head. "I didn't even know they knew each other."

"Do you do much reading, Arnie? Here, in the library?"

"If you mean the closed shelves, a little goes a long way. I prefer my own room with its ocean view and cuddling up with a current best-seller, unless something better comes along."

19

I MET HECTOR on my way to the garage. He tipped his cap and asked, "Do you have any more questions, *señor?*"

"Is Seth Walker in the garage, Hector?"

It was not the question he expected nor one he cared to answer. "I don't know, *señor.* I mind my own business around here."

"I don't blame you, Hector."

The garage was a four-car affair and like ours, had an apartment on its upper story. Seth could probably live there if he chose, but I imagined he would prefer The Breakers. As I drew near, I saw a woman come scurrying out of a side door and knew why my question had embarrassed Hector.

"Mrs. Peterson, I presume?" I called as she tried to bolt past me without acknowledging my existence.

"Yes. I'm sorry. I was just seeing if I had left one of the grocery bags in my car. I did the shopping this morning and seem to be missing a few items I know I bought."

She was a few years younger than her husband, which still left her past her prime. I attributed her trim figure to a metabolism in a constant state of overdrive rather than to a conscious effort at diet and exercise. Her hair was a shade of reddish brown that did not appear on Mother Nature's color chart.

Eyeing her empty hands, the fingers of which fluttered as if she were manipulating a string of invisible worry beads, I said, "I take it you didn't find what you were looking for."

"No, I didn't. If you'll excuse me . . ."

"Is Seth in the garage?"

"Seth?" She suddenly looked as if she were about to cry. "How would I know?"

"Well, you just came from the garage, Mrs. Peterson, and I'm looking for Seth Walker."

"He might be in there. I didn't notice. I just went . . ."

"Yes, Mrs. Peterson. You told me why you were in the garage. By the way, I'm Archy McNally."

"Yes, I know. Or I assumed that's who you were. I really must be getting back to the house now . . ."

"I've met your husband and Arnold."

She began to march in place, giving the impression that it was the loo she was desperate to get back to. Poor thing. I imagined her husband would find her excuse to visit the garage as lame as I did. Knowing that Peterson was tied up with me in the library, had she made a quick run to the garage to bring Seth a goody from the kitchen? Herself, for instance?

"Are you at all curious as to what I'm doing here, Mrs. Peterson?"

"I'm sure it's none of my business, Mr. McNally. We were told to expect you and to answer any questions you wished to put to us." Very little seemed to be the business of Mr. and Mrs. Peterson.

"However, Mrs. Peterson, I did not ask you what you were doing in the garage, did I?"

"No, but I . . ."

"But you thought you would tell me anyway. How kind. What items were missing from your grocery bags?"

Between her busy feet and her hands, I thought the woman was gearing up for a marathon. "I was missing . . ." She threw her hands in the air and exclaimed, "I don't know what I was missing." She began to weep.

"Mrs. Peterson. Really. You must get a grip on yourself. I have no wish to cause you distress, and I could not care less what you were doing in the garage, or anyplace else, for that matter."

She removed a tissue from the pocket of the very plain gray dress she wore and dabbed at her eyes. "Forgive me. I've not been myself lately." Then she took a deep breath and said, "I went to the garage to tell Seth you had arrived."

"May I ask why, Mrs. Peterson?"

"Because he asked me to."

"Seth Walker asked you to alert him to my arrival?"

The tissue had been rolled into a ball and was now hidden in her clenched fist. "No harm, I'm sure. We were all curious about you, and Seth asked me to let him know when you got here."

"You could have called. I'm sure there's a phone that connects the garage to the kitchen and other rooms in the house."

She looked a bit startled and answered, "I never thought of that." And I almost believed her.

"Did you and Seth discuss what might be the purpose of my visit?"

"Why, we all did," she stated.

"And what did you all conclude, Mrs. Peterson?"

"That you're here because of the murder."

Now it was my turn to be startled. "You mean the murder of Geoff Williams?"

She nodded. "Who else? Unless there's been another murder on Ocean Boulevard."

"What connection would Mr. and Mrs. Fairhurst have with the murder of Geoff Williams?"

"They were good friends at one time— Mr. and Mrs. Fairhurst and Mrs. Williams and her first husband. They were very close, in fact. Not so much after Mr. Manning died and the widow took up with Geoff Williams. The Fairhursts didn't care for him. And the whole world knows you've been helping Mrs. Williams's daughter."

Geoff's murder was the talk of the town, and thanks to my television appearance with Veronica, I was now associated with the case. Ergo, I should have known that the Fairhurst household would think I was acting for Melva and not their employer. And I had inadvertently played along by asking both Peterson and Arnie what they knew about Geoff's connection with Seth Walker.

Neither man had the boldness, as did Mrs. Peterson, to confront me with the purpose of my visit, so Arnie said a lot about nothing and Peterson said a little about the same thing. Unless those guys thought I was looking for the Mystery Woman among Fairhurst's collection of erotica, they must now be wondering how Seth Walker fit into Geoff's murder. Some can of worms I had opened around here, and I did it without half trying.

But I immediately sensed that the misconception could work to my advantage. If my presence was otherwise accounted for, the blackmailer would have no idea I was hot on his trail. So why not add a little more mis- to the conception? "Did you know Seth was a friend of Geoff Williams, Mrs. Peterson?"

She began shredding the piece of tissue between her fingers. "I did not. Is that why . . ." She stopped in mid-sentence.

"Is that why he was worried about my arrival?" I finished for her.

"I didn't say Seth was worried. He was just curious like all of us. How friendly was he with Geoff Williams?"

"Sorry, Mrs. Peterson. I ask the questions."

That got her back up as high as it was ever going to get. "What else would you like to know, sir?"

"The answer to my first question. Is Seth Walker in the garage?"

"Yes." And without a by-your-leave she hurried off, her walk turning into a trot before she had taken ten steps.

The garage contained three cars, the Rolls and two less impressive vehicles. Just as I was about to conclude that Seth Walker had made himself scarce, I saw something move inside the Rolls. I ambled over and peeked in the back window, where I saw a young man seated with his nose in a magazine whose glossy cover depicted a young lady clad in bikini briefs and nothing else. I tapped on the window.

The young man rolled down the glass and looked at me as if I had come to sell him a subscription to *National Geographic*. "Yeah?" The word came out sounding like "get lost."

"Are you Seth Walker?"

"Who wants to know?"

Arnie's thumbnail sketch was right on the mark. Young, handsome, not too bright but with street smarts written all over his pretty face. The face reminded me of an actor of yore, but I was too angry at the moment to place it. It would come to me.

"You know damn well who wants to know. Mr. Fairhurst told you I was coming and Mrs. Peterson just informed you that I had arrived. Now put that magazine down and step out where I can see all of you."

He tossed the magazine onto the classy leather seat and after opening the door of the Rolls, he stepped out. The punk spread his arms wide and did a complete turn-around for my inspection. In lieu of a cap at a rakish angle, he was crowned with a head of brown hair, perfectly cut and layered.

When he had finished exhibiting himself, he exclaimed, "Look all you want. More than that you can't afford."

"Keep a civil tongue in your head or you might find yourself unemployed."

"Touchy. Okay, I'm at your disposal, Archy."

"Mr. McNally to you."

"Whatever. How can I help you, Mr. McNally." He had a way of making the more proper address sound degrading. But I felt certain that when speaking to his employers, he sounded as shy and ingratiating as a two-year-old looking for an ice-cream cone. What a package was Seth Walker.

"Do you get to Miami often?" I asked. And why not? He had no idea what I was after.

"South Beach, when I feel like slumming."

"And when you don't feel like slumming?" I tried again.

"I stick close to home."

"Where's that?"

"In Palm Beach. South of here."

"South of here goes all the way to the Keys."

"Not to mention South America. Could I know what all this is about?"

"No."

"Can I smoke?"

"They're your lungs."

He wore the black suit and tie of the chauffeur, but on Seth Walker the outfit looked vaguely military—a naval officer who had forgotten to sew the chevrons on his sleeve. He pulled a pack of Camels out of his jacket pocket and lit one.

"What do you know about the Fairhurst family?" I watched him closely as I spoke, but he never betrayed what was going on beneath that perfect head of hair. Seth Walker wasn't a stranger to being interrogated.

"Their checks don't bounce."

"Have you ever been inside the main house here?"

He inhaled deeply and blew smoke out the corner of his mouth. The boy must have been raised on gangster films. "When I was interviewed by Mr. Fairhurst I was in the house."

"Where did the interview take place?"

"In his office. It's in the back, on the ground floor. Why?"

"Don't keep asking me why, because I'm not going to tell you. Get it?"

"Hey, mister, I'm cooperating, and for this you're giving me a hard time."

"Were you ever in any of the other rooms in the house?" I questioned.

He puffed on his cigarette, pretending to think. "I've been in Arnie's room. He's got a suite. Nice."

"What were you doing there?"

"Socializing, I think it's called. Why do you want to know where I've been in the house? Did someone pinch one of the knickknacks?"

"You know better than that." All I was doing here was treading water while watching the hooligan grin at me. "What did you do before you got this job?"

"Waited tables in South Beach."

So, there was a link to Miami. "When was the last time you visited the old haunts?"

"Not since I started here. More than a month ago."

"How'd you get this job?" If I thought this was going to put a crimp in his style, I was wrong.

"Finally," he said, "the reason you're here. Why didn't you just say it up front and save us all this painful bull? You know how I got this job. Mr. Fairhurst told you, I'm sure."

"Now I want you to tell me."

"Geoff Williams put in a good word for me with Mr. Fairhurst. That make you happy?"

"What would make me happy, pal, would not make you happy, believe me. What's your connection with Geoff?"

"None, I hope. The guy is dead, isn't he?"

I wouldn't mind seeing Seth Walker in the same condition. "How did you two meet? And I want the truth."

He stuck his free hand in his trouser pocket and looked at the ceiling. "He was an acquaintance of my mother's."

No surprise. It was just as I thought. Geoff doing a lady friend a favor. And Seth Walker was a surly blob who would one day choke on his own bile.

But now I had something else to think about. Was Seth's mother our Mystery Woman? Melva said that she had been a young woman, but that was just a fleeting impression. Even Lady Horowitz, who was over seventy, had the figure and grace of a much younger woman. I had to keep reminding myself that I was here to locate a blackmailer, not Geoff's last paramour.

"Geoff was in Palm Beach about a month ago, long before the family moved down for the season. Any idea what he was doing here?"

"No."

"Did he see your mother?"

"He could have."

"Is your mother in Palm Beach?"

"That's as much as I'm saying about my mother, and you can tell Mr. Fairhurst I said so. You wanted to know how I got this job and I told you the truth, so don't push your luck, Mr. McNally."

"Don't push yours, Seth—and by the way, is that your real name?"

"Yeah. Is Archy McNally your real name?" He dropped the cigarette on the concrete floor and ground it out with the toe of his shoe.

I turned to go, paused, and turned back to face him. "Did you enjoy your chat with Veronica Manning at the Horowitz reception?"

"Christ, man, are you living in my back pocket?"

"Did you know she was Geoff's step-daughter?"

"I knew she was the best-looking chick in the room, and that's all I cared about."

"Don't let Arnie hear that. He might lock his door the next time you go to his room to socialize."

He took a step toward me, one fist raised, but thought better of it and expressed his anger with a few well-chosen cuss words.

Quitting while I was ahead, I waved bye-bye and was history.

Aside from how the blackmailer might have learned the Fairhurst secret, I wasn't a step closer to collaring the miscreant.

I went back to the house to report to Mr. Fairhurst before leaving. Peterson led me to the den, where I found both Mr. Fairhurst and his wife busily engrossed in the afternoon newspapers. Lolly's rag, I noticed, featured on its front page the blank outline of a woman's face with a huge question mark where her nose should be.

Mr. Fairhurst introduced me to his wife, who acknowledged me by removing her glasses and eyeing me stem to stern before saying, "How do you do, Mr. McNally?"

Mrs. Fairhurst was what is often described as a handsome woman, meaning she was not now a beauty nor had she ever been. A bit horsey, one might say, with rather prominent teeth but a lovely complexion and a poise born of confidence in one's self and her husband's fortune. She wore the uniform of her class and generation—dark skirt, white blouse, and a beige cashmere cardigan.

"Have you finished here?" Mr. Fairhurst asked.

"Yes, sir, I have, but I'm afraid I have very little to report at this stage, aside from what I have already pointed out to you in the library."

"I didn't think you'd learn anything from my staff, Archy. And I've told Mrs. Fairhurst about your discovery."

"Quite a shocker," Mrs. Fairhurst admitted. "It was very clever of you to catch it, Mr. McNally."

"Thank you, ma'am." After glancing at the door, I asked if I could speak freely.

"Of course," Mr. Fairhurst quickly put in. "Our servants don't listen at keyholes."

"You've mentioned your confidence in your staff before, sir, but I'm afraid I must remind you that someone in this house has surely been listening as well as looking."

Mrs. Fairhurst, who had been pretending to read her paper, dropped the pretense and looked up.

"I don't understand, Archy," Mr. Fairhurst said.

"Well, sir, as we discussed, our letter writer may have figured out that your grandfather did not die on the *Titanic* by comparing the dates on the portraits. However, that does not explain how he knows that your ancestor got off the boat in drag. I beg your pardon—disguised as a woman."

Mrs. Fairhurst began to fuss with her newspaper. Was it my crude language or something else? John Fairhurst III seemed oblivious to her reaction, but then, he seemed oblivious to everything that went on in his home—except, perhaps, the handsomely bound writing secreted away on the closed shelves.

"Good lord," he cried, "I never thought of that. Did you, Emily?"

"No," she said to her husband, "I didn't." After fidgeting a bit more in her seat, she added, "John, do you think we should drop this investigation?"

"Drop it? Why, whatever do you mean?"

"I mean," she said, "drop it. Pay the horrible person the money and forget it ever happened."

"Absolutely not," Mr. Fairhust nearly shouted. "There's no guarantee the man will stop with this one payoff. He'll have us by the throat for the rest of our lives."

There was no question that Mrs. Fairhurst was looking decidedly uncomfortable. "Then let him go to the press and tell his story. What proof does he have but that brass plate? We can have it changed tomorrow," she pleaded.

"My dear Emily," her husband explained, "my father's birth date is a matter of public record. We can't change that."

"But why has no one ever noticed the discrepancy before now?" she questioned.

"Because, ma'am," I cut in, "I imagine no one ever cared enough to compare those dates. What I mean is, whoever heard of checking the date of a man's death against the birth date of his son? As long as they aren't years apart, to be sure. In this case it's a mere three months and the years coincide.

"Now, a very devious person has gotten hold of the information and intends to grow rich on the knowledge. I must ask you both if at any time you discussed with anyone how your grandfather got off the *Titanic?*"

"Never," Mr. Fairhurst exclaimed.

His wife did not answer. Did her husband speak for both of them?

In deference to her, I asked, "Do you want me to continue with the investigation, sir?"

"Of course."

"Then," I advised, "all we can do now is wait for the letter telling us where and when to deliver the cash."

"I'll let you know as soon as it arrives," Mr. Fairhurst assured me.

"It was a pleasure meeting you, Mrs. Fairhurst. I'm sorry it wasn't under more pleasant circumstances."

"Thank you," she said, "and I'm sorry if I sound a bit rattled. First that letter and now poor Melva. Have you seen her, Mr. McNally?"

"I have. If I said she was fine, it would be a lie, but she's holding up and her lawyers are confident."

"Mystery Woman!" Mrs. Fairhurst blurted. "There was never any mystery about that man's indiscretions. He deserved what he got, I'd say."

"Emily, please," Mr. Fairhurst scolded.

"Tell Melva we're thinking of her, Mr. McNally, and if she needs us, we're here." Mrs. Fairhurst got in the last word on the subject.

"I will, ma'am. And now I must be going."

"We have confidence in you, Mr. McNally," Mrs. Fairhurst said with a royal wave of her hand.

"Thank you, ma'am," I responded, wondering whether she placed her confidence in my success or in my failure.

20

MY AFTERNOON AMONG the Fairhursts' servants told me more about them than I cared to know, but nothing regarding the purpose of my visit. The brass plates under the portraits of the Fairhurst men told me that the current John Fairhurst had goofed royally when he ordered his father's dates etched in metal. I'm sure he had actually come to believe the story of his grandfather's gallantry, hence it had never occurred to him to alter his father's birth date.

The lesson learned here is that the only way to perpetuate a lie is with more lies.

I also learned that Mrs. Fairhurst was concerned with the blackmail threat but for reasons different from her husband's. I doubt it was the Fairhurst name she was anxious to protect, but her own. Mrs. Fairhurst clearly did not want the guilty party brought to justice. I wonder why. During the last great war, government posters reminded citizens that "Loose lips sink ships." Did Mrs. Fairhurst forget this warning? I would have to have a chat with the woman without arousing her husband's suspicions. I didn't relish the chore.

Back home, I got out of my investigative garb—proper suit and tie—but beneath, the real Archy pulsated in red briefs and blue T-shirt, don't-you-know. If I added a cape, Lois Lane wouldn't know me from the real article. Instead, I donned my Speedos, yellow for this lovely late afternoon, and an ankle-length terry robe with hood. Cars paused for me as I crossed the A1A, thinking that a white monk was on his way to bless the waters.

The Atlantic was calm and welcoming, if a bit nippy, but then we were approaching the winter solstice. I completed my two-mile swim and was back in my digs in just over one hour. For my evening date, I selected yellow linen trousers, a lime-green sport coat of the same fabric, and Bally loafers. Thanks to Veronica's less than complimentary remark regarding my berets, I ventured forth bareheaded.

There was still a small crowd in front of Melva's gate looking for photo ops, and in the waning twilight they edged forward to see who was seeking admittance to the murder scene. I had purposely raised the Miata's top to maintain as low a profile as possible and not one flashbulb popped as I gave my name to the security guard.

Veronica, looking lovely in a simple white pique shift with a matching short-sleeved jacket, greeted me at the door. "Hattie is bringing mother a tray," she explained. "Do we have time for a drink?"

"We have all night," I answered, following her into the drawing room, where a portable bar had been set up. On a lovely evening such as this, the solarium, with its glass walls and view of sky and ocean, would have been the ideal place for cocktails, but I assumed that room was still off-limits by choice rather than police insistence.

"You still have company out front," I told her.

"I know. We're prisoners in our own home and the only reason the phone is not ringing is because I've unplugged them again, just as Hattie did the other day. It's horrid, Archy, just horrid."

"We could hire Meecham's yacht and use the back door."

"And have them descend from the air? No, thanks."

"It's nothing that we didn't expect," I said, moving to the bar. "What's your poison? It'll help steady your nerves as long as you don't make it a habit."

"Vodka martini, please." She sat in the chair usually occupied by her mother. As she crossed her stockingless legs, names like Grable, Charisse, and Miller popped into my mind.

I reached for the Sterling vodka—the rich know how to separate the hype from the real thing—and began mixing two perfect martinis.

Behind me, Veronica was still complaining. "And the television news is relentless on the subject. If World War Three broke out, it would get a ten-second mention between 'The Hunt for the Mystery Woman' and a commercial for acid indigestion."

"I never watch television, and I would advise you to do the same, young lady. I hope you're not subjecting your mother to that vast wasteland."

"She spent most of the day in her room. I'm worried about her, Archy."

"As well you might be. She's had a shock and it will take time to wear off. Her medication is also keeping her down. Why don't you call Dr. Pearlberg and see if she can't come in and have a look at Melva." I served her drink.

"Thank you, Archy. Maybe I'll do that." Veronica raised her glass and toasted, "Cheers, if that doesn't sound too absurd."

"It does, but cheers anyway."

After taking a sip of the clear brew she stared at me as if the drink had suddenly cleared her vision. "My God, Archy, you look like a lime rickey."

Am I to be spared nothing from this divine creature? "We're in Florida, not drab New York," I told her.

She smiled, then laughed. "You're the best medicine in the world, Archy. Cheers, again."

* * *

Thanks to Veronica, our exit was much more of a media event than my entrance had been. The popping flashbulbs turned night into day long enough to blind me. While waiting to recover my sight, I rolled down the Miata's window and shouted to the security guard closing the gate behind us, "We're going to Ta-Boo' and should be back before midnight."

I pulled out onto the A1A and headed south. "I take it we're not going to Ta-Boo'," Veronica said.

"You take it wrong. That's exactly where we're going."

"And they'll go to every restaurant in Palm Beach except Ta-Boo'." Veronica got the point.

"Give the lady a cigar."

I decided on Ta-Boo' because we could eat in the bar, at those absurdly small round tables, and avoid the prying eyes of those in the main dining room. That was my first error of the evening. The bar was crowded with the young of Palm Beach—those who weren't at Hillcrest this evening—and most of them knew Veronica. The sudden hush as we entered was quickly followed by a ripple of polite but rather strained chitchat. Deciding that we were the floor show, the hostess led us to a table that was in plain sight of the bar. All that would be lacking, I mused, was a spotlight. I pointed to an empty table in a rear corner and she quickly changed direction.

"Sorry," I whispered to Veronica as we sat.

She shook her lovely blond tresses. "It would be the same no matter where we went," she pointed out. "In fact, this corner table is what's known as Siberia in café society circles. Perfect for us, I would say."

Our waiter informed us that his name was Eric in a manner not unlike an overblown thespian reciting "The Charge of the Light Brigade." I ordered two stand-up Sterling vodka martinis and asked for menus. "We'll dine here," I told Eric, who did an about-face with military precision.

"Waiting tables is something they do between the Actor's Studio and winning an Academy Award," Veronica observed.

"I was in a restaurant with Binky Watrous one night and he asked our waitress if she were an 'expiring' actress. She said, 'I hope not,' and Binky said he could have sworn she was."

Veronica looked amused. "How is Binky? All over his rabies scare?"

"Yes, but now he's suing Hobo."

"Poor Hobo," Veronica lamented.

Poor Melva. Poor Hobo. What a town this was. Didn't anyone in Palm Beach feel sorry for the victim? Eric brought our drinks and menus, and trailing him was a young lady who was tugging on the elbow of a man in uniform like a mother delivering her son to the dentist.

"Veronica," she cooed, bending to kiss Veronica and almost dunking her nose into a Sterling martini. To me, she said, "Please, don't get up. I just couldn't leave without saying I'm so sorry."

I had as much intention of getting up as she had of revealing the reason for her sorrow.

"This is Fitz," Veronica informed me, but I already suspected that here was the famous Elizabeth Fitzwilliams. And what a knockout was Fitz. A brunette with blue eyes and a figure that would cause a ninety-year-old Buddhist monk to regret his vows.

"Archy here," I introduced myself.

"Hello, Archy," Fitz said. "And this is Ensign Douglas Wilson."

So, the ensign came to dinner and walked off with the dessert. Douglas looked as if he had just stepped off the cover of *Military Life.* Crew cut, square jaw, and tight-lipped. He nodded but thankfully did not salute.

"We won't interrupt," Fitz babbled on, "but couldn't leave without saying—well, you know. I've been trying to get you on the phone all day, Veronica. It's always busy."

"I pulled the plugs," Veronica told her.

"How exciting," Fitz once again cooed. She sounded as if she might run home and implore her mother to shoot her father so she, too, could unplug the phones. "Then call me," Fitz said, moving away and taking Douglas with her, "we must catch up."

"I will," Veronica promised. As we watched them gyrating their way through the maze of round tables, Veronica whispered, "What do you think of Fitz?"

"Lovely. But gentlemen prefer blondes."

"Not Douglas, and from the way she's hanging on to him I expect they'll be engaged before the night ends."

"So soon?"

"Not for Fitz. She gets engaged at least once a month. The last one was a quarterback from Purdue."

"What happened to him?"

"He was demoted to third string due to chronic exhaustion."

"Oh my, that was naughty," I chided.

"It was. Let's order, I'm starved."

"We'll not have the green linguine," I said, opening my menu.

"Why not?"

"Because everyone has the green linguine and I refuse to amble along with the herd."

I summoned Eric and he rattled off the evening's specials with a flourish. Veronica settled on the grilled pompano and I chose a rib eye. For openers, we both went for the crabmeat cocktail.

The bus person (who was a he) supplied us with bread and rolls and as we eagerly buttered up, I made my second error of the evening by asking, "What did you think of Seth Walker?"

"Who?"

"Seth Walker," I repeated. "He introduced himself to you at Lady Horowitz's reception."

"You mean the Fairhursts' chauffeur?"

"None other."

Veronica nibbled on her roll. "Adorable. That's what I think. And how do you know he spoke to me at that awful woman's party?"

Poor Lady C. Really, she wasn't that bad. "My friend Connie Garcia is secretary to Lady Horowitz. She told me she saw you talking to him and remembered because Lolly Spindrift called her after the party to ask who the boy was." I purposely left out Mrs. Marsden as the person who had identified Seth for me.

Veronica helped herself to another bite of her roll. I do so like a girl with a hearty appetite. "He crashed the party, you know. Seth, that is, not Lolly. Strange how Lolly and I seem to attract the same men."

"No, my dear. You attract the same men Lolly is attracted to. Did Seth invite you out?"

She patted her lips with her napkin. "Why am I being interrogated?"

"Maybe because I'm jealous. Did he ask you out?"

"Do you know him?" she asked, as if the possibility had just occurred to her.

"We've met."

"Where?"

"Sorry, I'm not at liberty to say."

She finished her martini before saying, "Neither am I."

We had come to an awkward impasse, thanks to my clumsy inquisitiveness, which was saved by the arrival of our crabmeat cocktails. "I'm sorry," I said. "I didn't mean to sound like a mole for the CIA. I'm doing a job for John Fairhurst and I was at the Fairhurst house today and met Seth. I remembered the connection between him and you and Lolly. Now let's enjoy the crabmeat. It's too expensive not to."

She picked up her cocktail fork and dug right in. "Connections," she repeated. "That's the story of Palm Beach, isn't it? Everyone is connected. A chauffeur to an heiress to a gossip columnist to a private investigator. Well, we're an eclectic band of rogues, I'll say that for us."

On that note we ate our crabmeat, careful not to imbibe the lettuce beneath the fish, which would have been gauche. No sooner had our bus person removed all traces of our appetizer than who should appear—all six feet, two inches of him—looming over our table, but Buzz. The bar was swarming with those of a nautical bent.

"Hi, Veronica. Hi, Archy."

"I thought we were in Siberia," I said to my tablemate. "But it looks more like Grand Central Station to me."

"Oh hush, Archy," she rebuked me. "How are you, Buzz?"

"I was seen by twenty million viewers," he proudly told us. "I checked the ratings."

"Then shouldn't you be home answering your fan mail?" I asked him.

"I didn't get any yet," he said, sounding certain that the morning mail would contain a thousand requests for autographed photos. "Have you heard about the ball?"

"If you mean Lady Horowitz's ball, how did you hear about it?" I countered.

"Everyone is talking about it. A masked ball, and Lady Horowitz has asked me to be a page. I'm being fitted for silk breeches."

I remembered *Adventures of a King's Page,* published in London in 1829, and shuddered. "When did you meet Lady Horowitz?"

"Today. Lolly brought me to her place for tea. Some house."

Tea, indeed. There was a name for men who introduced people for the purpose of cohabitation, and I'd remind Lolly Spindrift of that fact the next time I saw him. "Lady Horowitz's ball is not a very pleasant subject for Veronica, you klutz."

Buzz looked as contrite as he knew how, which wasn't very repentant. "I didn't mean to offend," he apologized.

"It's all right, Buzz," Veronica said. "That woman's party is not your doing, and I still appreciate what you did for me the other day." Veronica had a weakness for handsome, young men.

"Thanks," Buzz said and, feeling vindicated, he bounded off with a wave, a grin, and nary a trace of egg on his face.

Our dinner arrived and not a moment too soon. I ordered a white Burgundy for Veronica and a Beaujolais for *moi*. Eric poured the customary dollop of wine from each bottle for us to taste and after we both gave it the nod, he filled our glasses. My steak was what is known in some gourmand circles as "Pittsburgh." Black on the outside and red within. I trust the name came from those iron mills pioneered by Andy and John I. Eric tossed our salad—

oil, vinegar, and a sprinkling of finely grated Romano—and we began this delightful meal in the middle of which Veronica dropped a bomb.

"You've met Seth before today," she informed me.

"I doubt it. I never forget a face. What makes you think so?"

"He was with me at Hillcrest—in the chat room. I believe you exchanged words."

I was fast losing my appetite. "You went there to meet him? Why?"

"Because he invited me."

"Do you always go where people invite you?"

"No. Only when I want to."

That seemed to say it all. We continued eating in silence. I couldn't help thinking how foolish pretty, young girls could be, and judging from Veronica's pleased expression, she was thinking that the grilled pompano was delicious. By the time our coffee arrived, she once again opened up to me.

"Archy, I went to the Horowitz reception with Fitz and her parents. Like all those so-called charity events, it was one big bore, and suddenly there was Seth. So attractive, I thought, and daring. And he never pre-

tended to be anything than what he was—
the Fairhursts' chauffeur. Of course, the only
reason the Fairhursts were there was
because the reception benefited some children's hospital where Mr. Fairhurst is on the
board of directors. That Horowitz lady knows
how to pull in the big fish. And that's it."

No, I thought—that isn't it. "And he invited
you out?"

"Yes. I saw him again the following
evening."

"And the night after that you met him at
Hillcrest?"

"I just told you I did."

"Have you seen him since?"

"How could I? I spent the next day and
night with you, and I've been with my mother
ever since. And I have no intention of seeing him again. I've grown up in the past two
days, Archy, and Seth Walker no longer
amuses. Now, can we drop the subject?"

"With pleasure," I said.

One very clever paparazzo was waiting
for us outside Ta-Boo', but we didn't even
say "cheese" when he took the picture that
would make the front pages of the morning
tabloids.

* * *

When I took Veronica home, I made my third error. I kissed her good night. Not a brotherly kiss, but the kind of kiss mothers warn their daughters against, especially when indulged in convertible cars with their tops up. I pulled up in front of Veronica's door at eleven-fifteen. She left the Miata at five minutes to midnight.

21

"WELL, IF IT isn't our celebrity of the day." Lady Cynthia Horowitz was sitting poolside in a recliner, protected from the noon sun by a humongous beach umbrella. Many women her age in Palm Beach never showed their face in the bright light of day, but Lady C. seemed to enjoy doing just that, adding to her mystique as a genuine local "character." She had a long nose with a droopy tip and a pointed chin that curved upward. No, she wasn't a witch—but she was certainly no beauty.

Upon meeting her for the first time, I could not understand how she had managed to snare five husbands of great wealth and one Brit with a title. But when a national tabloid printed an article on this Palm Beach "character," it was accompanied by photos of Lady C. in her prime, and while even then she had a face that could stop a clock, below was a body so voluptuous that photographers and artists vied for her services as a model. Her first nude photographs had caused a sensation and started her on her many trips down the aisle to great wealth and, ultimately, a title.

It was rumored that even Picasso had painted her, turning her goddesslike form into a stack of shingles that was greatly admired by art lovers throughout the world.

Now, at age three score and ten—at least—she had somehow managed to retain the body that had made her fortune. Wearing white shorts, white blouse, white turban, and white wedgies, she brought to mind Lana Turner in *The Postman Always Rings Twice,* and I'm certain the analogy was intended. She had also retained more moxie than any woman—or man—had a right to possess. Most noticeable among her numerous pet peeves were cigars, dogs, men who wore pinky rings, and air conditioning. She was short-tempered and, if elbowed, foul-mouthed.

On the table beside her were the remains of a late breakfast and the morning paper, which featured yours truly and Veronica Manning emerging from Ta-Boo'. I must say, we made a fetching couple.

"Pull up a chair, lad," Lady C. said with a wave of her hand. "Can I offer you a coffee?"

"That would be nice," I answered, accepting both offers.

Lady C. poured. "Help yourself to cream and sugar. I'm not going to do it all for you." As I did, she tapped the front page of her newspaper with a forefinger whose nail was polished with a colorless gloss. "She's young enough to be your daughter."

"She's twenty-two." I was growing weary of reminding people of this fact.

"How old are you?" she asked, without a trace of timidity.

"Old enough to know that this masked ball idea is absurd. A play for publicity that's destined to backfire."

"Your girlfriend told me I might hear from you on that subject. By the way, Connie is very unhappy about this." Once again the newspaper was prodded with Lady C.'s polished digit.

I had figured as much. On my way in, I had tried to see Connie, but she was on the phone and shooed me off like a pesky fly. Not a good sign.

"And I'm old enough to tell you that you're wrong," Lady C. said. "I'm suddenly getting invitations from people who've shunned me in the past, and do you know why? Because they want to come to my ball, that's why."

That was not entirely true. If Lady C. had been shunned, it was because she did not enjoy dining in other people's homes or public restaurants. She gave great parties and those who attended knew that she would refuse any attempt at reciprocation. Her love affair with society was so one-sided because that's the way she wanted it to be. However, the upper, upper strata of Palm Beach society did not approve of Lady Cynthia Horowitz—as in the Fairhurst crowd—but I could not imagine them wanting to attend the upcoming masked ball. She was merely being cantankerous, which was par for most conversations with Madame.

This was not going to be easy, but then, I never thought it would be.

"Lolly put you up to this, didn't he," I asserted.

"Give me some credit, lad. Oh, Lolly added a few touches, but the idea was all mine."

"Buzz's silk breeches, for instance?"

Lady C. smiled, making a thin line of her mouth, which seemed to bring her droopy nose and the upward tilt of her chin into alarmingly close proximity. "How news travels in our community. Yes, that one was Lolly's. And I can't wait to see Buzz wearing them. Royal blue they'll be. Would you like to be a page, Archy?" Lady C. eyed my jeans provocatively. The woman was a menace.

"No, Lady Cynthia, I would not. What I would like is for you to cancel the ball."

"Not possible. We are moving full steam ahead, and if the scuttlebutt is any indication, we'll get national coverage with this one."

"Lolly's television appearance has certainly gone to his head," I countered. "Anything less than national attention will no longer do."

"Oh, it's not only Lolly." Indicating the newspaper with a nod she continued, "We're all aboard the gravy train. Veronica Manning is some catch for the sole proprietor of Discreet Inquiries."

I let this go. What she wanted was a knockdown, drag-out fight to vindicate her party, and she wasn't going to get it from me. "I was looking after Veronica as a favor to her mother. Melva needs all the help she can get." The point, I'm sure, fell on deaf ears.

"And you look different, lad," she went right on as if I hadn't spoken. "More— what's the word? Conventional?" I was wearing jeans, polo shirt, seersucker jacket, and loafers. "You look like a prospective son-in-law."

Aware that my relationship with Connie made this last statement a direct kick in the *cojones,* she took great delight in administering the blow. Tit for tat, I responded, "And in case you don't know it, Buzz belongs to Phil Meecham. He's Phil's first mate."

"Was Phil's first mate. After Buzz's television appearance, thanks to you, he's given up the yachting set for a career in films. Buzz will reside here and a drama coach will come in daily to round him out."

Lady Cynthia had had live-in tennis instructors, live-in backgammon instructors, live-in bridge instructors, a Swami, a leftover flower child, and a man who claimed to be the illegitimate son of Prince Philip and Cobina Wright Jr. Excuse the pun, but it was inevitable that an aspiring actor was waiting in the wings.

"Buzz has all the charisma of a dead fish," I told his ardent patron.

"He has other attributes."

"Such as the ability to fill out a pair of silk breeches?"

"You said it. Not me." This seemed to please her.

Having inflicted her wounds, the Lady now began sprinkling them with salt. "Connie tells me we're getting inquiries about the ball from New York, Los Angeles, and Sardinia," she boasted with great relish.

"Sardinia? Who in Sardinia?"

"The Aga Kahn, of course. And his lovely sister, Jasmine."

This was preposterous. "Lady Cynthia, Melva is fighting for her life. This ball would make her situation a travesty."

"I owe Melva Ashton Manning Williams nothing. She never had the time of day for me, but she certainly had time to spare when she spotted Geoff Williams on my tennis court."

Lady C. was known for never forgetting a slight, real or imagined, and striking back when the iron was hot. Now, the reason for this ridiculous party was crystal clear. Lady C. couldn't have Geoff back, but she could have her masked ball, see Melva humiliated, and ogle Buzz in silk britches. A sort of grand slam vendetta.

"I did you a favor once," I reminded her.

"And if blood is indeed thicker than water, I paid you back handsomely. Don't twist my arm, lad. We don't want to bring my lawyer into this, do we?"

I got the message, loud and clear. Case closed! "I wouldn't think of it, Lady Cynthia. When is the happy event?"

"Ten days from today. It's the best I can do. The invitations are being printed on parchment scrolls. They'll be hand delivered to exactly two hundred people. You're on the guest list."

"I'm not honored, I'm sure." Knowing I couldn't fare any worse, I decided to stick a pin into the Lady's balloon. "What happens if the real Mystery Woman shows up before the ball?"

"Then I eat crow," she said. "Or do I eat a buffet dinner for two hundred all alone? Either way, lad, it would be the pits. But there are those who say the Mystery Woman is pure poppycock. Melva's rather racy excuse for ending what had become a tiresome marriage."

"Don't believe it, Lady Cynthia. The police are very close to identifying the Mystery Woman. In fact they may do so before the ink dries on your parchment scrolls. I would put the brakes on your running footmen, not to mention Buzz's silk pantaloons."

The lie was worth the effort. Finally, I had her looking worried. She sat forward and stared at me, long and hard. "Are you serious?"

"I've never been more serious in my life, Lady Cynthia. Cross my heart and hope to die."

Lady C. gave God a good half minute to strike me dead, and when He didn't, she leaned back in her chaise longue and said, "I don't believe you." But she wasn't sure. I knew she wasn't sure. I rose, thanked her for the coffee and left her a little less cocky than when I had found her. It wasn't a grand slam, but I had managed to trump her ace.

I had been rebuked by Lady C., but as dear old Al Jolson used to say, "You ain't seen nothin' yet." What I had not seen, yet, was Consuela Garcia. When I did, I wished I had followed my nose to the front door and onward to the Pelican where I could drown my failure with Lady C. in suds and a medium-rare steak tartare.

Connie, naturally, was on the phone. A disembodied voice filled the office. "I highly recommend the cherry tart flambé. The waiters bring it in at midnight, trays aloft, to the accompaniment of 'The Grand March' from *Aida.* For a few extra bucks you can have an elephant."

"I don't think we want an elephant with dessert, Sam, and I'm not too sure about *Aida.*"

"What about 'Lara's Theme' from *Zhivago?*" was Sam's immediate comeback. "It's very big at weddings with the burning cherries."

"At midnight?" Connie cried. "No way. They'll all be drunk and start crying."

"Okay," Sam said, "I'll put you down for the cherry tart flambé and pencil you in for either *Aida* or 'Lara.' And Connie, thanks for talking her out of the baked Alaska. Baked Alaska for two hundred is pure hell."

"My pleasure, Sam. We'll talk later."

"You have a fascinating job, Connie," I told her as soon as she had cut Sam off.

"Not as fascinating as yours. I've never been televised on a yacht from a helicopter, nor did I ever make the front pages of every newspaper in Florida simply by walking out of a restaurant." Her tone implied that she was more disgusted than fascinated with my chosen profession.

Seeking sympathy, I cried, "I've just had a dismal interview with Lady C. She flatly refuses to give up the masked ball. She even threatened to complain to my father if I insisted on putting the screws to her. And if the Master had to choose between me and Lady Cynthia Horowitz's annual remittance, guess which he would choose?"

"Poor Archy. All that and caught in the act, too." Once again, I had Lolly Spindrift's rag waved in my face.

"Caught? What's that supposed to mean? I wasn't trying to hide."

"I thought you were finished with baby-sitting Lolita."

Just one hour after high noon and the day was going from bad to worse. "Melva asked me to take Veronica out to dinner. She's been a prisoner in her own house since Melva got out of jail, and it's obvious why Melva didn't want to come with us."

"Melva seems to be literally throwing her daughter at your feet. And another point I'd like to make, Archy, is that Veronica Manning is not the innocent you seem to think she is. It was put about last season that she was something of a loose cannon, in fact."

"I've heard that about all of the young and restless in Palm Beach, and so have you, Connie. You're being unfair."

With a look of stark determination I had never seen on the face of Consuela Garcia before, she read me the riot act. "Lolita or me, Archy. That's my ultimatum and your choice."

"But, Connie . . ." I tried pleading.

"One more date with her and our relationship will be for whom the bell tolls." As if applauding her stance, all the lights began flashing on her telephone console. "Now get out of here, I have to work."

"Before I go, may I say just one thing?"

She shrugged hopelessly. "Make it fast, Archy."

"Instead of 'Lara's Theme' from *Zhivago,* why not 'Laura's Theme' from *Laura?*"

"Get the hell out of here, Archy McNally!"

Dinner that evening was low key, but with an air of expectancy that owed its existence to my much publicized date with Veronica Manning. Mother noted, more than once, how happy we looked emerging from Ta-Boo'. I told her it was due, no doubt, to the fine quality of our meal, but she would have none of this. "I think you are both happy to be in each other's company," Mother insisted. "I noticed that when she dined with us the other evening, Archy."

Over Ursi's ribs of beef, oven-roasted potatoes, and white asparagus with a light hollandaise, Father also extolled the merits of Melva's offspring without bluntly stating the vast wealth of the family. *Mon père* had selected a very fine Bordeaux from the Médoc region for our wine—an indication that he felt more than just a good dinner wine was apropos to the occasion.

Was marriage, like death, inevitable? And if I had to ponder a choice, was I really in love with either candidate? And last, but surely not least, let us consider that neither "candidate" had thrown her hat in the ring.

"Mother," I said, "I want a girl, just like the girl that married dear old Dad.' "

"Oh, Archy," mother giggled, "she's too old for you."

Mother went off to the kitchen to "help Ursi," as she enjoyed calling her nightly sitcom fix. Father and I adjourned to the den for our brandy. "So," father began, removing the cigar box from his desk drawer as I poured our brandy into crystal snifters, "tell me what's happening with the Fairhurst situation."

"In fact, sir, it's just the subject I wished to discuss with you." I refused a cigar in favor of an English Oval, and after giving father his drink, I took my seat. "But first, is there anything new in Melva's case?"

Father indulged himself in the ritual of snipping off the end of his cigar before putting it to the flame of a lit match. "Not much. Every effort will be made to find the so-called 'Mystery Woman' before Melva's lawyers begin plotting the defense. As you know, how the defense will proceed will depend on whether or not they can come up with the woman to back Melva's testimony."

"And if they can't find the 'Mystery Woman,' sir?"

Father puffed thoughtfully on his cigar. "Allow me to put it this way, Archy. It would be a much easier case for the defense if they could produce the woman and she cooperated, but not finding her wouldn't necessarily spell doom for Melva."

"I see, sir."

"Between your contacts and your club affiliation, you get around, Archy. Have you any idea who the woman is?"

"No, sir. Not a clue."

Father sighed audibly. "Then we'll just have to wait and see, won't we? Now, what about Fairhurst?"

I described my visit to the Fairhurst house, giving him as detailed a description as possible of the staff and the principals and my impressions of them.

The brass plates beneath the portraits elicited a one-eyebrow lift from the Sire. "What fools these mortals be," he said. I assumed he quoted Shakespeare because Dickens never said as much in so few words. "And you think Mrs. Fairhurst knows more than she's saying?"

"I do, sir. In fact, I think it was quite obvious. And if her husband were a more astute man, he would think the same."

Father did not like maligning a client, so disregarded this with a sip and a puff. "And what do you suggest, Archy?"

"I want to interview Mrs. Fairhurst, alone, without her husband's knowledge."

He was silent for so long I thought he had fallen asleep. When he finally answered, it was brief and to the point. "I'd rather you wouldn't."

"But, sir . . ."

"John Fairhurst is our client, Archy. Our first—no, our only—obligation is to him. We must keep the client apprised of every action we take in his case. I cannot sanction a clandestine meeting between you and our client's wife."

"I am trying to learn the facts and save Mrs. Fairhurst what could prove a great deal of embarrassment."

"Learn the facts, Archy, but do so without going behind John Fairhurst's back."

I hoped Melva fared better with her judge and jury.

22

ALTHOUGH I WOULD have gladly left the chapter out, I dutifully recorded the day's events in my journal. My three major encounters having ended in defeat, I resolutely rejected humble pie in favor of a pony of brandy, my lone English Oval of the day, and offensive optimism.

Regarding Lady C., I could not stop her from having her wretched ball, but I could still hope that the Mystery Lady would turn up in time to douse Sam's cherry tart flambé.

Regarding Connie, Lady C.'s masked ball was a masked blessing. From long experience I knew that the party would keep Connie so busy, she would have little or no time to badger poor Archy. I would soon have to make a decision regarding my erstwhile fiancée, but not immediately. Therefore, I could while away the next week or so with Veronica before that decision had to be made.

Regarding the Fairhurst affair, I would deal with the *Seigneur* in true epic fashion by ignoring his order in favor of protecting, if I could, Mrs. Fairhurst. Until I had my talk with Mrs. Fairhurst and until we received the blackmailer's second letter, there was nothing I could do to salvage Grandpa Fairhurst's reputation. That left Melva and the hunt for the Mystery Woman.

I knew why Melva thought the car returning on that fateful night was Geoff and not Veronica, and I knew why she had Veronica's exact location in writing, ready and waiting to hand over to me.

What I still didn't know was why the alarm at Melva's front gate had been turned off, and what Hattie had said that still nettled me. The enigma of the alarm would remain just that for now, but I thought I knew where I might jump-start my mind in recalling Hattie's testimony—short of going directly to the source. I had to remember that my only obligation to Melva was to look after Veronica in her mother's absence, and I had fulfilled that obligation. I had no right to cross-examine poor Hattie, or anyone else involved in Geoff's murder.

In the morning I lingered in my quarters long enough to be assured that father had gone off to his office and mother was hard at work in her garden. Jamie was at the kitchen table, enjoying his coffee and his newspaper as I hoped he would be. While Ursi prepared my French toast and turkey sausage, I began priming the pump in hopes of getting a steady flow of coherent sentences from Jamie Olson.

"Remember the day I returned Veronica Manning's car to her and you followed me in the Miata?"

In response, Jamie showed me the front page of the morning paper. The blank face with the question-mark nose was once again on display and below it, in three-inch black type, was the word "REWARD." So, they had finally done it. Was it strictly the newspaper's ploy or was Melva guaranteeing payment? Either way, the police were going to be inundated with Mystery Women.

"How much?" I asked.

"A hundred thousand," Ursi answered, as she presented me with cranberry juice and coffee.

"Why don't you give yourself up, Ursi, and take the money and run?" I recommended.

"If I thought I could get away with it, I would," she answered.

Turning once again to Jamie, I reminded him of the day we drove in separate cars to Melva's.

He nodded.

"I believe you spent some time in the kitchen, talking to Hattie."

"She made me a cuppa," Jamie admitted.

Five words. I was making progress. "Hattie told you what happened that night?"

"She was in tears," Jamie remembered.

This was more than I had hoped for. "Do you recall exactly what she told you?"

Jamie seemed to be looking for the answer to my question on the obit page of his newspaper. Not a good sign. Knowing better, I did not repeat my request but waited patiently for Jamie to see who in Palm Beach was no longer interested in the long-range weather forecast.

"You mean about the robbery?" he asked, turning from the obituaries to the comics.

"What robbery?"

"Hattie thought they were being robbed. First the shouting woke her, and before she was out of bed she heard the gun go off. She figured the bandit had killed the family, and she was afraid to leave her room for fear he would get her, too."

The hair on the nape of my neck rose. Ursi placed my breakfast before me, and the odors of cinnamon and vanilla assaulted rather then assuaged my appetite. I already knew the answer when I asked Jamie, "Why did she come downstairs if she was so afraid?"

"Because she heard the car drive off. She knew the bandit had fled."

Melva said she fired at Geoff after the Mystery Woman had fled.

"I heard her car drive off and wondered if she was still naked and what a scandal there would be if she were stopped by the police. Then I think he noticed the gun I was pointing at him."

Hattie told me she heard the gunshot and then she heard the car drive off, and Jamie had just confirmed that fact.

I now knew why Hattie's statement had kept me awake that night, but I took no comfort from the solution. Wasn't it just as easy to believe Melva as it was to believe Hattie? No! Because Hattie was a very frightened woman who would never have budged from her room if she hadn't heard the car leave after the shot was fired. Had the shot come last, Hattie would have correctly reasoned that the person doing the shooting was still downstairs and she would have remained in her room.

But what did it mean? That the Mystery Woman had witnessed the shooting? If so, why had Melva lied? To protect the Mystery Woman? To absolve her of any firsthand knowledge of the crime? And what else was Melva hiding and why? I didn't know. What I did know was that I didn't like it. Not in the least.

I called the Fairhurst residence and got Peterson. When I asked to speak to Mrs. Fairhurst, the butler asked who wanted her. "Archy McNally," I said, guessing that the guy had recognized my voice and to lie would only add to whatever speculation was going on among the staff.

"Mr. McNally," Mrs. Fairhurst began, "I should say I'm surprised to hear from you, but we both know that would be a lie."

"Yes, ma'am."

"I trust you would like to see me, Mr. McNally."

"I would, Mrs. Fairhurst. Alone, if that's possible."

"Yes, it's possible. And, as I'm sure you know, it's also preferable. You can't come here and I won't come to your office," she stated, leaving no doubt that she meant it.

"The Alcazar Lounge at The Breakers?" I suggested.

"You have a date, Mr. McNally. It's eleven now. Shall we say in one hour?"

"We shall say, ma'am."

As I dressed in slacks and blazer I thought of Lady C.'s accusation that I had gone conventional in my garb. Prospective son-in-law was her theory for the change. Had I capitulated to custom since Veronica's arrival in my life? I didn't think so. Conformity, in either direction, is conformity. Variety remained my hallmark, and may the bluebird of happiness unload on Lady C.'s white turban. But just in case, I passed up the wing tips in favor of sneakers.

I arrived early and took a seat at the bar, ordering a vodka and tonic with lime. The pretty barmaid presented me with a bowl of salted nuts along with my drink. The lounge was less than half full, but it was a tad early for the ladies who lunch. Right now I was surrounded by tourists and those who were breaking their fasts with juice laced with hard liquor.

Mrs. Fairhurst spotted me as soon as she came into the room and didn't pause a moment on her way to my perch on a bar stool. Today she wore a navy blue suit with a bit of white fluff at the neck, and blue and white spectator pumps. Her good skin and trim figure belied her age, and her shapely legs told you why she probably never wore pants.

I got off my stool to greet her. "Mrs. Fairhurst," I said with a nod, "I appreciate your time."

"My pleasure, Mr. McNally." She made a move toward the stool next to the one I had just vacated.

"Would you rather we sat at a table?"

"Heavens no. I never get to sit at the bar in public places, and I never have secret rendezvous with handsome young men. If I'm going to break the rules, I insist on breaking all of them."

I liked this lady. We settled in, side by side, and I moved my bowl of salted nuts to a position that would afford both of us easy access. When the barmaid appeared, Mrs. Fairhurst ordered a gin and tonic in a stem glass. "It looks more respectable," she explained.

"You drove yourself?" I asked.

"Yes. It's one of the few things I do well."

We watched the barmaid mix her drink as if we were intent on memorizing the recipe, and our banter ceased until Mrs. Fairhurst had sampled the finished product.

"You wanted me to set up this date, didn't you?" I asked.

"Oh dear. Are you being Freudian? Do you mean I subconsciously sent out signals asking you to call me?"

"I thought it was rather overt. I'm only surprised your husband didn't notice your quandary."

Mrs. Fairhurst was sipping away at her gin and tonic at a rather rapid pace. Nerves,

I suspected, notwithstanding her noncha-
lant chatter. "If I thought my husband would
notice, it wouldn't be necessary for us to
meet, Mr. McNally."

The old story, but it's new when it happens to you. A husband more interested in
himself, his lineage, and his "library" than in
the woman he married. I was sure Mrs.
Fairhurst had all the creature comforts one
could ask for—and more—accompanied by
a marital relationship that would chill the
heart of a penguin.

"You're going to think I'm a very foolish
old woman," she said.

"Try me."

If her stem glass had a gauge, it would
register dangerously close to E. "When the
children were home I had a lot to occupy my
time. I mean, Mr. McNally, I had a reason
for living. When they left the nest, John and
I suddenly looked at each other like
strangers in a physician's waiting room,
each wondering what was wrong with the
other. Our children had filled a void my husband had never occupied. He was never
unkind. Just never very thoughtful. His
upbringing precluded any show of emotion,
and I'm afraid he learned his lessons well.

I am, you see, a living cliché." She paused before asking, "May I have another drink?"

"You may, and I'll join you." I motioned for our barmaid to repeat our order and as she did I said to Mrs. Fairhurst, "You need not bare your soul, ma'am. I think I understand the situation."

"Just cut to the chase. Isn't that the popular expression?"

I smiled, and so did she. There was a twinkle in her eyes and I felt very, very sorry for this poor rich lady. However, I felt just as sorry for her mate. Look at all he was missing. "Then along came Arnold," I prompted.

She took a small sip of her fresh drink and I did the same with mine. We both continued to ignore our salted nuts.

"You are either very clever, Mr. McNally, or my tale is as old as the proverbial hills. Yes, and then came Arnold Turnbolt. You see, John and I became involved in so many charities, many of which we founded, that a secretary was more a necessity than a luxury. So, we took on Arnold, and I was hooked from the moment he came into our home. Arnold made me laugh. He made me remember that life was to be enjoyed, not endured. On his own time he escorted me to the theater, museums, restaurants, and social functions John refused to attend." She paused, thought a moment and said, "And he was safe—if you know what I mean."

I nodded. "An openly gay man," I said, "and therefore above suspicion. You wouldn't be the first woman of substance to employ a 'walker,' Mrs. Fairhurst."

"But Arnold is so much more than a paid or convenient escort. He's a friend. We consult each other on everything—mostly my clothes and his boyfriends." Again the twinkle and smile.

"And you told Arnold about grandpa's less than heroic exit from the *Titanic.*"

She took another sip of her drink, pacing herself more carefully on her second gin and tonic. Smart gal was Mrs. Fairhurst. "Like you, Arnold noticed the dates under the portraits and when he pointed them out to me I told him the whole story."

"But you never told your husband about the dates?"

"Heavens, no. There was no reason. If no one besides Arnold had ever noticed them we assumed that no one ever would. And then along came Archy McNally."

"I'll take that as a compliment," I said. "You also didn't tell your husband because he would have asked you exactly what you told Arnold following his discovery. This would leave you two choices—lie or fess up that you had confided in your secretary. It was easier to keep quiet."

She raised her right hand and said, "Guilty." Then, before I could ask, she stated, "Arnold is not blackmailing us, Mr. McNally."

"Are you sure?"

"I am. And not just because I trust him implicitly but because I confided in Arnold, as you call it, over five years ago, Mr. McNally. Why would he wait until now to do such a dreadful thing?"

"I believe you, Mrs. Fairhurst. Does Arnold know about the blackmail scam?"

She shook her head adamantly. "No, he does not. Or I should say if he does, he didn't hear it from me."

"Do you know that your new chauffeur, Seth Walker, has visited Arnold in his rooms?"

"Mr. McNally, I have said all I came here to say."

"But Mrs. Fairhurst, Seth is the new kid on the block and if he's been intimate with Arnold . . ."

"Please, Mr. McNally. I don't want to hear any more. I've told you all I know about this insufferable business, and I have no intention of saying anything more."

That twinkle had been replaced with tears. If Seth was the culprit and I connected Arnold to Seth—however unwittingly Arnold had acted—it would be the end of Arnold's job and Mrs. Fairhurst's dear friendship. That she had told me as much as she had was a testimony to her allegiance to her husband—who didn't deserve it—and her belief in justice, regardless of the consequences to her own person. A very noble lady, indeed.

"I respect your position, Mrs. Fairhurst. This conversation ends here and will never go beyond us."

"Thank you, Mr. McNally. You are a gentleman, but I'll pay for the drinks."

"No," I insisted. "I'm on an expense account, and this will get charged to your husband." Her smile told me she liked the idea.

"Anything new with Melva's situation?" she asked.

Plenty, but not for publication, I thought. Aloud I told her what little I knew. "Have you spoken to her, Mrs. Fairhurst?"

"No. But I will. In fact, I want to ask her to dine with us one evening soon. You know, we were very close to Melva and Ted, but never really took to Geoff."

"Yes, I know. And I think she would appreciate your call."

"You and Veronica are something of an item, I understand. Or at least that's what Arnold says."

"I'm keeping an eye on her as a favor to Melva. That's all."

"Melva is very lucky to have you on her side, Mr. McNally."

"Thank you," I answered, wondering if that were really true and not liking myself for the thought.

"I respect Melva," Mrs. Fairhurst told me.

"Respect, ma'am? Why?"

"Because she had the nerve to do what she did."

After that, there was nothing left to say.

* * *

If Seth Walker wasn't my pigeon I'd eat all four of my silk berets, with my pith helmet for dessert. But how to prove it, was the question. And did I want to prove it? Yes, dammit, I did. It was my job to do so, and neither rain nor sleet nor snow nor Arnold's soft job would stop me. I had done all I could to protect Mrs. Fairhurst, but when we left the Alcazar Lounge we both knew that we had arrived at a meeting of the minds. She had done her duty, and now I had to do mine. If Arnold was implicated, even secondhand, it would be up to him to shield Mrs. Fairhurst, and I strongly suspected that he would.

23

I DROVE THE Miata into the underground garage of the McNally Building and waved to Herb in his glass booth. He immediately picked up his phone, no doubt alerting Mrs. Trelawney to my arrival. My presence in the McNally Building is rare enough to warrant such recognition. I maintain an office here that is the size of a handkerchief, and as it makes my claustro phobic I avoid it assiduously.

I took the elevator to my warren and set to work compiling my expenses for the week. I had had the good fortune of being treated to dinner at Ta-Boo' by Melva, saving McNally & Son a considerable sum, so didn't feel the least perturbed when I presented the outrageous bill for drinks at the Alcazar Lounge for my unauthorized meeting with Mrs. Fairhurst. My rationale for this was that McNally & Son was coming out ahead.

Mrs. Trelawney accepted my rendering with, "Thank you, Archy. I was in need of a good laugh."

"Happy to oblige, Mrs. Trelawney. When may I have a check?"

"I'll take this right to accounting," she said.

"Petty cash would be more fitting," I told her.

"There is nothing petty about your swindle sheet, Archy. And your father would like to see you."

"How does he know I'm here?"

"Guess," she called over her shoulder as she toted my expense account to the keepers of the privy purse. "You can go right in, he's expecting you."

Father was seated at his desk, outfitted in a single-breasted blue tropical worsted suit with vest and Countess Mara paisley tie, looking every inch the sovereign of his domain.

"Anything new on the Fairhurst business?" father asked as I sank into a leather visitor's chair.

"Nothing concrete, sir, but after my visit there I'm more certain than ever that the chauffeur, Seth Walker, is our blackmailer."

"The young man recommended by Geoff Williams?"

"One and the same."

"What was his connection with Geoff, Archy? Sorry, but I forgot."

"He's the son of one of Geoff's lady friends. No secret there. The boy readily admitted it. I told you Geoff was in Palm Beach about a month ago when he ran into John Fairhurst and recommended the boy."

"What was Geoff doing in Palm Beach alone?"

"Visiting with Seth's mother, I assume, which resulted in Seth's being taken on by Fairhurst. By the way, the boy hates the job. Thinks it's beneath him."

"I see," father mused. "How do you think this boy, Seth, learned the facts? He's only been in John's employ for several weeks."

"True. But Seth struck up a quick and close friendship with Mrs. Fairhurst's secretary, Arnold Turnbolt, who has been a member of the household staff for ten years. Turnbolt and Mrs. Fairhurst have become very close during that time, and I've learned that Turnbolt noticed the dates on the portraits some five years ago."

Father didn't need a road map to tell him where this was leading. He had stated our position regarding a private meeting with Mrs. Fairhurst and would never again allude to the subject. If Prescott McNally was Dickensian in his literature, he was Machiavellian in his politics. When it came to business, the end justified the means, and if the means were contrary to policy, so be it, but never discuss it. Father would never ask how I knew what I knew.

"Can you prove the boy's involvement in this business?"

"No, sir. I'm hoping to link Seth to the letter detailing where and when to deliver the loot."

"Can you lean on this Turnbolt to see what he may have passed on?"

"I'd rather not," I answered. "He's a very astute man, and if I said too much I would be giving my hand away and our pigeon might fly the coop."

"Do you think Turnbolt would warn this Seth?"

I didn't pause a moment before saying, "No, sir, I do not. I believe Turnbolt would confront Seth, and that could prove dangerous."

Father was taken aback but he did not raise an eyebrow. "Are you being rather dramatic, Archy?"

"I don't think so, sir. Seth Walker is a bad seed, but thanks to his connection to Geoff, he and the rest of the Fairhurst staff think I'm investigating Geoff Williams's death. I'd like to keep it that way until we get the second letter."

Father leaned forward in his king-size swivel chair and placed both hands, palms down, on his desk. "I have a bit of news regarding Melva's case. The Mystery Woman has given herself up to the police."

I tried to feign surprise but had all I could do to stifle a yawn. I had no idea why father was acting like a kid on Christmas Eve. "I know about the reward, sir. How many Mystery Women do the police have in tow?"

Father did not take kindly to my under-handed slap at his sagacity. "The usual kooks, publicity seekers, and gold diggers turned up, but so did the genuine article."

Chastised, but still skeptical, I muttered, "How did they separate the wheat from the chaff?"

Triumphant, the Master leaned back in his chair and teased me with his silence. He gloated for a full minute before telling me. "As I understand it, the police put three key questions to any would-be Mystery Woman. Those who answered two correctly would be granted a more in-depth interview. Until now, none have gotten past step number one."

"And I take it this one did," I said, my interest fading fast. The law of averages would account for at least one impostor to guess two out of three correctly.

"The young lady came to the police," father went on, "and identified herself as the woman they were seeking. Then, before they could question her, she said she would sign a statement waiving all rights to any reward." Father looked at me intently. "Are you hooked, Archy?"

"I'm hooked," I admitted. "Please go on, sir."

"She then answered all three test questions correctly and was detained for further questioning."

"When did you learn this?" I asked.

"About an hour ago. Melva's lawyers received a call from the police with the information I have just given you, and they immediately went to the station house. They are there now."

My first thought was that I had unintentionally predicted this in my conversation with Lady Cynthia Horowitz. Archy the soothsayer. My second thought was that I didn't believe it. "I'm troubled, sir."

"Why, Archy?'

Here I related the discrepancy between Melva's story and Hattie's story.

"Couldn't Hattie be wrong?"

I explained why I believed Hattie but father wasn't buying it, and I can't say I blamed him. I believed Hattie but I had no reason not to believe Melva. There was simply no logical reason for Melva to lie.

Melva had given her statement to the police the night of the murder. So had Hattie. The police must have been grappling with the same problem, and I was sure Melva's lawyers were in possession of both accounts, too. It seemed there was only one way to settle the case and father verbalized my opinion.

"This woman's statement will corroborate either Melva's story or Hattie's, and I'd put my money on Melva. Hattie, by her own admission, was not feeling well all day, was rudely awakened out of a fitful sleep, and was petrified. Not a very good witness, Archy."

"But what if the woman says she beat it after Melva fired at Geoff?"

Father shook his head. "When Melva's lawyers left here, the lawyer who told me the news said that the woman the police were holding had confirmed Melva's account of the events of that evening."

That seemed to be it, but I insisted on going one more round. "And that gate alarm still bothers me, sir. If Veronica turned it on when she went out, who turned it off?"

"It's my guess Veronica forgot to turn it on," father said. "It's as simple as all that."

"There is nothing simple about this case, sir."

* * *

I swam my two miles, which got the kinks out of my body but not the questions out of my mind. Back in my room the telephone was ringing. I mentally ran down the list of possible callers.

Lolly Spindrift to ask if it were true that the Mystery Woman had been found?

Binky Watrous to apprise me of the pending suit against Hobo?

Connie to tell me she was eloping with Hector?

Lady C. to call me a party pooper?

Buzz to tell me he had split a seam in his blue silk breeches?

It was Veronica, inviting me to dinner.

I dressed casually yet traditionally in gray slacks, a white turtleneck, and blue hopsack blazer. Just for the hell of it, I added my white beret. On my way out, I stopped in the den where I knew mother and father would be having cocktails before dinner. Father frowned at my beret but mother beamed when I kissed her downy cheek. When I explained that I'd been invited to Melva's for dinner, father's frown mellowed into a benevolent smile.

"Melva will have heard the news," father

said, "and be much relieved. Her lawyers are very optimistic at this juncture. Tell her I was asking for her, and, Archy, we must have Melva and Veronica to dinner very soon."

"Yes," mother joined in. "That would be nice. And you know your sister and her family will be here for the holiday, Archy. Have you thought about inviting anyone to Christmas dinner?"

"I have, mother, but I've made no decisions."

"If Melva and her lovely daughter will be alone, they are certainly welcome here. And Connie, of course." Mother, it seemed, couldn't care less which one I hitched to as long as I hitched.

But Veronica and Connie were a lethal combination I didn't want to think about, so I said, "Yes, mother. I'll think about it." I told father I would deliver his greeting to Melva, kissed mother again, and headed for the garage. Hobo, perhaps thinking I was a process server, didn't come out of his house to see me off.

While they weren't exactly popping open bottles of Dom Pérignon at Melva's place, the atmosphere was certainly more upbeat than when last I visited. Hattie was exuberant in her greeting, running on about the wonderful meal she was preparing in my honor. Veronica was less demonstrative, to be sure, but I did get a peck on the cheek and a compliment. "You look adorable," she told me, forgetting that not too long ago she found my smart berets less than chic.

Melva, in her usual chair, opened her arms wide as I entered the drawing room. When I bent to kiss her she said, "I'm sure you've heard the news."

"I have."

"Isn't it wonderful!" Veronica cried. She wore black capri pants with a cream knit top that left her midriff delightfully bare. Having deprived me of the opportunity of gazing upon the full length of her legs, she had made up for it by offering her navel. What other possible delights did the future hold?

"Vodka martinis all around," Veronica proclaimed, filling a pitcher with Sterling vodka at the portable bar. "I'm playing bartender, but Archy will be our sommelier at dinner."

As she hefted a bottle of vermouth, I cautioned her not to bruise the Sterling. A wise man once defined happiness as "the sudden turn of events for the better," and this evening Melva and her daughter were living proof of that keen observation. Up to this very morning they had no hope of the Mystery Woman showing her face and presto!—she not only gives herself up, she also waves away the hundred-grand reward. How altruistic can you be without arousing suspicion?

We toasted Melva's good fortune just as Hattie appeared with a tray of goodies, including caviar on toast points with chopped onion and grated hard-boiled egg. The rich know how to live, and I, for one, am glad they do. "One cocktail, please," Hattie warned us. "Save your taste buds for my goose and homemade applesauce."

"If we don't," I announced, "our goose will be cooked."

When we settled down with our drinks, I asked Melva what she knew about the woman who had turned herself in.

"Nothing. My lawyer called to tell me the police were interviewing a woman they believed was the one with Geoff that night. Later, he called again to say he had seen her and questioned her and both he and the police were certain she was telling the truth."

Melva was wearing black again. Was it to be her color of choice from now until the end of this ordeal? A black dress and silver threads among the brown hair would go a long way in winning the hearts of a jury. "Do you know her name?" I asked.

"Why, no. I never thought to ask."

"And why would you?" There was a decided edge to Veronica's tone. She had once accused her mother of being too forbearing, and I suspected her retort was as much an answer to my question as a rebuttal to her mother's almost apologetic reply. "I doubt if her name would mean anything to us and besides, it will be in all the newspapers tomorrow."

Like a camel filling up at an oasis, I helped myself to another dollop of caviar. It can be a very long way between oases. "And your lawyers are pleased?"

"Oh yes," Melva said. "Wasn't it you who told us how important this woman's testimony would be in my case? I'm feeling very sanguine, Archy, and I'll never forget what a good friend you've been through all of this."

I wanted to remind them both that while we may have scored a first down, we were still a long way from the goalpost. However, if they were in such a celebratory mood, who was I to play the naysayer? Let Melva's lawyers deal with Hattie's testimony, and, like my father, I'd accept the fact that Veronica forgot to turn on the alarm when she drove out that night.

"I was happy to help, Melva, and I toast your good fortune."

"Now that Horowitz person will have to cancel her masked ball," Veronica said with great glee.

Hattie's goose with a *foie gras* stuffing was as good to the palate as it was to the eye, and I was privileged to pour a Châteauneuf-du-Pape of excellent vintage. Alongside we also enjoyed a mushroom ragout with paprika and sliced red cabbage. Conversation, as opposed to the meal, was on the light side, and Melva excused herself right after the coffee and dessert. Taking my arm, Veronica led me out to the patio, where we sat side by side in deck chairs, puffing my English Ovals. My hand found hers as we gazed contentedly at the stars and listened to the ceaseless roll of the surf.

"Mother looks her old self again," Veronica said.

"She does. And I hope it's not premature."

"You're a pessimist."

"No," I told her. "I'm a realist. There's a long way to go before this is over and once the euphoria of today's news wears thin, you and your mother will have to dig in for the long haul."

"Couldn't we bottle the euphoria and drink it for courage during the passage?"

"What a charming thought," I told her. "You're not just another pretty face."

"I thought you'd never notice. Do you dance, Archy?"

"Only to music."

She got up and went to a table on which sat an object no larger than one of father's cigar boxes. A moment later, the perfect pitch of Ms. Dinah Shore filled the night air. "That's my kind of music, lady," I admitted with pleasure.

"I know," she said, and coming to me, she extended her hand and beckoned me out of my chair.

I took her in my arms. She was as light as air but far from ethereal. Her perfume reminded me of the night I escorted her home from Hillcrest. That night marked the beginning of our adult relationship. Was this night to be its climax?

Dinah sang about "Far Away Places" as a cruise ship, lit from bow to stern, moved across the dark horizon. We stopped dancing only long enough to kiss, and I had the eerie feeling we were being watched from above. Melva? Hattie? Or Clara, the neighbor's upstairs maid?

24

I WILL NOT reveal what happened between Veronica and me after our starlit kiss because a gentleman does not kiss and tell. Suffice it to say we are not officially engaged, and make of that what you will. On this overcast Palm Beach day, I had other things on my mind—and none of them had to do with love.

I called the "palace" on Country Road and got policewoman Tweeny Alvarez. I asked for Sergeant Al Rogoff, and Officer Alvarez wanted to know who was calling.

"His father," I told her.

A moment later Al was on the phone. "Hello, Pop."

"Hello to you, son. I thought I'd hear from you for Father's Day."

"You did, Pop. That was last June. Now it's almost turkey time."

"That's why I'm calling, son. I'm going shopping at Publix for our turkey. How big a bird should I get?"

"About twenty minutes—I mean twenty pounds."

"Twenty it is. Don't forget to wear your bulletproof vest at all times, son."

"I never take it off, Pop."

I drove into the lot of the Publix supermarket on Sunset Avenue, parked as far from the entrance as possible, and lit an English Oval as I waited for Al. When he pulled in beside me in his PBPD car, I got out of my Miata and slipped onto the seat beside him. "My father died a few years back, Archy," were Al's first words.

"I'm sorry to hear that, Al."

"Tweeny Alvarez attended the funeral," he went on.

"I see. Then she didn't believe it was your father calling?"

"With Alvarez you never know. She told me my father was calling long distance."

"From heaven?" I was astonished, but Al Rogoff often had this effect on me.

"She didn't say." He stuck the remains of the unlit cigar he was holding between his lips and began chomping on it. "I thought I would hear from you last night."

"I was otherwise engaged," I said.

"The blonde?"

"I got you here to ask the questions."

"Fire away, Pop."

"Please don't call me Pop."

Al was offended. "Why not?"

"Because you sound like Number One Son in a Charlie Chan movie."

"So I'll tell Alvarez it was Charlie Chan who called."

"Tell Alvarez anything you want, Al, but first tell me the name of the Mystery Woman."

Al pulled a notebook out of his bulging back pocket. This cigar-chomping man who murdered the King's English and loved the ballet and Beethoven was one of the shrewdest officers on the Palm Beach force. He had anticipated what I wanted to know and had carefully jotted down all the facts regarding the appearance of our Mystery Woman.

"That would be Linda Adams, with an address in Boynton Beach. I think she owns a trailer there."

It would be rude to scream "trailer trash," so I didn't. "What were the three test questions they asked the hopefuls?"

Al didn't have to consult his notes for this one. "First. What was Mrs. Williams wearing when she found you with her husband? Linda Adams knew it was a bathrobe and even told us its color.

"Second. What position were you and Mr. Williams in when Mrs. Williams came upon you?" Al pointed his cigar butt at me. "Archy, if you knew some of the answers these broads gave to this one, you would think they were raised in a cathouse."

"Some of them no doubt were, Sergeant. Linda's position was the correct one?"

"Check. How do you think . . ."

"Ask her," I cut him off. "Number three?"

"What was Mr. Williams wearing?"

"And she knew that, did she?"

"Right down to his jockey shorts, Archy. Most of the dames said he was wearing a tux. These broads think that's how the rich dress every night of the week. They've seen too many Fred Astaire movies on the tube."

Then Al told me this Linda described the solarium, its entrance from the back patio, the pool, etc., etc., etc.

"The lady has a photographic memory. How convenient. Did she say where she met Geoff?"

"One guess."

"Bar Anticipation."

"You know your turf," Al said.

"You should put a padlock on that place, Sergeant."

"Then where would we go when we were in need of someone to arrest?"

I watched one of the Publix boys gather stray shopping carts from the parking lot, nest them, and push them back to home base. The lad deftly maneuvered a train of nineteen carts. He could very well be the heir to one of America's great fortunes, or a high school dropout hoping to get promoted to a position at the checkout counter. This was, after all, Palm Beach.

"Did Linda say when she met Geoff?"

Not unexpectedly, Al told me she met Geoff about a month ago and he called when he returned to Palm Beach for the winter. Geoff had certainly covered a lot of ground on his hit-and-run visit to our tight little island several weeks back.

"And she picked him up the night in question?"

"That's right," Al said. "She picked him up, and they hit a few bars, had a meal, and went back to Geoff's place."

"When she picked him up, did she say how she got in the gate? I mean, was the alarm set?"

Al shuffled his pad's pages. "She didn't go in the gate. He met her outside, along the A1A."

"What time was this, Al?"

"According to her, about nine."

"Will you check the bars and the restaurant to see if anyone can ID them as having been there?"

"Oh, we will, but the places she gave us are dark as pitch and usually as crowded as a New York subway at rush hour. Their bartenders don't see nothin' and their clients see even less. They live by the 'don't rat on me and I won't rat on you' rule, and before you ask, the restaurant is a pizza joint in West Palm. No one will have seen them in any of these places, but no one will not have seen them, either."

"So the guy takes his date back to his own home where his wife is in residence? Why? And this ought to be good."

"This Linda broad says Geoff got drunk and refused to go to a motel or to her place in Boynton. He insisted they go back to his place and 'live dangerously,' as he put it. She seems to think he wanted to goad his wife and didn't care if Mrs. Williams caught them at it."

That was too much. Linda Adams's testimony would make Melva look more like the victim than the perp, as Al would have it. "So why did she agree to it, Al?"

"He said he would give her a nice present."

"Clever. Just short of calling herself a pro. What's your feeling about all this, Al?"

"My feeling is that your society broad had good reason to kill the punk."

"You don't think Linda's account is too letter-perfect?"

He shrugged. "Whose side are you on, Archy?"

Melva's, I thought, but I also had a passion for learning the truth, and I seriously doubted if that's what we were getting from Linda Adams. However, Al's question did make me feel something of a heel. Everything looked great for Melva and Veronica, so why was I rocking the boat?

Al was chewing on his cigar butt and mumbling as he idly thumbed the pages of his pad. "What did you say?" I asked him.

"She said the alarm at the gate wasn't set when they returned that night."

I leaped on that one. "Who asked her about the gate alarm?"

"Far as I know, no one asked her. She just said it when she was talking about coming back to his house."

"Were you present at the interview?"

"Sure. How do you think I know all this?"

"Why were you in on the interview?" I pressed.

"Because the interview was recorded on video and I work the camera, that's why."

"I never thought to ask," I blurted.

"You're no Charlie Chan, Archy."

I guess I deserved that one. "Al," I said, "no one but me ever questioned the fact that the gate alarm wasn't set that night, right?"

"Right. We never made it an issue because there was no break 'n' entry

attempt. The victim and the perp both lived
there. What's your point?"

"My point, Sergeant, is that Linda Adams
answered a question she wasn't asked
because—maybe—it was on her list of
memorized answers. I know only three people who knew the alarm question might be
asked because I had harped on it since the
night Geoff got his comeuppance. Melva,
her daughter, and my father."

"You smell a rat, Archy?"

No, I wanted to tell him, I smell Veronica
Manning's expensive perfume. Had that girl
hired someone to commit perjury to save
her mother's life? It was insane, but with the
young and the restless one never knew. But
how would a girl like Veronica find a dame
like Linda Adams of Boynton Beach? They
were as far apart as the Ice Age and the
Space Age.

But someone like good old Buzz would
know where to find a Linda Adams and
Buzz just couldn't be more ingratiating to
the rich of Palm Beach and points north.
Was my para- being too noid or was the
green-eyed monster egging me on?

"Veronica Manning was the first one out
that night," I told him. "And she should have

set the alarm. Her mother told me it was a house rule. Now this Linda says the alarm was never set."

"And what does Veronica say?"

"She told me she can't remember if she set it or not."

"So I guess she didn't," Al concluded. "Maybe she had a hot date that night and setting alarms wasn't a top priority on Blondie's agenda. Some dish, that broad, eh Archy?"

My mind was spinning like a whirling dervish in a Marrakesh sideshow, which is not conducive to drawing logical conclusions. "She did have a date that night," I confessed. "With a guy at a place called Hillcrest."

It was Al's turn to do a double take. "The house down near Manalapan Beach?"

"You know it, Al?"

He shook his head in wonder. "You sure do come up with the doozies, you do. We got the place under surveillance."

The Publix boy was once again collecting carts. Did he ever find one with a toddler left behind after the groceries had been loaded into the family car? I wouldn't bet against it.

"Drugs?" I guessed.

"Among other things. Is Blondie into anything heavy, Archy?"

"Nothing heavier than a good-looking stud that caught her interest, but it seems he couldn't hold it. A flash in the pan, Sergeant."

"Or so you hope." He grinned at his own wit. "Come on, Archy," he said, giving me a nudge with his beefy elbow. "She forgot to set that alarm because she was hot to trot and hightailed it out of her driveway."

I heard Jamie's voice describing Hattie's version of events that night as if he were sitting in the backseat and had just decided to put in his two cents' worth. *"What with the shouting and the fireworks and the car driving off, burning rubber like it was racing in the Indy 500 . . ."* A lot of people seemed to have made quick exits out of the Williams manse that night.

I seemed to be faced with two choices—again. Leave well enough alone and God bless Melva, or stick my nose in where it wasn't wanted and who knows what I'd sniff out? This was harder than choosing which female to hitch to.

* * *

I drove to the McNally Building to compare notes with father who, I assumed, must have received a full report on Linda's interview. When I pulled into the underground garage, Herb stopped me at his glass house. "I got a message for you, Archy," he said, "from your father." He pulled a scrap of paper out of his shirt pocket and read aloud, " 'Go directly to the Fairhurst house. It arrived.'" Then he looked at me and added, "I don't know what 'It' is, Archy."

I did.

25

"WE WERE EXPECTING you, *señor,*" Hector said excitedly as he opened the gate to my red Miata. "*El Patrón* say to go directly to the house."

"Do not pass Go, do not collect two hundred dollars," I replied.

"I do not have two hundred dollars, *señor.*"

"Neither do I, Hector."

Peterson, looking his old cheerful self, led me to *El Patrón,* who was nervously pacing about his office. "Archy, I'm glad you're here. That will be all, Peterson."

"Very good, sir." Peterson made a reluctant withdrawal.

I wasn't invited to sit, but then I once read that Queen Victoria had kept Disraeli standing for twenty years. "I understand 'It' has arrived, sir."

He nodded, grunted, and handed "It" over.

Same drill as the first letter. Miami postmark. Cheap copy paper. Typewritten and terse. The money, in bills none larger than fifties, was to be placed in a shoe box and delivered two days hence to an address in Boynton Beach. "The BB Trailer Court— Number Nine."

The dervishes were back with a vengeance, only this time they were chanting, "Stupid, stupid, stupid." While I'm not the fainting kind, they say there's a first time for everything. Had my time come? "Do you mind if I sit, Mr. Fairhurst?"

As if abashed at forgetting his manners, *El Patrón* made a sweeping gesture with his hand to indicate that I could alight wherever I chose. I chose the nearest perch and read on.

The messenger was to knock. The door would be opened wide enough for the box to be placed on the floor. The messenger was to depart. There was a reminder that should the police deliver the shoe box, Mr. Fairhurst would save twenty-five G's, but the family secret would no doubt become the central theme of the next *Titanic* film. For John Fairhurst III, it was a no-win situation.

For Archy McNally, it was *Il Momento de la Verdad,* as dear Connie would say. The Moment of Truth. If Seth Walker was the blackmailer and Linda Adams lived in trailer number nine at the BB Trailer Court, then Linda was Seth's partner in crime. Ergo, Veronica didn't go to Buzz to find a convenient Mystery Woman; she went to Seth. At this point, it was all pure speculation. I didn't know for certain that Veronica had gone shopping for a Mystery Woman, and the Boynton Beach trailer connection could be nothing more than an extraordinary coincidence. It was so extraordinary, I had no choice but to follow through on my assumptions.

I was officially on the Fairhurst case and unofficially trying to help Melva. Now it seemed the former was at cross-purposes to the latter. If I exposed Seth Walker as the blackmailer and Linda Adams as his accomplice, would I also come up with the fact that the Mystery Woman, Linda Adams, was as phony as a three-dollar bill? I would become, in effect, a witness for the prosecution in the case of the State of Florida vs. Melva Ashton Manning Williams. Rather than faint, I decided to think about that tomorrow.

Naturally, I wasn't going to tell John Fairhurst that I strongly believed his blackmailer had his sticky fingers in more than one pie. Nor was I going to tell him the bum might have those sticky fingers on the steering wheel of the family Rolls. It might be a tad too premature for both those assumptions, don't-you-know. But I was curious as to exactly what Fairhurst had in mind regarding the final warning in the second letter. It seemed it was also *Il Momento de la Verdad* for John Fairhurst III, and if I feared the worst I wasn't going to be disappointed.

"Mr. Fairhurst, when you came to us you said you didn't want to capitulate to the blackmailer, correctly assuming that he would not stop his demands for money after the first payout, blackmailers being a more greedy lot than other malefactors. You also said you did not want the police brought into this, for obvious reasons. Now we know where we can contact the blackmailer or his accomplice. If we don't deliver the money, he will sing. If we bring in the police, he will sing. If we give in to his demands, you'll never get him off your back. If I manage to apprehend him, I have no power to arrest him or to guarantee that he will quietly back off with his tail between his legs. In short, sir, where do we go from here?"

It didn't take Fairhurst long to reject all my options and answer my question. "I hired you, Archy, to locate the blackmailer and name him. That's all."

"That's all, sir?"

"Yes. You have a contact point and forty-eight hours to finger the bastard."

"And then, sir?"

"And then you submit your bill and I write you a check."

Archy, the angel of death!

26

IN THE FINAL reel of the old Andy Hardy films, a contrite Andy would be summoned to the family den, where his father, the Judge, would censure the brash young man for whatever wrong he had committed in pursuit of keeping the film's plot aboil and the audience entertained. The scene was inevitably a learning experience for both Andy and his faithful followers.

The Judge and his offspring did not enjoy a glass of port, as did father and I. I could not, however, help but compare McNally & Son to Judge Hardy & Son as we sat in our den on this rainy November night, due, I imagine, to the solemnity of our conversation.

At dinner, mother had talked of nothing but Dora's impending visit for the Christmas season, and now she was in the kitchen with Ursi, no doubt discussing, for the hundredth time, the logistics of putting up a family of five and keeping three children entertained while awaiting Santa's descent down the chimney. In the den, father and I discussed more weighty matters.

Although I find domestic chatter tedious, I would rather, at this moment, have been in the kitchen than the den.

After I had outlined the situation to father, I concluded by saying, "Please remember, sir, that as of now I have proof of nothing. I don't know if Veronica Manning purposely set out to hire a woman to impersonate the Mystery Woman, and I don't know if Seth Walker is the blackmailer. All I have to connect the two is this Linda Adams and an address in Boynton Beach."

"But the connection is more than Boynton Beach, Archy. It's specifically a trailer court in Boynton Beach. That shortens the odds considerably."

"I agree," I told him.

"In law, as you know, the accused is considered innocent until proven guilty. In this case, I think we have to assume Veronica and Seth are guilty until, and if, you can prove them innocent." Father sipped his port before continuing. "Do you think Veronica realized how harmful hiring a witness for her mother could be to Melva's defense once the prosecution learned of the deception?"

I thought about the lovely girl I had held in my arms as Dinah took us to faraway places. How easy it would be to run off with Veronica Manning with nary a backward glance nor a moment's regret. "No, sir. I'm certain her only thought was to do all she could to help her mother and, given her upbringing, hiring help was the easiest way out. And I don't doubt I had something to do with her decision."

"You, Archy?"

"Oh, I never suggested conjuring up a phony witness. But I did tell her, more than once, how important the Mystery Woman was to Melva's defense. Veronica soon suggested offering a million-dollar reward for information leading to the Mystery Woman."

The rain was coming down in torrents now, pelting our windows and, for the moment, diverting our attention from the business at hand. It was a true Florida winter downpour.

"If Veronica had used this Seth to engage a witness, I would guess it would be for a considerable amount of money," father now said.

"No doubt about that. Not a million, I'm sure, but a large sum nonetheless."

"Then why would he want to jeopardize a sweet deal with this blackmail scam? I would imagine he'd have enough to worry about with prepping this Linda Adams for her role."

"I thought about that," I answered. "Veronica told me the last time she saw Seth was when I picked her up at Hillcrest, the night of the murder. If she did contact Seth again, about finding a Mystery Woman, it would have been a few days after that night. Fairhurst got the blackmailer's first letter the day before Geoff's murder. What I mean, sir, is that Seth didn't know he would have a more lucrative job when he sent the blackmail note."

"I can appreciate that," father quickly put in, "but why didn't he abort the blackmail scheme when he came into better pickings, or at least change the venue where the money was to be delivered so as not to connect it to the Mystery Woman's address?"

I had thought about that, too. In fact, I had thought about nothing but these two cases since leaving the Fairhurst house this afternoon. "Because he's a wise guy and wise guys are often very stupid when it comes to lining their wallets. However, if we want to give this wise guy the benefit of the doubt, I would say he either forgot to tell Linda Adams not to give the police the Boynton Beach address, or someone other than himself, Linda, for instance, was in charge of posting the second letter and he forgot to either cancel it or change the delivery address.

"And let's not forget that Seth has no idea that I, or anyone else, is investigating the blackmail plot. He, and all of Fairhurst's staff, think I questioned them on Melva's behalf, thanks to Seth's tie-in to Geoff Williams." Even as I spoke I remembered my reaction to Fairhurst's comment that Seth Walker had been recommended to him by Geoff Williams. Odd as it now seemed, these two cases had a common link even before Veronica sought the help of

Seth Walker—if she sought the help of Seth Walker.

"Maybe Seth got a bit too cocky and thought Fairhurst would just hand over the money. If no one was wise to the blackmail scam, no one would connect the two crimes with the Boynton Beach address," I added.

"So many questions, Archy, so many questions." The rain had abated and we sat in silence, cogitating for a few moments, before father spoke again. "And I don't like what John Fairhurst might be up to, either."

Now that had to be the understatement of the century and we had very little time left to top it.

"I don't think there's any question of what he intends to do, sir," I insisted.

"You think he'll put a contract out for the blackmailer?" Father was in a tizzy over the thought of one of Fairhurst's ilk acting like a gangster in a B movie.

"I beg your pardon, but I think men like John Fairhurst do what they must do to maintain their privileged positions in our classless society. He was the keeper of the family secret and when he gets that final date etched on his portrait's brass plate he doesn't want to be remembered as the guy who lifted grandpa's skirts to expose boxers instead of bloomers."

Father winced. "You do have a colorful vocabulary, Archy, if a bit vulgar at times."

"Sorry, sir. I think Seth Walker is a punk who deserves what he gets, but I don't think he, or anyone, deserves to dive into Lake Worth wearing cement espadrilles. I also think Fairhurst wants to ask the blackmailer a few questions, such as where he learned what he knows."

"If Seth Walker is our man, you think he received the information from the secretary, Arnold Turnbolt?" father reiterated what we had discussed earlier, clearly avoiding the subject of where Arnold Turnbolt had come by his information.

"I do. I think he told Seth to impress the chauffeur with his knowledge of family lore. Arnold, as I've already mentioned, was quite taken with the boy."

"And if John Fairhurst learns this, you fear for the secretary, Arnold Turnbolt?"

"No, sir. I fear for Mrs. Fairhurst."

Another silence. There were moments in my conversations with father when the silences were more poignant than our words.

"Do you think you should confront Veronica and Seth directly?" father asked.

"No, sir, I do not. I don't want to tip our hand before I have all the facts."

"I agree," father said. "Also, if Linda Adams is a plant, do you think the real Mystery Woman will show up to refute this Linda's claim?"

"No way. If the real Mystery Woman hasn't turned herself in by now, she never will. Geoff Williams rubbed shoulders with the cream of Palm Beach and New York society, and I believe the woman he was with that night is a well-known figure in either or both groups—or even a friend of Veronica's. When she learns a Mystery Woman has shown up, she'll no doubt be relieved that she can keep her nose clean with a clear conscience. Both she and Melva are saved."

"Then wouldn't Melva have recognized the woman?"

"Not necessarily, given the circumstances. The woman fled minutes after Melva came into the room and Melva was in a blind rage, as they say."

Father, staunch defender of the rich and noble, asked, "Why would a woman from that social set go back to the house with Geoff, knowing Melva was there?"

"Why did two heiresses and a movie star marry Porfirio Rubirosa?"

To his credit, father did not blush. Instead, he finished his port and enjoyed his cigar. "And you don't think the woman was Seth's mother?"

"Melva said the woman was young, and Seth is twenty-five at least. His mother can't be young. Also, a woman like her would have come forward the moment the reward was announced. That type doesn't have to save face."

"I see," father sighed. "What do you intend to do now, Archy?"

"First, I'm going to scout that Boynton Beach trailer park and see if I can learn who hangs their hat in *numero* nine. If the blackmailer was foolish enough to give us his address it's because he doesn't believe anyone is on his tail. I think I have a good chance of learning what we want to know there."

"And then, Archy?"

"And then, sir—I don't know. I honestly don't know."

"That's too bad, Archy, because neither do I."

A red Miata convertible pulling into a trailer court would be as subtle as arriving in a Sherman tank. Therefore, I borrowed mother's Ford station wagon for my trip to Boynton Beach. Last night's rain had cleared the air, but not the skies. It was a brisk, breezy gray morning that showed no promise of change in the foreseeable future. Boynton Beach is due south of us, situated between Palm Beach and Delray Beach. The old reliable Ford made it to the center of Boynton in less than thirty minutes.

Linda Adams had gone to the police two days ago. Yesterday's papers reported only that the police were questioning a woman they believed was the Mystery Woman. This morning's papers said the Mystery Woman had been identified and gave her name as Linda Adams of Boynton Beach. The police had wisely not given out her street address. With any luck, I would be the only snooper at the BB Trailer Court.

The court was a miniature city laid out in a grid and inhabited, no doubt, by snowbirds in the winter and a smattering of year-rounders. Too early for the snowbird migration, the court was very quiet this early afternoon, with few cars evident in the one parking space allotted each trailer. I entered beneath an arch supported by brick pillars. The words BB TRAILER COURT were emblazoned across the arch. I cruised up the main street, which was lined on both sides with trailers mounted on slabs of concrete.

In a concerted effort at individuality, every trailer was painted a different color—mostly pastels—leading me to believe that if I clicked my heels together three times I would awake in Kansas in the loving arms of Aunty Em. All of them came with a wrought-iron railing guarding two steps and a patio just large enough to contain one tacky mesh beach chair, and a front door painted in a shade not remotely resembling the trailer's facade. Quite a few of the trailers boasted window boxes containing dead flowers. The BB Trailer Court, to my mind, gave new meaning to the epithet "Florida Modern."

Number nine was right on the main drag, toward the rear, and devoid of a car in its parking space. I took advantage of this by filling the void with the Ford wagon. Mounting the two steps, I knocked on the door with a brass knocker in the shape of—what else?—the number nine. Cute.

I did not get a response from within, but I did catch a glimpse of a café curtain being parted in the window of number nine's neighbor. I continued to pound the knocker, knowing that if I did so long enough the curious neighbor would leave the window and come out of her door on some pretext or other. I did, and she did. She emerged, wearing what I believe is called a housecoat, knee-length, upon which were printed nursery rhyme characters. At a glance, I spotted Jack 'n' Jill; Mary, Mary, Quite Contrary, watering her garden; Jack Horner and his Christmas pie; and a lad jumping over a candlestick. On her feet were pink mules. On her head were blue curlers. In her hands was a green bath-size rug she began shaking over her wrought-iron railing.

I knocked and she shook. Sooner or later one of us had to give, and it was the shaker, not the knocker.

"You a reporter?" she called in a northeast accent too often attributed solely to residents of Brooklyn—which is unjust. The other four boroughs and northern New Jersey also harbor those brandishing inflections that should be deemed assault weapons.

I hadn't yet decided how I would present myself in Boynton Beach, but a reporter was as good a calling card as any other, so I called back, "Yes. How'd you guess?"

She smiled, displaying a fine set of false teeth. "I played a hunch. I always play hunches. My husband says it's either gonna make us rich or homeless."

Judging from her current situation, homeless might be an improvement. She laid the limp green rug over the railing and made a move to retreat into her trailer. Knowing she couldn't resist, I stood my ground, not saying a word, until she gave up all pretense and shouted, "You looking for Linda?"

"How'd you guess?"

"Like I told you. I play hunches. The papers didn't give her address, so how did you know to come here?"

"We have our methods," I said.

"Yeah. I know what you mean. She ain't in."

"Do you know where she is?"

"I don't know if I should be answering questions about Linda. Looks like she's in trouble, an' I don't want no dealings with the police."

"I'm not the police, miss . . ."

"Angie. Everyone calls me Angie."

"I'm not the police, Angie." I left number nine and ambled next door. Once there was nothing but the green rug between Angie and me I removed my wallet from the breast pocket of my jacket and slowly extracted a hundred-dollar bill. "I'm just looking for a few facts about Linda Adams, Angie, and as you know, a reporter never reveals his sources."

She couldn't take her eyes off the greenback in my hand. "Yeah, that's what I read in the newspapers," she said.

"And sometimes we look for people to write feature articles about subjects they know intimately. For this a reimbursement of several thousand dollars is not unheard of." This was a line, of course, but it was music to Angie's ears.

Playing a hunch, Angie said, "Would you like to come in?" I wasn't sure if this was addressed to me or the hundred-dollar bill, but seeing as my hand was attached to the bill, I followed Angie into her trailer.

These boxcars are divided into mini-rooms and for obvious reasons bring to

mind the old railroad flats of New York tene-
ment fame. We entered through the kitchen,
which featured a dining area big enough to
hold a bridge table and two chairs. I declined
the offer of coffee but did take a seat at
Angie's table. If her husband was in the
trailer, he didn't make an appearance.

I folded the bill and placed it between salt
and pepper shakers in the shape of white
poodles sitting on their haunches. Having
paid my dues, I began to extract my
money's worth. "When was the last time you
saw Linda?"

"A month ago. Maybe a month and a few
weeks. I don't keep no records, you know.
Just mind my own business." Angie helped
herself to a cuppa from a Mr. Coffee machine
mounted beneath one of her cabinets.

"You mean she just left one day and
never came back?"

Angie lit a cigarette and then asked me
if I minded. When I told her I didn't, she blew
out her next line along with a cloud of
smoke. "They all left."

"Who are they?"

"Tina and her son Jeff and Linda."

"They all lived here? Is that what you're
saying?"

Angie's hair rollers bounced off one another when she nodded her head. "Yeah, mister. It was Tina's trailer, and Linda was Jeff's girl."

"You mean Geoff Williams? She was Geoff Williams's girl?" I couldn't believe Geoff would shack up in a trailer with two women, but then, there's no accounting for taste.

"You talking about the society guy Linda got caught in the sack with?" Angie cried. "The one whose wife bumped him off? Forget it, mister. She was Jeff Wolinsky's girl. J-E-F-F, that is. Not Gee-off like the society guy."

I almost fell off my folding chair. "Did you say 'Wolinsky'?"

Angie sucked on her unfiltered Pall Mall. "Yeah. That's what I said. Number nine is Tina Wolinsky's trailer. Tina and her son, Jeff."

"How long have they lived next door?"

Angie shrugged. It wasn't a pretty sight. "I been here ten years and they was here when I came. Jeff was just a teenager back then. Good-looking brat, he was."

"When did Linda appear?" I had to grip the seat of my chair with both hands to keep from leaping around the room like a ballet dancer with ants in his tights.

"Maybe a year ago. Like I said, I don't keep records. She was Jeff's girl, so I was surprised to read that she got caught in the sack with that society guy, Gee-off. But then Linda did have a rovin' eye, like they say. Once I saw her and Lou Mintz from number six out by the picnic area and believe me, mister, they wasn't munching Chinese take-out. It's a wonder Linda didn't take a bullet where it counts, too. This Gee-off's wife shoots first and asks questions after."

"Do you know why they left here?"

"All I know is that one day Tina tells me they're going away. She don't say where. Just that they're going to greener pastures."

"What did you take that to mean?" With someone like Angie, it was better to ask than to take anything for granted.

"Personally, mister, I don't think it meant anything. You see . . ." Angie stuck her thumb in the air and then pointed it at her lips.

Playing a hunch, I said, "Tina drinks."

"Like a fish," came Angie's reply. "Look, I ain't no prude. Me and the ol' man put away a few on Saturday nights and around the holidays, if you know what I mean. But Tina drank like every night was Saturday night, not to mention every afternoon. You had to catch Tina right after breakfast if you wanted to get a sober word out of her."

"So one day, about a month or so ago, all three of them are gone. Just like that." I snapped my fingers, but owing to their dampness, the gesture was literally mute.

Angie finished her coffee and got up to pour herself another cup. Her Pall Mall had been smoked down to where it was too short to hold. She dropped it in an ashtray shaped like a huge clamshell and allowed it to expire of its own volition.

"Gone," she repeated. The word must have brought to mind a closure because Angie quickly picked up the bill from between her poodle shakers and put it in the pocket of her housecoat. "I could tell you a lot about what went on next door over the past ten years. Tina was no Hannah Home-maker, let me tell you. You think your paper would be interested?"

I still hadn't fully recovered from the shock of learning who lived in number nine, and answered Angie's question with a question. "Are you sure their name is Wolinsky?"

"Sure as I'm Angie." She gave me another look at her false teeth. "Linda the Mystery Woman. I never thought I would be living next door to no celebrity. I told you all I know, mister, but I guess there's no chance of me getting that reward."

"No, Angie, I'm afraid there isn't." I rose, a bit unsteady on my pins, and took three steps to the door.

Angie was clutching the hundred-dollar bill in her housecoat pocket. "So long, mister. And thanks."

"So long, Pandora."

"What did you say . . ."

27

WOLINSKY! THE NAME kept playing in my
head like a vinyl record with the needle
stuck in a groove. Wolinsky! When Geoffrey
Williams showed up as Lady Cynthia
Horowitz's tennis instructor, no one had
questioned his roots. Handsome men in
tennis shorts were constantly arriving, and
departing, in Palm Beach. But when it
looked like Geoff was going to be around for
the long haul, the rumors began making the
rounds that in another life, he was Geoffrey
or Jeffrey Wolinsky. Why?

The answer must be that someone knew
him by that name. While rumors are seldom

based on fact, neither are they conjured up out of thin air. Geoffrey Williams was not a tennis pro or a golf pro or a Russian prince or pauper, but if I played hunches like Angie, I would say he was connected in some way with the name Wolinsky. How?

It had never been proven that Geoff Williams was a Wolinsky, but then, neither had it ever been disproved. And Seth Walker's identity remained a mystery, but not for long if I had anything to do with it. When I met with Seth Walker, I thought he reminded me of someone but couldn't match the familiar face to a name. Now I could. It was Geoff Williams.

On the drive north, rather than have my mind run amuck up and down cul-de-sacs, I mentally constructed the journal entry I would dutifully record later that day: About six weeks ago, Geoff Williams made a trip to Palm Beach, alone, and met Linda Adams in Bar Anticipation. He also ran into John Fairhurst, and, upon learning that Fairhurst was looking for a driver, Geoff recommended Seth Walker.

Geoff then returned to Palm Beach for the season with his wife, Melva, and his stepdaughter, Veronica.

At a social function, Seth the chauffeur introduced himself to Veronica. She went out with him the following evening.

That day, John Fairhurst received the first blackmail letter.

Veronica had a second date with Seth, at Hillcrest, the evening after their first date—which was the night of the murder. Veronica left the house to go to Hillcrest to meet Seth. When she left, both her mother and stepfather were at home. Thinking that her friend Fitz might want to join her later, Veronica left the Hillcrest address with her mother to give to Fitz, should Fitz call. Being the first one out for the evening, Veronica was responsible for turning on the gate alarm when she drove out. However, she can't remember if she did.

That same night, Geoff and Melva were invited to a party aboard Phil Meecham's yacht. Melva did not choose to go. Geoff decided he would attend alone and told Melva he would leave her the car because Lolly Spindrift was picking him up and driving him to Phil's. Actually, Geoff had a date with Linda Adams. She picked Geoff up outside the gate of his home, about nine o'clock that night. We still don't know if the gate alarm was set or not set by Veronica.

Geoff took Linda back to the house, where their tryst was interrupted by Melva. Linda fled and Melva killed Geoff. Or, Melva killed Geoff and then Linda fled, depending on whose version is correct, Melva's or Hattie's. That a car, in a great hurry, left the scene immediately before or after the shooting, is a fact.

I told Veronica how important the newly dubbed Mystery Woman was to Melva's case. A few days later, Linda Adams came forth claiming to be the Mystery Woman. She can answer correctly all the questions put to her regarding the scene of the crime, and her story of the murder jives with Melva's version.

Linda Adams, unasked, told the police that when she and Geoff returned to the house, about eleven, the gate alarm was not set.

When Melva summoned me to the house that night, shortly after midnight, the gate alarm was not set, concurring with Linda's story.

Veronica said that after their meeting at Hillcrest, she had never seen Seth Walker again.

At the same time, Al Rogoff gave me the Mystery Woman's name and her address—the BB Trailer Court, number nine, Boynton Beach.

Fairhurst received the second blackmail letter and was told to deliver the ransom money to Linda Adams's address. Specifically, trailer number nine at the BB Trailer Court in Boynton Beach.

I scouted out the BB Trailer Court and learned that Linda's address is the home of Tina Wolinsky and her son, Jeff, and that Linda is Jeff's girlfriend.

Six weeks ago, Tina, Jeff, and Linda left the trailer court for "greener pastures."

Six weeks ago, Geoff Williams arrived in Palm Beach, alone, and met Linda Adams at Bar Anticipation.

The circle is completed—I'm back to square one. Odd from a geometry point of view, but I think you know what I mean.

Tired and shopworn, I drove directly to my Pelican Club where Simon Pettibone mixed me a vodka gimlet, straight up. One sip and I was a new man, albeit a new man with the same problem. Wolinsky! Geoff and/or Jeff. "What's in a name?" the bard had written. A hell of a lot, that's what.

"You heard about the Mystery Woman, Archy?" Simon Pettibone asked.

"Yes, Mr. Pettibone. Did anyone win the pool?"

Priscilla came up to the bar to pick up a drink order and acknowledged my presence with a wave of her lovely hand. Today she wore a gardenia in her hair, and I was reminded of Dorothy Lamour in *Typhoon.* I hoped this wasn't a harbinger of tomorrow's weather forecast.

"No one won, Archy, but if you read the names that were submitted it would turn your hair gray."

"More likely green with envy, Mr. Pettibone. What happens to the money in the pot?"

"It's going toward a down payment for a new Garland range for Leroy. He wants to expand the menu."

"If he sticks to the steak tartare, a stove seems unnecessary."

"We're doing very well with the tartare," Mr. Pettibone boasted. "Since it went on the menu we've seen a sharp increase in our lunch receipts. Most people like it medium rare."

"Another gimlet, please, Mr. Pettibone," was the only reply that came to mind.

The club was in full swing, with most tables occupied by those who like their steak tartare medium rare. As my second gimlet was placed before me, none other than Binky Watrous took the stool next to me. "Hi, Archy."

"Well, well, well. Are you here under your own steam, Binky? No walker, no ambulance, no velvet slipper? Are we to assume you will live?"

"I'm feeling fine, Archy."

"A beer for Mr. Watrous," I called to our bartender. "And you shouldn't say you're feeling fine, Binky. It could be used against you in your civil suit. I will say, however, that Hobo is to undergo oral surgery next week."

Binky sipped his beer, the foam of which added thickness to his limp mustache. I must give serious thought to talking him into shaving the foolish thing.

"I'm not going to sue, Archy," he said with a smile.

Finally, a sudden turn of events for the

better. "And the Duchess knows of this momentous decision?"

"We struck a deal," he answered.

"A compromise?" I dreaded to think what the Duchess had extracted from poor Binky in return for not trying to squeeze a million out of McNally & Son. "What did you promise her, Binky?"

"That I would be gainfully employed before the end of the year."

Now there was a feat on par with a camel passing through the eye of a needle. "How do you intend to live up to this bargain, Binky?"

When Binky was employed as a bank teller, his debits and credits never tallied, not even once. When he toiled in a pet store, all the pets, big and small, mistook him for their dinner. At Kmart, he caused an entire display of jarred jelly beans to tip over, landing on a woman shopper, who, on last report, was still under a doctor's care. As a cab driver, he was constantly getting lost, and as a waiter he spilled a bowl of hot consommé down the décolletage of a grand Palm Beach dowager. Need I add that Binky Watrous was in short supply of referrals.

"I already have the job," Binky announced.

"Really? Where?"

"The toy emporium in West Palm. It's called Toys R Noyes."

I wondered if Mr. Pettibone had put something funny in my gimlet—like a hallucinogenic substance. "Toys that make noise? I would think parents would shun them like the plague."

"No, Archy. Fred Noyes is the shop's owner. Get it? Toys R Noyes."

I got it, but I didn't know if I wanted it. In fact, I was sure I didn't. "What will be your function at Toys R Noyes, Binky?"

"I start the day after Thanksgiving. I'm their Santa Claus."

Now I wished Mr. Pettibone had put a dash of cyanide in my drink—it might have spared me this news. "You are going to take children on your lap and ask them if they've been naughty or nice?"

"I'm very good with children," Binky proclaimed with a certainty born of blind faith.

"How do you know, Binky? You've never had any."

"Remember how good I was with little Darcy last year?"

"You overdid it, as I recall. You filled him so full of candy kisses we had to purge the poor lad well into the New Year. Besides, you don't weigh a hundred and fifty pounds, fully clothed."

"The Santa suit comes padded. I already tried it on."

I felt duty bound to spare Mr. Noyes the sight of toddlers falling headfirst off Santa's lap and ending up in intensive care like that poor Kmart shopper. "You do realize, Binky, that this is a dead-end position. I mean, by definition, your job ends on December Twenty-fourth. Then what? Do you go to the North Pole and cavort with the elves until next year?"

"Mr. Noyes said if things work out he would take me on as a salesperson."

Poor, unsuspecting Mr. Noyes. "Binky, my boy, do you know the difference between Barbie and Ken?"

Binky gave this much thought. He tried hard. He really did. Finally he had to confess, "I give up, Archy. What's the difference?"

"That's just what I want you to do. I want you to give up the idea of playing Santa at Toys R Noyes. It's demeaning."

Binky got that hurt look on his face. The look that always got me where I lived. "I'm doing this for you, Archy. Remember?"

That did it. I resolved there and then to find Binky Watrous a position more suitable to his capabilities before Thanksgiving, although I had no idea what those capabilities were. Meanwhile, to assuage my guilt, I scolded, "None of this would have happened if you had followed directly behind Veronica and me that night. We would have all arrived at my house together, and Hobo would not have felt threatened. No bite, no lawsuit. No lawsuit, no Santa suit. But no, you had to hang around to cohabitate."

"No way, Archy. I came out right behind you, but I had to wait for Steve. You know, my friend who was driving my car. He had to follow me because he didn't know where you lived, so I had to wait for him."

"What was his problem?"

"My car was the problem. We got there early and I parked way down at the end of the driveway, near the garage. The jerks that came after all the parking spaces were taken just left their cars in the driveway. We had to find the owners and get them to move their cars before Steve could get my car onto the highway."

I didn't say a word. I just sat, staring at Binky. Mr. Pettibone mixed drinks, Priscilla waited on tables, and all around me were the sights, sounds, and smells of people enjoying their noonday meal. I was at once a participant and an observer of the scene—I was *"Hic in incorpore sed non spiritum"*—here in body, but not in spirit.

When I had recovered somewhat, I asked, "You had to wait for Steve?"

"That's right," Binky nodded.

Knowing the next question would change the course of many lives, including my own, I asked, "And where was Veronica's car?"

"Oh, right near the front door. Didn't you see it when you drove in?"

No, I hadn't seen it. As a matter of fact, there was a lot I hadn't seen that night, and for many nights after. There's an old Chinese proverb that says, "If you can't baffle them with brilliance, dazzle them with beauty." Veronica had done just that, and I fell for it. I hadn't been merely dazzled—I had been blinded.

Veronica had arrived at Hillcrest a very short time before me. In fact, I might have been trailing her. *That a car, in a great hurry, left the scene immediately before or after the shooting, is a fact.* Was that car a silver Mercedes convertible with a blue canvas top?

"You having lunch, Archy?"

"No, Binky. I just lost my appetite."

After retrieving my Miata I drove directly to the McNally building. I had to see the *Seigneur* and tell him what I knew. He would have to speak to Melva's lawyers, and they would have to convince Melva that only the truth would set her free. What was the truth? I shuddered to think.

Mrs. Trelawney informed me that father was in conference with a client and could not be disturbed.

"Any idea how long he'll be?" I asked her.

"The client arrived not more than ten minutes ago. An estate planning is on the agenda, and that could take hours."

"I'll wait in my office," I said.

"While you're there, you could answer this call. It came about an hour ago."

She handed me a message memo. Al

Rogoff wanted me to call him ASAP. Now what?

In my cubbyhole I dialed the "palace" and got Tweeny Alvarez. This was not my day, not by a long shot. "Is this Al's father?" she asked, recognizing my voice.

"That's correct."

"You're pretty vocal for a man in your position," Tweeny observed.

"De mortuis nil nisi bonum," I snapped right back.

"What does that mean?" Tweeny's second language was obviously not Latin.

"Say nothing but good of the dead," I translated for her.

"I didn't mean to offend."

"As we say up here, you are forgiven, child. Now put my son on the line, as I'm calling very long distance."

"Pop," Al came on and got right to the point. "We need to buy another turkey."

"How big, son?"

"Fifteen pounds."

"I'm on my way."

I got to the Publix ahead of Al Rogoff and watched the boy collect shopping carts. I think my brain was on overload because it refused to do anything more profound than count the shopping carts the kid was nesting. Only fourteen this time. He was falling down on the job.

After Al pulled in, he hopped out of his car and joined me in the Miata, puffing on a stogie the size of a blimp. "Remember I told you we were checking the Hillcrest place?"

I acknowledged that he had.

"The Hillcrest place is what the kids call a party house. They pass around cheap wine, sometimes to minors, and sell drugs. Pot mostly, but some hard stuff for those who can afford it."

"Nothing I don't know, Al."

"The house is a rental, and the guy on the lease is Geoffrey Williams."

How much more could I take? "And he rented it about six weeks ago, I believe."

"How did you know?"

I could have told him I was playing a hunch; instead I said, "I learned a few things today that I will pass on to you as soon as I know they're true and figure out what they mean. Trust me, Al."

The Miata was so full of cigar smoke my eyes began to tear. I was sorry I hadn't put the top down, but the threat of more rain still hung over Palm Beach.

"Sure, Archy. No sweat. We're seeing if there's any link between Hillcrest and the murder."

So am I, I thought. "Do you know who actually lives in the house, Al?"

"No. Do you?"

"Could be a lady who thinks it's greener pastures."

"What does that mean?"

"I'll tell you when I know, Sergeant."

"I have another piece of news for you, Archy. I didn't tell you that day I was guarding the murder scene because it wouldn't have been kosher. But today we told your friend Melva's lawyers that we found a second set of prints on the murder weapon."

I held my breath and asked, "Did you ID them, Al?"

He waved his cigar in a negative gesture. "No. They were blurred. Only partial prints, and we gave up trying to match them, but we're legally bound to tell Melva's lawyers what we know."

Was I legally bound to tell Al Rogoff that those prints could belong to the person who left the scene in a big hurry? The person who was not Linda Adams but Veronica Manning? If I wasn't legally bound, I was certainly duty bound to my friend Al Rogoff. However, I needed to fill in a few missing pieces before I could present the police with a picture that wasn't full of holes, and very often a partial truth could do more harm than a spiteful lie.

"Like I said, Al, I have some information that might help, but until I separate fact from theory I'll keep it to myself. When the time is right, you'll be the first to know."

"I understand, Archy, and if I'm not around when you're ready to talk, pass it on to the lieutenant."

"What do you mean, if you're not around?"

"I got some time off," he confided, "an' I'm going up to New York."

"Why?"

"To see *Swan Lake.* The new one with male swans." It cost him a lot to admit this, but we were breaking down barriers.

"Where are you staying?" I asked.

"Don't know yet. Why?"

"Tell me when you're going. I'll book you into the Yale Club."

"Thanks, Archy."

"Shirt and tie, Al. It's a classy joint. No chomping on cigar butts, and keep your mouth shut or they'll think you're a spy from Harvard."

"Shove it, Archy."

And he was gone in a cloud of smoke, leaving behind an aroma more compatible to beer halls than Miatas.

28

I DROVE SOUTH again, this time only as far
as Manalapan Beach, to Hillcrest. It started
to drizzle as I left my car. Does the sun ever
shine on this place? There was a doorbell
that produced no sound when I pressed it.
I waited a minute or two, then knocked with
similar results. I turned the big brass knob,
pushed, and the door opened. I went in, out
of the rain.

The place looked and smelled like a
nightclub the morning after, before the
cleaning people come in to put Humpty-
Dumpty back together again. All around me
were dirty glasses, empty wine bottles,

overflowing ashtrays, and parquet floors covered in grime, discarded tissues, and cigarette butts ground into the wood by the nightly visitors. There is nothing as depressing as grandeur gone to seed. If I had my druthers I would rather be in the BB Trailer Court. It made no pretense of being anything other then what it was and succeeded admirably. Hillcrest was greener pastures covered in cow dip.

"You from the police?"

She appeared in the dark passage beyond the grand staircase. In the gray light of a rainy day, I saw a slim woman in a shapeless print dress and bedroom slippers. Her hair had been cut into a mannish bob and dyed a strange shade of red with what looked like one of those "shower in the color" shampoos.

"No. Were you expecting them?"

"They were here yesterday on some half-assed pretense or other. What they were doing was casing the place." She spoke slowly, enunciating each word with great care. A drunk, pretending to be sober and thinking she was getting away with it. "So, who are you?"

"Archy McNally."

"What's your business, Mr. McNally?"

"I'm an investigator representing John Fairhurst."

"The guy Jeff is driving for?"

Score one for Archy. Seth Walker was Jeff Wolinsky. It wasn't totally unexpected news, but I was moving out of the realm of speculation and into the world of facts, a situation long overdue.

"Do you mind if I come in?" I advanced a few steps toward her.

"You are in."

"I mean, can we sit down and talk?"

"First tell me what you want to talk about, Mr. McNally." She stood her ground, hands on her hips. Her dress had seen better days and so had her face, which, like Hillcrest, showed vestiges of beauty gone to pot.

"I believe your son is blackmailing Mr. Fairhurst. It's a very serious charge and I'm here to see if we can avert calling in the police, who I know are interested in your son for other reasons."

"Christ!" Her shoulders slumped in a gesture of pure despair, a gesture that seemed as familiar to her as a smile is to the more fortunate. "Come on in."

She turned and walked down the passage toward the chat rooms. I followed, and she made a left at the end of the passage into what I had guessed the other night was the sun room. I was correct. The west wall was composed entirely of French doors that opened to a narrow balcony overlooking Lake Worth. Both sky and lake were gray and not one craft appeared on the choppy water.

"You're Mrs. Wolinsky?" I began.

"How'd you know?"

"I talked to Angie at the trailer court."

"That one! Then you know my life history. You get around, Mr. McNally."

"I told you I was an investigator."

"Yeah, so you said." She didn't ask how I had traced her to the trailer court. Either she didn't care, or her brain was unable to make the connection. Perhaps the truth was a little bit of both.

Like the rest of the house, the room was only partially furnished. It held a divan fronted by a coffee table and two side chairs that might be called Danish modern. There was a sideboard against one wall, and on it was the inevitable bar set-up: ice bucket, assorted bottles of liquor, and mini fridge from which Mrs. Wolinsky removed a can of beer. "Can I get you a drink?"

"No, thanks." I sat on one of the Danish moderns.

She popped the metal tab and poured her Bud into a pilsner glass. I suppose I should say I was grateful she didn't drink it right from the can. She stood by the bar, her hand rubbing the smooth surface as if it were the head of a pet dog.

"Why does your son call himself Seth Walker?"

"Because his father told him to change his name for the Palm Beach social set, that's why."

"Where's his father now, Mrs. Wolinsky?"

"In the morgue, or don't you read the newspapers?"

Another speculation gave way to fact. I was certainly learning a lot about Geoff Williams, né Wolinsky, at John Fairhurst's expense.

Half the beer in her glass was gone. She turned and poured herself a neat rye—downed it, and chased it with her Bud. This was some heavy hitter.

"You have to excuse me," she apologized. "It helps my nerves. I'm very nervous. I got problems, and I figure the liquor is more sensible than pills. Pills kill, you know. Marilyn Monroe took pills and look what happened to her."

"You had a child with Geoff Williams?"

"Why the hell not? He was my husband. Is that a crime?"

So Geoff Williams, or Jeff Wolinsky, had been married to this woman and had had a son with her. No wonder he didn't want the boy parading around Palm Beach with the name Jeff Wolinsky. When I asked the supposed Seth Walker what his connection was to Geoff, the boy had said, "He was an acquaintance of my mother's." Well, he hadn't lied, I'll give him credit for that.

"Geoff rented this place for you when he was in Palm Beach alone, about six weeks ago. Is that right?"

She finished her beer and refilled the glass, emptying the can of Bud. "Not for me. I was happy in the trailer. It was the kid, little Jeff, like we used to call him, who has big ideas. The kid was crazy jealous with the way his father was living while we were marking time in Boynton. He told his father that if he didn't improve our lot—that's what he said, improve our lot—he would rat on his father." She poured herself another neat rye without apology.

The kid was a born blackmailer. "You mean he'd tell Geoff's wife that Geoff had an ex-wife and a son?"

"You're a laugh and a half, Mr. McNulty." I didn't bother correcting her because I doubt if she would know what I was talking about. "Ex-wife, my eye. We were never divorced. I'm the only legal wife J-E-F-F Wolinsky ever had. So if he left an insurance policy . . ."

I couldn't have been more stunned if she had hit me on the head with her bottle of Four Roses. I sat there in what I believe is called a state of suspended animation as she droned on in a drunken rage.

". . . He started giving tennis lessons. Oh, man, he was good at tennis. Only, all his students were women old enough to be his mother, and after a hot day on the court they retired to a hot time in the bedroom. He changed his name for professional purposes. How do you like that one? Professional purposes. Geoffrey Williams . . ."

The story unfolded like a soap opera scripted by the Marquis de Sade, and as I listened all I could think of was Melva. Poor, poor Melva. As if murderess wasn't bad enough, she would now also be known as the second wife of a bigamist. Geoff Williams—or Jeff Wolinsky—had gotten off easy.

"...I had the kid and my nerves were bad. They always were." She poured herself another shot of Four Roses, but her beer glass was empty so she chased it with yet another shot of Four Roses. How much longer could she stay on her feet?

"Then he gets married again. Can you beat that? To a rich bitch, no less. So what am I supposed to do? Put him in jail? Then who'll support us? Me and the kid. Tell me that, Mr. Mac. Tell me that."

In her own befuddled way, she had a point.

"...bought us the trailer and gave me a thousand a month. A thousand. In cash. Every month. Hey, who's complaining? Not me. All I had to do was keep my mouth shut, an' I did. But not the kid. Oh, no, not him. When he's old enough to know where his father is, he don't pass a restful night until he gets what's coming to him. What's coming to us. Me, too. The kid says his father owes us, and the kid bugs him until we end up in this mausoleum on a lake."

"Geoff got the boy a job with Fairhurst?" She ran her hands through her hair and groaned. "That job. A driver for a rich guy. Little Jeff was angry, let me tell you. Angry, like he wanted to kill his old man. But big Jeff says the job is just a stepping-stone, and he talks the kid into doing it for now, because big Jeff wants the kid to see how the other half lives, like the job is a freaking finishing school. Big Jeff could talk even better than he could play tennis. But he couldn't talk the rich bitch out of shooting him."

"So your son decided to blackmail his employer," I said, bringing the subject back to the original purpose of my visit. But then, how often does one get sidetracked by a tale of bigamy, booze, and betrayal in sunny Florida?

"I don't know anything about that, Mac. I swear." Again, she didn't appear to be even remotely interested in what her son had on John Fairhurst to threaten him with blackmail. "An' little Jeff ain't got nothing to do with the crap that's been going on around here. He got in with a bad crowd in Miami, my kid. When we moved in here they muscled in on him an' started throwing parties almost every night, looking to cash in on the rich Palm Beach brats. My kid ain't in on it, but he owes them, you see—so they moved in on us."

"I'm not interested in that," I said. "I told you I was here on behalf of John Fairhurst." Then I asked, not on John Fairhurst's behalf, "If little Jeff is not in on the drug scam, how do you propose to pay the rent on this house? When your husband died, you lost your benefactor."

She started laughing—one octave below hysteria. "He left us an annuity. That's what the kid said. You know what an annuity is, Mac? A steady income, that's what."

"I don't believe Geoff Williams was in a position to leave anything. He was being supported by his wife. Or the woman who thought she was his wife."

She screeched like a parrot as her arms began conducting an unseen orchestra. "That's what little Jeff said. An annuity. He got himself killed, and that makes it an annuity."

Tina Wolinsky was now listing, like a ship taking on water. It was only a matter of time before she would sink. She was completely *non compos mentis,* but I had to at least try to make some sense out of the connection between Geoff's death and her annuity. "Murder isn't an annuity," I told her. "What are you talking about?"

She picked up her pilsner glass and put it to her lips. A moment later she realized the glass was empty. "Screw you, Mac. He got killed and that makes . . ."

"SHUT UP. YOU HEAR ME. SHUT UP."

The glass shattered when it hit the floor. Little Jeff was standing in the doorway, pointing at his mother, and screaming.

29

FOR THE FIRST time since coming to Hill-crest I feared for my safety. The boy was in a rage and the poor woman, completely disoriented, reacted as if a chicken hawk had flown into her coop.

"Shut up," he kept shouting. "Just shut up! Don't you know who he is? How many times do I have to tell you to keep your mouth shut around strangers? You don't know what you're saying, so keep your mouth shut!"

I stood up. "Take it easy, kid. She's not responsible for—"

"Who's asking you?" Now his fury was transferred to me. "Who's asking you, eh?

Can't you keep your puss out of where it's not wanted?"

His mother began to sob, the sound both forlorn and unnerving. Little Jeff went to her and took her hand. "Okay. Okay," he repeated, trying to quiet her. "It's going to be okay." His anger vanished as quickly as it had erupted, and now he spoke to his mother with the compassion of a parent reassuring a frightened child. He even made a vain effort to explain the reason for his verbal barrage. "This guy works for *her.* He's sniffing around about the old man's murder. Don't you get it? He's trying to pump you. He's trying to prove a case of justifiable murder."

He led her to the sofa and gently lowered her to a sitting position, but as soon as he let go of her arm she slumped over, her head hitting the armrest. The boy took a pillow from the back of the couch and gently raised her head and then lowered it onto the cushion.

His movements were as professional as that of a nurse. Little Jeff had probably been a caretaker from the age of ten or eleven, and the scene I had just witnessed—the explosion followed by the remorse—an everyday occurrence. I wanted to walk out of the room and out of the house. Turn my back on Hillcrest for the last time and let these people sort out their lives as best they could. She would sleep it off and little Jeff would—would what? End up where he'd been heading since the day he was born, thanks to his father. Oh, yes, Geoff Williams, or a rat by any other name, had gotten off easy.

But I had a job to do and no choice but to tell little Jeff just what that job was. "I'm not working for any *her,* I'm working for John Fairhurst, and I've been to trailer *numero* nine."

I saw his shoulders slump just as his mother's had. A family trait based, no doubt, on a lifetime of having their schemes, aspirations, and petty intrigues squashed just short of fruition. He looked at me as if he were sizing me up, trying to determine how much bull he could send my way. Then he headed for the bar. On his way there he said, "Tell him to forget it. It was a joke. I don't give a crap about his fag grandfather. And I'm not going back to that house. Tell him that, too."

A confession, an apology, and a resignation, all wrapped up in one neat package. A good try, but it wouldn't work and he knew it.

"It's too late for that, Jeff. I told you I wasn't formally involved in your father's murder investigation, but thanks to your second letter, I find myself in it up to my chin."

He helped himself to a Bud from the mini fridge, but didn't invite me to join in. "You know who I am," he said, then nodded in the direction of the sleeping woman. "Sure you do. What else did she tell you?"

"Everything. Quite a tale."

"Yeah, like I should go on Oprah, right? Or how about *Family Feud?* Hey man, that show must have been named for us."

The boy wasn't stupid—and more's the pity.

"Look," he was saying, "it was a joke. Tell Fairhurst it was a joke. A joke that got out of hand."

"Sorry, Jeff, but after mailing the second letter the joke was on you. It wasn't supposed to be sent, was it? When Veronica Manning came into your life, the twenty-five grand you wanted from Fairhurst began to take on the appearance of loose change.

Who mailed that second letter, Linda Adams?"

He carried his beer over to one of the chairs and sat. Pulling off the tab, he drank straight from the can. His mother started snoring, and he looked at her when he answered. "No. I left it with a guy in Miami. I forgot to tell him not to mail it."

"I'll bet you did. You had a lot on your mind. You want to tell me about it?"

"I don't want to tell you dick, Mr. McNally."

"Tut, tut, son. Let's watch the language and listen carefully to what I have to say. I might be your only hope out of this mess."

That got his attention. Hope! Little Jeff knew the word well. It was the story of his life summed up in the only four-letter word that wasn't naughty.

"First, you got your father to rent this place for you and your mother."

"Hillcrest. That's what they call it. How do you like it, Mr. McNally? He took us out of a little dump and put us in a big dump."

"Then your friends from Miami came up north and moved in with you."

He stood up, removed his jacket and put it over his mother, touching her head gently. She snorted and mumbled in her drunken sleep. When he took his seat again, he said, "I owed them money, but I'm not involved in what they're doing here. I'm clean on that score."

I explained yet again that I wasn't interested in what was going on here. Little Jeff would have to convince the cops—not me—of his innocence in the goings-on at Hillcrest.

"Then Geoff, as I know him, got you a job with Fairhurst."

"The final insult, right? Driving Fairhurst's Rolls in a monkey suit." Little Jeff was infuriated. "Your mother said your father promised you better things if you took the job."

He drank from the can again, not really enjoying the brew. He pulled a pack of Camels out of his shirt pocket and lit one. "He wanted me to look and learn. You like that, eh? So I looked and learned."

"You learned the Fairhurst secret from Arnold Turnbolt."

"Yeah, he told me. With a guy like Turnbolt all I had to do was smile pretty to learn all the Fairhurst gossip."

"I don't think I want to know that, Jeff."

"Oh, no, you don't want to know that. Too raunchy for you, eh? You people think life is a freaking rose garden. Well, some of us have to soil our hands to make a living."

Feeling I deserved it, I took out an English Oval and lit it. Jeff eyed the package with curiosity, but didn't ask what they were for fear of appearing ignorant of life in a rose garden. "You wrote the blackmail letters, took them to Miami, mailed one and left the other with your pal to mail on a given date. That was your first mistake, little Jeff."

"Mr. McNally, my first mistake was selling pictures from girly magazines to my sixth-grade classmates. I didn't come into blackmail at an entry-level position."

I begrudgingly admired him his sense of humor. He might have made it as a stand-up comic or a rap artist, an art form I have long thought should get a C before the R-A-P. "You spotted Veronica Manning at the Horowitz party and introduced yourself to her."

"Why not? We're practically kin."

"What did you tell her?"

"Everything my mother told you," he said, "only I was sober when I let her in on our family secret."

"Why?" I asked. "She's just a kid."

"Hey, man, she could teach you a few things."

She could and she had. "Did you intend to blackmail her or her mother?"

"It crossed my mind. But what I really wanted to do was stick it to my old man. He played with us too long. Too many promises he never kept. Putting us in this overgrown flea bag and dressing me in a chauffeur's uniform. So, thanks to him, his son is told to stay in the kitchen with the help, while his stepdaughter is lapping up the champagne and caviar. Something snapped inside me, Mr. McNally, so I made a date with Veronica and played out my hand. It wasn't hard. She knows a good-looking stud when she sees one."

Modesty was clearly not the boy's long suit, and now I knew what the row was all about in Melva's solarium on that ill-fated night. "Your disclosure probably led to your father's death."

For the first time since coming in the room, he smiled as if he sincerely meant it. "I hope so."

We were both quiet, smoking our cigarettes, the only sound coming from the congested lungs of Tina Wolinsky. I wondered if he was anticipating my next salvo. "But when Veronica came running here the night Geoff was killed and asked you to swear that she had arrived before the murder, you forgot all about blackmailing Fairhurst and started blackmailing Veronica, only this time around you called it an annuity."

"You can't prove a thing, Mr. McNally."

I ignored the comment, because it was very close to the truth, and asked, "What time did Veronica get here the night Geoff was killed?"

"Nine, give or take ten minutes." He didn't look at me as he lied. Instead he ground his cigarette out in a glass ashtray.

"Now that's interesting. She got here around nine and parked behind everyone who drove in after her. Did the latecomers fly over her Mercedes?"

He didn't answer, so I filled in the blanks. "She came here after the murder and told you what had happened. She also told you the clever plot she and her mother had cooked up about Geoff being with a woman that night. The so-called Mystery Woman. Their housekeeper was in her room all day and only mother and daughter knew what took place that night. You were to swear that

Veronica was here hours before the murder to authenticate Melva's story. What went on at their house that night, Jeff?"

"Ask Veronica."

He knew when to give and when to hold back.

"What was your fee for backing her story?"

He flashed me a look so insolent I almost knew what was coming. "Marriage," he spat out.

"I don't believe you," I said.

"Believe whatever you want, but she promised to marry me. Like father, like son, as they say."

Hence the annuity. I still didn't believe it, but there was so much about this case I wouldn't have believed before coming to Hillcrest this afternoon. "Wouldn't your girl-friend, Linda Adams, have objected to the marriage?"

He shrugged and grinned sheepishly. "Linda is very flexible. Especially if the price is right."

"When Veronica told you they had to have a Mystery Woman, you came up with Linda. And, not counting your sixth-grade porn enterprise, this was your second mistake.

From the night I came here to take Veron-ica home, you thought I was working for Melva and had no idea someone was inves-tigating on behalf of Fairhurst. You forgot to cancel that second letter now that you had a bigger fish on the hook, but you weren't too worried because you were so sure no one could connect Linda to the blackmail scam.

"You were so sure that it never even occurred to you to have Linda give the police an address other than the Boynton Beach one. Error number three, little Jeff, and you're out."

"Am I? Can you prove Linda wasn't with my father that night? Can you prove Veron-ica got here after the murder? Do you know how many silver Mercedes convertibles with blue canvas tops there are in this town, Mr. McNally? Don't count me out. Don't ever count me out."

"I got you on the blackmail rap," I reminded him.

"Fairhurst doesn't want the family secret to go public. He won't prosecute, and I don't want his money."

I wasn't about to tell him what Fairhurst had in mind for the blackmailer. Instead, I lied. "He will prosecute. He told me he would, regardless of the consequences."

I think little Jeff was the first to blink. I took advantage of the moment. "Twenty years," I said. "With the Fairhurst money behind him, he'll have you locked up for twenty years. And if Veronica does marry you, you'll be the richest guy in the stir. If you call that a consolation, it would be your fourth very serious error in this unfortunate caper."

He drank his beer, draining the can, and lit another Camel. "So, what's your offer?"

"You know the police are wise to what's going on here every night. They'll be moving in on the action any time now. I'll put in a good word for you, if it's true that you're not a part of the drug cartel."

"You have influence with the police?" He was back to his wise-guy mode.

"How do you think I knew the address Linda Adams gave the police which led me to your neighbor, Angie, at the trailer court? And how do you think I knew who signed the lease on this place and where to find you and your mother?" Not waiting for a reply, I continued. "Second. Take your mother back to the trailer court and see that she gets the help she needs."

"Don't you think I haven't tried?" he challenged me.

"Try harder. And call on me if you need help."

"Why are you doing this?"

"I thought you were a punk, and now maybe I'm not so sure. Please don't prove me wrong."

"You want Linda to go back to the police and tell the truth?"

"You got it, little Jeff."

"It will hurt your friend Melva."

"If she's the murderer. Is she, Jeff?"

"All I know is what Veronica told me. Her mother killed my father and they needed my help. The rest you know."

"Okay, but nothing could hurt the accused as much as bribing a false witness," I said.

But it was himself he was worried about. Not Melva or his incipient bride. "If I do what you say," he asked, "how do I know you'll keep your word?" Given his *curriculum vitae,* it was a fair question.

"You don't know," I told him. "But neither do you have a choice. Add conspiring to produce a false witness and perjury to the blackmail rap, and you'll spend the rest of your life in jail. Linda might get off with ten years, but then she's flexible, right?"

"What about Fairhurst?"

"That's my problem."

"Yeah? I thought people like you had no problems."

"Only the dead have no problems, little Jeff."

He thought about that for a minute and said, "So my old man comes out the winner again."

I rose and headed for the door. Jeff buried his handsome face in his hands and made a sound that could have been a sigh of relief or a sob. I didn't hang around long enough to learn how he felt about our private chat.

30

I KNEW WHAT I should do. Drive straight to the McNally Building and inform the president and C.E.O. of McNally & Son of the latest developments in the case of the State of Florida vs. Melva Ashton Manning Williams. *Mon père* would pass it on to Melva's lawyers who, according to Al Rogoff, already knew about the second set of prints on the gun. It would be up to them to learn the truth.

But just who was protecting whom when mother and daughter concocted the tale of the Mystery Woman? And why? Bigamy was surely a more justifiable reason for

murder—if murder could ever be justified—
than finding your husband in flagrante
delicto with another woman. Would Melva
rather be remembered as a murderer than
as the second wife of a bigamist? Would the
public remember Williams as a bigamist
who kept his legal wife and son in near
poverty while he and his supposed wife
lived an existence of "opulent extrava-
gance," as the press would label it.

Tina Wolinsky being a nonentity, only little Jeff could have made the Mystery
Woman story. It was easy to see that if little
Jeff demanded marriage to Veronica as his
price, she had no choice but to agree. And
it all might have worked if the boy's blackmail gambit hadn't sent them all tripping
over one another's lies, and if I had kept my
puss out of where it wasn't wanted.

So, Veronica's play for Archy was nothing
more than a diverting tactic. My ego was
bruised, but not mortally.

Next, I should go to see John Fairhurst. I
still wasn't sure what I was going to tell him,
but a plan was beginning to evolve that
might satisfy both my client and my conscience. However, for a variety of reasons,

Connie among them, my conscience was in tatters.

Melva had lied to me from day one, and so had her daughter. I owed them nothing. Therefore, I decided to bypass the McNally Building and the Fairhurst manse in favor of going to see Melva and caution her about what was afoot. Old friendships die hard, and that's as it should be.

Alpha and Omega, as the poets say. The beginning and the end. These were my thoughts as I drove through the gates of Melva's rented mansion. The same gates I had found unarmed that midnight because no one had left the house until after the murder, when Veronica sped off to Hillcrest, not stopping for a red light, let alone pausing long enough to set the alarm.

One look at Hattie's face as she opened the door told me that news of the day's events had preceded my arrival. The atmosphere here was in sharp contrast to my last visit, when we had celebrated the appearance of the Mystery Woman. Today we seemed to be mourning her disappearance. "Missy is in the drawing room and

Miss Veronica is upstairs," Hattie informed me. "What's happening, Mr. Archy? They tell me nothing."

"They told me nothing, too," I said, but the poor woman had no idea what I meant. "Is a cup of coffee possible, Hattie?"

"Oh, yes, Mr. Archy." And she hurried off to the kitchen, happy for something to do.

Melva was standing in the center of the room as if awaiting my arrival. "The sun is over the yardarm, Archy. What can I get you?"

"How about the truth, straight up."

Her skin was ashen and her eyes swollen from crying. Even her chic silk print dress looked shopworn, and I doubt if she'd had her hair done since the day she was set free on bail. "You know the truth," she said. "The boy, Jeff, is it, called and said the jig is up. Is that correct, Archy, the jig is up?"

"That it is, Melva. And you know the police found another set of prints on the gun, but they can't identify them."

She didn't sit, nor did she invite me to sit. I noticed that her hands were trembling as she strained to keep them at her side. "Yes, so I'm cold. Veronica tried to wrestle the gun out of my hand at one point, and that accounts for the smudged prints the police found."

"Did you tell your lawyers that?" I asked.

"Yes. I did."

"And who made up the story of the Mystery Woman? You or Veronica?"

"Why, I did."

"I find that hard to believe, Melva. It's so unlike you."

"I also brought you into it to help back my story. I did that because you're the only person in Palm Beach I consider a true friend, and if you find that a paradox I was wrong about you. Can you believe that?"

I could, and I didn't find it a paradox. When in need, one calls on friends, and that's just what Melva had done. "The paradox, Melva, is that I'm the guy who blew your cover."

She moved about the room, touching the tops of pieces of furniture as if checking for dust. "Don't think I haven't thought about that," she said. "You're better at your job than anyone suspects."

Was that a compliment or a slap in the face? I settled on the former and moved on. "What went on around here that night? And let's have the truth this time."

"Veronica went out with that boy, and you know what he told her. The next day she confronted Geoff and he denied it, but she didn't believe him. She said she would call our lawyers and have them check his past. Then she stormed out of the house."

"Where were you all this time?"

"In a state of shock, I think, and acting like a zombie. I swear to you, Archy, I can't recall with clarity what went on after Veronica told Geoff what the boy had said. It's like a bad dream that you can't recall in detail but you know was a horror."

I nodded. "I understand." Then I prodded her to continue. "When did Veronica get back?"

"Not till late. After ten, I think. I was frantic. I didn't know where she'd gone or what she would do. I refused to talk to Geoff. I didn't even want to look at him. I locked myself in my room with a bottle of Scotch and actually thought about taking my life. I either fell asleep or passed out. When I awoke it was dark, and the first thing I heard was them arguing. Veronica and Geoff. I think it was then I decided to kill him. I took the gun from the night-table drawer and went downstairs.

"They were screaming at each other. Or rather, Veronica was screaming at Geoff. I was sure Hattie would hear. They were in the solarium. I went in and pointed the gun at Geoff. That's when Veronica tried to stop me but failed. I shot him. Then we mapped out the clever plan that almost worked."

"You both undressed him, set the scene, then Veronica took off to where she knew she would find Jeff. Then you called me." I finished the story.

"And that's it," Melva said, simulating relief. "Now that you have the truth, are you sure you won't have a drink?"

Veronica joined us, entering the drawing room barefoot, her hair dishevelled, dressed in jeans and a man's shirt with the tails hanging out. She looked as if she had either just awoken from a drugged sleep or was drunk.

"Go back to your room," Melva ordered. "I told you to stay there until Bill gets here." Turning to me, Melva explained, "Bill Evans is our lawyer. He said he would come to take our statements before we gave them to the police."

"The charade is over, mother," Veronica announced.

"Go back to your room," Melva repeated. Her voice was as shaky as her hands, which she now clasped in a prayerlike gesture.

Looking at Veronica, I wondered if the beautiful girl who had taken me to faraway places the other night had remained abroad and been replaced by a Ms. Hyde. Had her eyes always been such an icy blue? The nose so sharp? The jaw set in stone? The voice so harsh and cynical? "He was my lover," she stated. "My lover. It began when I finished school and moved back home—"

"No," Melva cried. "Please, Veronica. Don't say any more. I'm begging you."

"He was going to leave my mother and marry me. Imagine that, Archy. He was going to be a bigamist twice over. So I killed him."

Melva was sobbing and pleading at the same time, "Now do you understand, Archy? Now do you see why I lied and why I must continue to lie? Why we must all continue to lie? Please, please, leave us and pretend you never heard any of this. I killed him—I killed him. The day I married Geoffrey Williams I pulled the trigger, and I'll pay for it. Not my baby. Please. Now do you understand?"

What a merry hell must have been going on around this place since the day little Jeff spilled the beans. But did the boy know the whole story? I didn't think so.

Veronica sank into a chair. "I did it, Archy. My mother wouldn't have the nerve and you know it." She closed her eyes and looked as if she were about to nod off.

I went to her and raised her head. Her eyes were closed. I shook her but she didn't respond. "She's dead drunk, Melva."

"That can't be. She hasn't had anything to drink all day." Melva was whimpering and looked more bewildered than ever.

I thought I was going to have two comatose women on my hands when Hattie came in with my coffee. "It's time for your pill, Missy," she was saying, "but I can't find them. They're not on the night table in your room and . . ."

Melva let out a cry just as Hattie put down the coffee tray. When the housekeeper spotted Veronica slumped in the chair, she joined in the histrionics.

"She's breathing." I shouted above the wailing. "And I doubt if there were enough pills in that small bottle to kill her. Now, keep your heads, both of you. Melva, dial 911, right now. As Veronica said, the charade is over."

I used the gate phone to announce my arrival at the Fairhurst house. Hector must have been off because Peterson, not looking pleased, came down to let me in. I offered him a ride back to the house which he accepted with little grace. Mrs. P. played butler at the front door and told me her employer was in the first-floor office, awaiting my appearance. It was Peterson, however, who led the way and announced me.

I was surprised to see both Mr. and Mrs. Fairhurst in attendance. As soon as he dismissed his butler, Mr. Fairhurst said, "You remember my wife, Archy."

"Of course," I answered, with a nod toward Mrs. Fairhurst. She smiled a "how-do-you-do," but didn't offer me her hand. Both she and her husband were seated when I came into the office and Mr. Fairhurst stood to greet me.

"What do you have to report, Archy?" Mr. Fairhurst looked as anxious as an expectant father hovering outside the delivery room.

"I know who the blackmailer is, sir."

I could see Mrs. Fairhurst's eyes widen, but other than that, she gave no indication that she was in any way concerned with my news. Mr. Fairhurst looked as if he couldn't wait to get his mitts on the trespasser.

"And he's dead." I allowed this bomb to drop as casually as I dared.

"Dead?" Mr. Fairhurst couldn't believe that someone had usurped him of the deed.

"It was Geoff Williams, sir. The man you knew as Melva's husband."

The two of them looked at me in amazement as I related the story that would become public knowledge by tomorrow morning. "He must have seen the dates on the portraits when he was here with Melva and did a little research to learn the truth. I assume the fact that your grandfather wore woman's clothing to escape the ship was a wild guess on Geoff's part, and it worked."

Mrs. Fairhurst had tears in her eyes as she shook her head and repeated again and again, "Poor Melva. Oh, that poor woman."

"He was a bastard and a four-flusher," Mr. Fairhurst said. "I knew it from the day he arrived in Palm Beach."

"He had no money of his own, as you know," I continued, "and thought he had struck gold with his knowledge."

"But the second letter came after he was killed," Mr. Fairhurst suddenly recalled.

"That's right, sir. The man we knew as Geoff Williams mailed the first letter himself and gave the second to his son, whom you know as Seth Walker, to mail."

Mrs. Fairhurst let out a little cry as her husband pounded his fist on the surface of his pedigreed antique desk.

"He planted his son in this household to keep an eye on things and, I imagine, for future reference. As you said, sir, he wasn't about to stop after one try. He was looking for a steady income. And," I quickly added, "the boy knows nothing. I traced him and his mother through the address in Boynton Beach. I'll give you a full report of what happened after that. Suffice it to say for now that the boy confessed to mailing the second letter given to him by his father and swore he did not know what was in the letter or what his father was up to. I believe he's completely innocent, sir."

"How can we be sure?" Mr. Fairhurst demanded.

Here, my relief pitcher stepped in, and not a moment too soon. "I believe Mr. McNally, John, and so should you. A man like this Geoff Williams, or whatever his name is, wouldn't share what he knew with anyone. He was a greedy and despicable person. Let it all end here. It's Melva and her girl we have to think about now."

Reluctantly, John Fairhurst nodded his head in agreement with his wife. "So be it. You did well, Archy. My check will be in the mail as soon as I receive your bill."

"Thank you, sir." I turned to Mrs. Fairhurst. "It was a pleasure seeing you again, ma'am."

"The pleasure, Mr. McNally, was all mine."

De mortuis nil nisi bonum. Say nothing but good of the dead. And, in my own way, that's just what I had done. Posthumously, I allowed Geoffrey Williams, or Jeffrey Wolinsky Sr., to do the right thing by his family. The heroic gesture was long overdue.

31

IT WAS ALMOST dark when I arrived back home. Too late for my swim, I settled for a shower, a small marc, and an English Oval. Then I called Consuela Garcia.

"Archy? What's going on? Rumors are flying up and down Ocean Boulevard faster than the traffic."

Already? But of course. Hattie must have been on the horn with Mrs. Marsden before the ambulance, the police, and the lawyer, Bill Evans, arrived. "I'll tell you all about it when I see you."

"When will that be?" she asked.

"Tomorrow night. How about dinner at your place?"

"How about dinner out," she countered, "and not the Pelican Club."

"Cafe L'Europa?"

"I accept," she answered, faster than rumors, traffic, or a speeding bullet.

I could feel my wallet beginning to bleed as I said, "I assume Lady C.'s masked ball is history."

"Don't be ridiculous, Archy. The invitations are out and the masked ball is very much on. Only now it's going to be a 'who-done it?' extravaganza. A theatrical agency in Miami has been hired to put it together. They orchestrate the mystery cruises for one of the big lines operating out of Fort Lauderdale. There will be a murder or two, and an investigation with Buzz in the role of Sam Spade."

"What about his silk breeches?"

"He wears them as a disguise when he mingles with the guests, who are all suspects."

"You must excuse me, Connie. I have to ring off now."

"Why?"

"Because I'm going to jump out the window."

"Archy . . ."

My father sequestered me in the den before dinner, and I related my day from start to finish. He nodded from time to time but otherwise didn't interrupt the story. When I finished, he said, "The girl has a good chance of getting off easy. Bigamy and sexual abuse will be the defense's trump cards and they'll play them for all they're worth."

"That's what I've been thinking, sir."

"And John Fairhurst was satisfied with your explanation and conclusions?"

"He was." And as I knew he would, father didn't pursue the subject.

"You've done very well, Archy."

"Thank you, sir." After a moment's pause, I said, "I was wondering if you would be taking on any extra help for the holidays. You know how busy it gets this time of year with mail, packages, errands, and what have you."

"Why do you ask, Archy?"

"Binky Watrous would be available if the need arose, sir."

Father raised one eyebrow, and I can't

say as I blamed him. "I'll give it some thought," he promised. "Now, why don't you prepare our cocktails. I expect your mother will be here any moment."

"Yes, sir." I went to the bar and began our ritual by filling the silver pitcher with ice. After preparing three perfect Sterling vodka martinis, I brought one to father and said, "Now that you know John Fairhurst's grandfather was a drag queen, I imagine you feel more amiable toward your father, Ready Freddy McNally of Minsky fame."

Prescott McNally was not amused.

According to Lolly Spindrift, Lady Cynthia's "who-done-it" was the premier social event of the new season. Phil Meecham was the "victim," which enabled him to spend most of the night in Lady C.'s boudoir, playing dead with a generous supply of food and liquor to keep him company. Lady C. was the murderess brought to justice not by Buzz, the sleuth in silk breeches, but by a young man said to be a clairvoyant with remarkable talent with whom Lady C. was most impressed—and so the season has officially begun.

Lolly, the official guru on our society murder, let us all know that Veronica was declared mentally unfit to stand trial, and has been hospitalized until such time as she is able to answer for her crime. Given the circumstances, father doubts that she will ever be found guilty of first-degree murder, but will most likely get off with a plea of temporary insanity, her time in the sanatorium to be applied to any sentence she may be given.

What Lolly doesn't know is that Melva, in spite of all her problems, has used her wealth and contacts to have the real Mrs. Williams placed in a private rehabilitation facility. She has also offered young Jeff support if he wishes to complete his education, with the goal degree in computer science, long a dream of this surprising young man.

Melva has gone back to New York, her rented mansion eerily empty, and she told me she doubted if she would ever return to Palm Beach. That remains to be seen.

It is also rumored that the Fairhurst family portraits have been sent out to be "cleaned and refurbished." Now there was an item I could have scooped Lolly on but chose professional integrity instead.

Binky is second in charge of the mail

room at McNally & Son, a de facto title as our mail room consists solely of old Mr. Anderson, a post-office pensioner who is very near to retiring a second time. Mrs. Trelawney, I am told, adores Binky. Those doe eyes will do it all the time.

And finally, my dinner with Connie at L'Europa cost a week's salary, but was worth every cent. Connie will also have Christmas dinner with us, where she will join in the traditional McNally yule toast, "God bless us, one and all."